The Queen
Who Became King

SHARON JANET HAGUE

Other books by the same author
Moses and Akhenaten: A Child's Tale
The Tutankhamen Friendship

For Wendy,
aunt and friend

Main Characters

Tuthmosis - King of Egypt (1506 BC - 1493 BC)

Ahmose - Great Wife of Tuthmosis

Mose - son of Tuthmosis

Wadj - son of Tuthmosis

Hatshepsut - daughter of Tuthmosis, Great Wife of Dhey, King of Egypt (1479 BC - 1458 BC)

Dhey - son of Tuthmosis and Mutnofret, King of Egypt, (1493 BC - 1479 BC)

Kitane - royal nanny, mother of Kalma

Kalma - artist, daughter of Kitane, friend of Hatshepsut

Leto - nanny to Dhey

Neferure - daughter of Dhey and Hatshepsut

Thutmose - son of Dhey and Iset, King of Egypt (1479 BC - 1425 BC)

Lord Senenmut - courtier

Hapuseneb - Chief Priest of Amun

Useramen - Chief Vizier

Ptah-hotep - Vizier of Lower Egypt

Itaja - son of Ptah-hotep, friend of Thutmose

CONTENTS

PART I

1.

"Hatshepsut! Put your sandals on, now!"

Nanny Aya's face was purple. Shoving on her footwear, the little girl rapidly obeyed. She leaned forward. Gleaming gold filled the harbour. Her father, King Tuthmosis, was arriving from the battlefields of Nubia. His queen, the Great Wife Ahmose, and Hatshepsut's brothers, Wadj and Mose, huddled together under the royal pavilion. In the chilly dawn, they could make out the ships. Wadj jostled his mother's skirts. Peering frantically across the water, he tried to spot his father. Mose was dignified and sat still. Hatshepsut put her hand in her mother's and smiled up at her. Tired, Ahmose did not respond. Having worried for months, she did not know whether her husband was returning to Egypt wounded or whole. Dangerous and unpredictable, the southern Nile cataracts had prevented regular updates from Nubia.

Now, with the crowds of common Egyptians, they awaited Pharaoh. Egypt's subjects knew Tuthmosis was conquering foreign lands and making his kingdom great. However, Ahmose was aware of a more homespun truth. The only reason her husband had endangered his life was because their country needed resources. The trip to Nubia was important. Egypt's economy was at stake.

Finally, the king's flagship swung into port, followed by his royal fleet. Cheering subjects crowded on the pier in the frosty morning air. With loud shouts, crew members flung ropes to men waiting on the shore. Sliding up against the bank, King Tuthmosis' ship docked as the sun struck the top of the palm trees. Hatshepsut wanted to rush forward, but the family had to remain seated under the protective awning of the royal pavilion.

Dressed in a white robe and carrying a staff, Vizier Ptah-hotep stepped forward. Catching the girl's eye, he inclined his head. She knew him well from visits to his home. It was a place where she could play with other children of her own age and where tasty cooking smells filled the air. Ptah- hotep's cooks were also better than the palace chefs. This morning, the vizier made her feel important. Hatshepsut sat up straight and the nanny's admonition rolled off her.

Crew lowered a wooden gangplank from the royal flagship. Porters carrying chests and sacks, disembarked. Officers followed. A group of prisoners in chains and wooden handcuffs shuffled onshore. Suddenly, Pharaoh appeared. Clad in a ceremonial kilt and war crown, Tuthmosis moved swiftly down the gangplank. He accepted his people's adulation while his bodyguards desperately tried to keep the unruly masses at bay.

"Daddy!"

Tuthmosis waved to his daughter. Excited, Wadj and Mose followed their sister's lead, calling out to their father. The king's officers disembarked and joined their leader. Finally, they moved as a group towards the royal pavilion to where the royal party waited. Tuthmosis scooped up his daughter into brawny arms. She smelled his myrrh gum, which he chewed to keep his breath fresh.

"Miss me, petal?"

Hatshepsut hugged his neck. Gently, he kissed the top of her head. The child relaxed and dangled her legs. Her sandals fell off. Rubbing noses with his wife Ahmose, the king stroked her long tresses. Wiping tears from her pale cheeks, he spoke softly. Then, deciding his family needed to get out of the morning chill, Tuthmosis headed for the palace, dragging everyone in his wake. Ptah-hotep, who had a speech prepared, picked up the hem of his garment and trotted behind them. Catching up to the royal party, he took Mose and Wadj by the hand. The princess gazed over her father's shoulder. The sun was still rising. On the jetty, empty boats lay in a long line. In the distance, she noticed a naked man hanging from the prow of the flagship. Rocking back and forth, he dangled upside down, hands bound behind him, an arrow sticking out of his chest.

Hatshepsut turned her head on her father's shoulder. Birds rose out of the marshes. Still as the royal fleet of ships, the Nile gleamed like a mirror. Up since an early hour, the child fell asleep.

***

2.

Inside the palace, Tuthmosis spent the morning with his wife and children, telling them of his adventures as he handed out gifts.

"What's this, Daddy?"

"Gold, Wadj."

"There's so much of it, dear!"

"Several ships, Ahmose!"

"Who was the man hanging from your ship's prow, Daddy?"

"An enemy, Mose."

"Did you kill him?"

"With an arrow to his chest. Then I strung him up as an example to others who dare disobey Pharaoh."

Crinkling her brow, Hatshepsut reflected on his words.

"Thinking about your future?" Aya smirked.

The comment was innocent enough, but for the first time, the princess fixed her with a stare.

I won't be a child forever.

Getting up, the woman moved to the other side of the room to where Wadj and Mose were playing with their new spinning tops. Tuthmosis ruffled his daughter's auburn hair.

"This is for you."

He opened one hand. A locket of gold, set in silver and inlaid with amethyst lotuses, glinted against red linen wrapping. Deftly, Tuthmosis hung it around his daughter's neck. Hatshepsut's surly mood evaporated in the warmth of his love.

***

3.

Wadj was the older boy. Hair slicked back, he refused to shave. The royal sidelock of youth for him was a tiny pigtail. Mose, on the other hand, was careful about everything. He followed rules to a fault. He would not hesitate to jump into the crocodile-infested waters of the southern Nile if his father told him to. Mose's hair was shaved so close to his scalp, it burned on a hot day. He always ensured his sidelock hung in a single sleek plait on the right of his head, down to his shoulder.

"Isn't it a shame you don't have the rest of your hair when you untie it at night, Mose?"

"I am the king's son."

"So am I – the eldest. Someday I'll be your king, and everyone will have to grow their hair. What do you think of that?"

"There will be a severe lice problem."

"I don't have lice."

"You shouldn't have long hair, Wadj."

The elder boy snickered. Grasping his walking stick firmly, he spun it into a blur. Mose had no such desire to show off. Sitting quietly on a grassy bank, he waited for their nanny. The old woman was forever losing the children. Wadj thought it was a great laugh. Aya was stern and unforgiving in front of their parents, a model disciplinarian. But every afternoon she had the same problem. She lost track of the princes. Fortunately, the boys knew where to wait. An hour after midday, Aya stumbled outside her apartments, weeping. She sat on the grass by the Nile. Suddenly, she looked up.

"There you are, you naughty boys!"

Wiping her eyes, she waddled over to the children and scolded them. Mose kept silent. He felt compassion for the woman. Everyone who lived long enough would grow old. Laughing gleefully, Wadj tossed his walking stick into the air. He caught it and spun it between his fingers. Aya turned away. Wadj stopped, suddenly bored. Without a reaction, there was not much point in continuing. The children sat together with their nanny, knowing she would eventually tell them a story. It was always about hippos or crocodiles leaping from the Nile to eat hapless boys. Then it was time for an afternoon nap.

Mose knew his sister was more knowledgeable than Aya. She had wonderful stories written on papyrus scrolls and neatly stacked on her shelves. He wanted another story besides one in which he became the next meal for a carnivore.

***

4.

Known as Dhey to his friends, Prince Djehutymes dutifully rubbed noses with his mother Mutnofret. As a secondary wife to the king, she lived in the harem away from the main section. Of lesser status than the Great Wife, Mutnofret still knew her child was one of the palace's most valuable commodities. Boys could not only inherit the throne, but were also a rarity at court.

After hugging her son close, she released him back to the world. Dressed in his white kilt and gold apron, Dhey trotted down the stairs of their small apartment to greet Nanny Leto. His governess was from Greece, and he was always pleased to see her. Smiling at him, she kissed his cheeks.

"How is my best prince?"

"My pleats itch."

Leto examined the apron, which she suspected was the culprit. Starched, it pressed down on the pleats, making it difficult to walk. Tugging on the child's belt to test it, she found it was too tight.

"It's a wonder you can breathe, little one." Quickly, she unclasped Dhey's belt. An audible sigh went up. "In future, if you don't like something, let me know."

The nanny took Dhey's hand, and they strolled down a winding path of hibiscus bushes. Leto felt that morning sunshine was good for a growing child. Pheasants pecked for worms on neatly trimmed lawns. A pond filled with brightly coloured fish, lay to one side of the path near the king's quarters.

Eventually, they arrived at court. Columns shaped like papyrus plants flanked a gigantic gateway. The pair walked across ceramic tiles which depicted the king's enemies crushed underfoot. Dhey liked bright colours. He never stopped to consider that the yellow, green, and red tiles portrayed subjugated images of non-Egyptians. Bound and forced to walk on tiptoe, Nubians, Syrians, and Libyans were not worthy to set foot in Egypt. Instead, they were fair game to be exploited, robbed, and killed. His nanny grimaced. Maybe the child would never think about the images and what they meant. Mostly, it was all lies. Everyone knew the Egyptians preferred to trade. Even Leto was here of her own free will. Her father was a rich wine merchant from Mycenae, her husband the cargo superintendent for Thebes. The ancient land of Egypt was more peaceful than Tuthmosis' propaganda would have people believe.

Now they were in a hall lined with more ceramic tiles, but these included scenes from nature. Fish swam among water lilies while birds rustled in thickets. Near the throne, scenes of Egypt's enemies once more played out in an endless demonstration of Pharaoh's power. The pair moved towards the back of the hall with the other children and their nannies. Careful to avoid Aya, whom she despised, Leto drew her shawl across her face. She led Prince Djehutymes to a small throne. It was in a place where they could see the ambassadors from foreign countries, but where it was private enough to chat.

When they had settled into their positions, Leto unhooked a linen pouch, which she kept under her robes. Opening it, she offered the boy the first of many tempting savouries and sweets.

"Now watch the ambassadors, Dhey. Who catches your attention?"

"Those men carrying big jars. Where are they from?"

"Crete. The Egyptians call them Keftiu. They live near my homeland of Mycenae. Those jars are made of glass."

"What's that?"

"It's like faience, except more valuable."

"Their belts are huge!"

"Cretans like to draw attention to their waists."

"At least they don't have itchy pleats."

Munching on spicy savouries, the pair were the envy of the other nannies and their charges. Bored, the youngsters took no notice of the foreign dignitaries. Most were restless. Toddlers constantly needed the toilet and whimpered, or bawled at the top of their lungs. Except one. The solemn little daughter of Tuthmosis and Ahmose observed each visitor's arrival at court. Eyeing her with curiosity, Leto thought the girl seemed to be keeping notes. In fact, she was! Palette and papyri in hand, Princess Hatshepsut was writing words. At least Leto *thought* they were words. They could have been childish doodles. Dhey tugged her sleeve.

"Why are you staring at my sister?"

"I'm trying to find out what she's doing. Let's spy on her!"

Dhey's eyes sparkled. They rose and made their way to the exit. It lay close to the toilets and was a good excuse to go for a walk. As they passed Princess Hatshepsut, the nanny looked over the girl's shoulder. Instead of childish scrawls, perfectly created hieroglyphs graced her papyrus sheet. Foreign ambassadors had names. Gift lists were described in minute detail. The girl could have been an accountant.

"Nanny, can you read hieroglyphs?"

"Enough to know your sister is studying our guests."

Picking up Dhey so he could see, Leto walked past his sister.

"She's making notes on everybody, Nanny!"

Now a Nubian delegation walked up to the throne. Dark as ebony, the men's teeth flashed in broad smiles. They laid a stunning array of gold necklaces at the feet of the king.

"Who are those ambassadors, Dhey?"

"Men from the south. We get gold from them."

As they approached the toilets, Leto noted there was already a queue. Hatshepsut threw the pair a suspicious look. The nanny remained in the line, even though her charge did not require the facilities. Zeus knew how that girl loved to talk to her father!

***

5.

It was afternoon. Prince Dhey was asleep in the nursery. His nanny checked on him, ensuring the fanbearers stirred the air around him, and the windows were open to the river breeze. As she walked down the cool corridor to her own apartment, Leto passed the rooms of the other princes and princesses. Both Wadj and Mose had colds and were absent from court. Drawing her veil over her head, the nanny reflected that the serious little girl with the writing palette was doing more than showing precociousness at court. Hattie was being trained.

Finally, Leto was in her rooms. Her husband was away on business, so she was alone in their home with nothing to do. She pushed open her cedar doors, which led out to a patio. A manservant, Nakht was asleep on his pallet in one corner. With the sun blazing over the garden, it was another sultry afternoon. A foreign ambassador had already complained of sunburn. Another envoy had gone mad with heatstroke at midday. His inappropriate murmurings before the Egyptian sovereign caused him to be tactfully, but forcefully, ejected from lunch. Servants rumoured he was recuperating in his rooms with a cold towel over his forehead.

With Hatshepsut studying, and illnesses affecting the boys, Leto knew she had to take special care of her charge. Besides, she thought affectionately, Dhey was a sweet boy. He never complained and always did the right thing. Nobody at court took much notice of him. But then there were also no assassins hiding in the bushes. Palace security guarded Wadj and Mose to the point where they had no privacy. Leto retired to the garden. Sitting in the shade, she listened to the cicadas.

Sometimes, she reflected, obscurity could be a very good thing.

***

6.

Wadj was in a bad mood. Oppressive afternoon heat weighed down on him. His head itched from lice. He was about to lose his curly locks to the royal barber. On the palace roof, he watched the bustling masses below. An angry sun beat down, relentlessly baking everything in its way. With the heat, the boy's mind wandered.

How were the pyramids built? Did their labourers work before sunrise? Did they take the afternoon off and resume in the early evening? His father thought the workers toiled all day under the hot sun, but then he was a soldier, trained for extremes. There were so many types of pyramids! Some were of pure limestone. Others were made of mudbrick and afterwards, encased in limestone shells. All were shiny, mysterious marvels. And all were heavily guarded.

Wadj's fevered brain turned to the guards around him. They were everywhere, even inside his bedroom these days. It was as if Egypt's burgeoning empire was paranoid. But even Wadj had his limits. One morning, he found a security officer in his bathroom, checking the ointments for poison. He screamed so loudly his father dismissed the man.

Now, the prince leaned over a parapet to catch a sultry breath of wind. In the streets below, mirages glimmered in the heat. A royal messenger once told him there was a place called Babylon in the north-east where two gigantic rivers weaved through mountains and plains. In that kingdom, there were terraced gardens. For now, Wadj decided he would make do with the palace rooftop. But, by Amun's beard, it was hot! He scratched his head vigorously, but it did not help. A cough behind him brought the boy down to earth.

"Why aren't you playing with us?"

"I have lice, Mose."

11

On cue, the royal barber approached the boys. His silver razor flashed in the sun.

"Come downstairs later, Wadj."

Mose found the barber blocking his way. Ducking under the man's arm, he fled down the steps. The barber studied Wadj's head.

"Close-shaven, it'll have to be. You'll be losing the sidelock, I'm afraid."

The prince gritted his teeth as the man set up the tools of his trade. At least his head would be cooler soon.

***

Both boys rolled in the sand. Mose struggled for a grip, but his brother had oiled his body to gain an advantage.

"It's a pity you can't tug my hair, Mose. You can't cheat anymore."

"It was always full of lice. Look, even your sidelock's gone!"

Wadj pushed his brother's head into the soft garden earth.

"I win!"

Mose scraped mud off his face and stood up.

"I'm sorry about your hair, Wadj."

"Are you looking for another drubbing?"

"You had nice hair. I mean it. Don't worry, it'll grow back."

Wadj rubbed his bald head.

"Unfortunately, it won't be the same colour when it grows back, Mose."

"How do you mean?"

"It'll be darker. That's what happens when you shave your head. The regrowth is a different colour."

"I thought that was an old wives' tale."

"Are you calling me an old woman?"

Before Mose had time to draw breath, Wadj threw him to the ground and pulled his sidelock for all it was worth.

"WHAT is going on here?"

The boys broke apart. Their scowling father loomed above them. Wadj mustered the courage to speak.

"Nothing."

Placing his hands under his son's armpits, Tuthmosis swung Wadj above his head. His biceps bulged under the jewelled armbands of Nubian gold. He laughed a deep, throaty laugh.

"Blood pumping to your heart yet, Wise One?"

"Put me down, Daddy!"

The king lowered him to the ground.

"Now, what were you fighting about?"

"Mose is always annoying me."

"You will be king one day. You can't be offended by everything."

"He has lice," Mose explained innocently.

Taking a seat on a battered garden chair, Tuthmosis gave his sons his full attention.

"How?"

"Because he's vain and grew his hair too long."

"Come here, Wadj."

The boy gave his sibling a withering look. Approaching his father, Wadj let him inspect his head.

"I only see sunburn."

"Are you sure, Dad? Mose scratched my head in a fight!"

Tuthmosis regarded both sons.

"There are only two of you. Be friends."

"I have friends."

"You don't have any, Mose," Wadj snickered.

"There's always Dhey."

"Nobody's friends with him!"

Tuthmosis dusted his hands off and rose gingerly out of the chair. Carved from a palm tree by one of the children in carpentry school, one leg was shorter than the others.

"You are the chief wife's sons. Respect each other. One day, you will have to work as a team."

"Is Dhey really illegitimate?" Wadj asked suddenly.

"He's my son, with another wife. Don't worry, your mother is my favourite."

With an absent-minded pat on his son's cheek, Tuthmosis departed.

***

7.

Leto snoozed on her couch. The entire household was resting to escape the afternoon heat. Suddenly, there was a commotion. Royal guards banged their spears loudly on the ground. The nanny stirred. Tuthmosis stood in the doorway. Not quite believing she was awake, Leto pinched herself.

"Don't get up."

The king crossed the floor covered in soft rugs. Sitting on a chair reserved for guests, he clasped his hands before him.

"Wine, Your Majesty?"

"Juice would be good. Where's your husband?"

"In Crete, on a business trip." Leto clapped her hands. "Nakht!"

Roused from his nap, the manservant emerged from the porch. Ignorant of royal etiquette, Nakht served savouries with sweets.

Paying no attention to his mistakes, which normally incurred the death penalty, Tuthmosis accepted the service politely, even complimenting the food. Taking a much-needed glass of juice from the man, he drained it.

At last, Nakht left the room to resume his place on the porch.

"How can I help Pharaoh?"

"Dhey must be properly educated. Does he read?"

"Since babyhood."

Drops of juice spilled on Tuthmosis' kilt.

"That's an exaggeration!"

"I assure you he can read, Your Highness."

"Dhey's never at court. How is he supposed to learn the business of kingship?"

"We attend every day."

"I never see you."

"We sit at the back of the hall."

"But Dhey's my son!"

"Not with the Chief Wife."

Tuthmosis rose out of his chair. Unlike the last one, all its legs were the same size.

"I'll arrange for extra seats next to me. Dhey's new tutor arrives next week."

The king departed with his guards in tow. Leto popped a piece of goat cheese in her mouth. The afternoon's lengthening shadows gave way to pink and purple tinges in the sky. Palm trees darkened from green to black.

On the balcony rails, a lizard flicked out its sticky tongue at a passing fly.

***

8.

Mose and Wadj sauntered into the nursery. They ordered staff to place their toys in the middle of the room. Princess Hatshepsut was in a corner, writing. Acknowledging their noisy presence with a perfunctory nod, she continued her work. Her brothers sat in their miniature thrones as though they owned the world.

"I wish we could get another nanny, Mose."

The princess' ears pricked up.

"What's wrong with Aya?"

Wadj wrinkled his nose.

"What's right with her?"

"Is it because she's old?"

Mose rolled his eyes.

"No, Hattie!"

"She's mean," Wadj explained. "You know that."

Hatshepsut pondered the problem.

"I could speak to Dad."

***

The royal couple met in the morning before attending to their duties. As usual, the Great Wife checked the nursery on the way to her husband's office. Today, the children were playing at the feet of a young lady who wore an embroidered waistcoat and layered skirt. Her unusual garb could only be from Crete. Deciding to check with her husband before asking questions, Ahmose continued her walk down the chilly corridor.

In the king's office the royal couple rubbed noses in greeting.

"I passed the nursery on the way here. Where's Aya?"

"Home, in the Delta, Ahmose."

"We need a nanny."

"We have Kitane."

17

"The foreigner in the nursery?"

"She's from Crete."

"I thought you wanted our children raised by Egyptians."

"Egypt has strong diplomatic ties with Crete. I have to think like a monarch these days."

Helping herself to a handful of figs, Ahmose crunched in silence. Her husband had just returned from battle, not simply as a warrior but as the nation's king. Being careful not to encroach on Tuthmosis' new position was one of her priorities. It was hard enough now they were royals. Five years ago, the childless King Amenhotep nominated his cousin, General Tuthmosis, as successor. Father to more than one son, it was hoped Tuthmosis would take the dynasty into a new era. His military prowess would protect and extend Egypt's borders.

After several hundred years of foreign rule, the Hyksos invaders were gone. Ousted by Ah- Moses, a Theban prince from the line of Se-kenre-Tao, their fortifications in the Delta were destroyed. Egypt was once more a unified country, ruled by Egyptians, but it was also a kingdom which sought to extend its borders. Nubia, in the south, would be conquered for its gold. In the north-east, Syria, Palestine, and Mitanni were ripe for the picking. King Tuthmosis also had his eye on Kadesh. Egypt was about to be contender for first place on the international stage as a military superpower.

Picking up a cup of milk, Ahmose sipped her beverage. Gazing out at the Nile, she reflected that, while kingship was important, nannies were not.

***

9.

A week later, it was Hatshepsut's seventh birthday. Her doting parents were involved in its preparation. Bemused, she watched them huddling in corners. Several times she thought she saw her father's kilt vanishing behind the columns of their apartments, as he tiptoed past with a parcel. On her special day, the family gathered in a private living room where Hatshepsut stood in front of a cedar table laden with sweets, fruits, and flowers. To her puzzlement, there were also papyri sheets and water pots. Attendants stood in the corner, ready to serve. Wadj and Mose pinched each other before being separated by their nanny.

King Tuthmosis stepped forward and presented his daughter with an oblong box made of sycamore.

"What is it, Daddy?"

"A scribe's palette."

Sliding the cover across the box, Hatshepsut was delighted. Cakes of brilliant blue, red, yellow, and white lay against reed brushes. Her father pointed to one of the water pots on the table.

"Do you want to paint a hieroglyph?"

Taking a new reed brush from the box, Hatshepsut bit the end to separate the fibres. Dipping it in the water, she dampened a cobalt blue cake and sketched a perfect hieroglyph. Her father drew himself up proudly to his full height.

"Did you see that, Ahmose? Our daughter is a scribe!"

"I can hardly believe my eyes. Do you know the alphabet, Hattie?"

"I started learning when I was *four*, Mother."

"Nanny Aya didn't tell me. Now I see why your father replaced her."

She glanced with gratitude at Kitane who was holding the squabbling boys apart. Swiftly, Hatshepsut drew more hieroglyphs for her mother.

"See?"

"That's my name, Hattie. You're so clever!"

19

"Let's have sweets to celebrate." Tuthmosis gestured towards the waiting servants. "You're quite the diplomat," he whispered to his daughter.

"Like you, Daddy."

Smiling, the child helped herself to a piece of fruit instead of a sweet.

***

Ahmose shuffled off her sandals. She sat at the end of a long couch covered with the pelts of lions her husband had hunted. Sinking into the cushions at the other end of their couch, Tuthmosis ordered servants to pour fortified wine. Ahmose removed her earrings. Dismissing the help with kind words, the king offered his wife a cup.

"Our daughter enjoyed her party, Tuthmosis."

"Did you see her self-discipline in choosing fruit for a snack?"

"I was busy eating those delicious milk sweets. Where are they from?"

"Mitanni. How are your feet?"

"My bunions are killing me."

Moving across the couch, Tuthmosis took his wife's dainty feet onto his lap and started massaging them. Her painted nails gleamed under the pressure of his strong fingers. Ahmose took a gold vial from her robe and mixed poppy into her drink. The concoction hit her brain. Soon, she slipped away from the world into a land of dreams.

***

10.

The office contained a mat and two water pots. A hook-nosed young man bowed low before the visitors. Dhey clutched Leto's hand, and shrank back. His nanny smiled brightly.

"Dhey, this is Tchanan, your new tutor."

"It's dark in here."

"Don't be afraid. Greet him."

Dhey marched forward and stood before his tutor.

"My father tells me you are the best writing teacher in Karnak. I'm honoured to be your student."

"The honour is mine."

Leto left the pair and made her way back to the nursery. As usual, Wadj and Mose were rolling about, practising their wrestling moves, which consisted of illegal thumps and eye gouges. Oblivious to her brothers' rivalry, Princess Hatshepsut wrote at the speed of a court scribe. Leto calculated the girl would cost a fortune in papyrus by her wedding day. Rolling her eyes, she turned to leave.

And had an idea.

***

Struggling with his paternal emotions and sense of duty, Tuthmosis paced his audience room. Truly, his son's nanny was as demonic as any enemy he had fought.

"But I can't tell Tchanan what to do!"

"You're King of Egypt."

"Teaching is his job. He trained at the temple for years. I can't dictate the curriculum. I wouldn't know what was appropriate for a child's learning."

"Did you know Hatshepsut writes?"

"My daughter sits with me at court every day, scribbling."

"Do you know what she's writing?"

"I'm too busy receiving foreign emissaries."

"But you clearly know what she's doing."

Pharaoh's eyes focussed on the woman before him. Fearlessly, she returned the gaze.

"What exactly are you implying?"

"She's being trained."

"Princess Hatshepsut will be the next Great Wife. It's not a state secret!"

"Dhey can read. He can even read what Hatshepsut's writing."

"Good for him!"

"The princess writes as well as a scribe."

"Good for her!"

Leto took a breath. Verbal exchange with a warrior pharaoh, accustomed to bludgeoning his enemies to death, was not what she expected.

"My suggestion is that Tchanan be sent back to Karnak, Your Majesty."

"Why?"

"Nobody writes as fast as Hatshepsut. I doubt even Tchanan can keep up with her. It might be an idea to put the children together."

"Whatever for?"

"To prevent later rivalry."

"But don't you want Dhey to have a trained teacher?"

"Hatshepsut can be his teacher. I've watched her. Dhey will learn from her. It'll do her good to share her knowledge."

The two stared at each other for several moments. At last, Tuthmosis spoke.

"But Hatshepsut is only seven!"

***

11.

It was a hot afternoon at the palace harem. Birds chirped sleepily under the eaves. Most tucked their heads under their wings, too tired to try. Everyone was sleeping or playing desultory games of *senet,* a favourite Egyptian board game. Hatshepsut's younger brother stood under a miniature date palm. Knowing his sister was about to walk across the portico to her room, Mose was in position.

***

For her part, Hatshepsut could not gain access to her mother. To make matters worse, her father referred to Ahmose's need for rest as part of the "change of life", but did not explain himself further. Deciding to visit Kitane for an explanation, the child found she had picked the wrong time. Her nanny was engrossed in her favourite occupation, that of remaking the children's beds.

In Crete beds were made up differently to their Egyptian counterparts. For Kitane, the Cretan way was the best way. Humming to herself, the woman fluffed up pillows and turned mattresses. Taking a deep breath, Hatshepsut asked about her mother's condition. The nanny did not reply. Instead, she folded a bedsheet.

"Why won't you tell me what it means?"

"You'll know when you become a woman."

"I am a woman!"

Sitting down on the bed she was making, Kitane laughed until tears sprang to her eyes. Hatshepsut wanted to stamp her feet. But the nanny was so pretty and fun, unlike Aya, she forgave her.

Leaving her governess to her housework, the child made her way back to her apartment. A welcome Nile breeze rustled through the portico.

23

"Will you play with me? We can go to your room. I'd like to see your books, too!"

"I'm busy, Mose."

Escaping to her bedroom, the annoyed princess pulled out a papyrus scroll and began to read. It was a story about a man called Sinuhe. Everyone in class would have to know it. Like most of the girls in her family, the princess attended Scribe School. Even her mother wrote and practised hieroglyphs in the evening.

There was a knock on her door. Kalma, daughter of Kitane, was an artist and Hatshepsut's age.

"What are you up to, Hattie?"

"Reading for next term."

"But *The Tale of Sinuhe* isn't part of the syllabus until the planting season of Peret!"

"I like to keep ahead."

"Would you like to see one of my paintings?"

"Why not? I know this story, anyway."

Throwing her book aside, the princess slipped on her sandals. Leaving the royal apartments, the girls made their way through the gardens. Chattering happily, they rounded the corner of the nursery where the princess suddenly pulled up short. Painted on a wall was an unusual scene. Ladies wearing short jackets and wide layered skirts, danced in fields of saffron and poppies. Miniature bulls leapt and sported with gazelles and big cats. Everything was in glorious bright colours, full of movement and grace.

Awestruck, the princess studied the painting. Running her hand over the leaves and swaying lilies, Hatshepsut felt as if she were part of the exotic scene. Taking in the many details, she explored the forest of gaily painted trees and shrubs.

"Look! Monkeys!"

And there they were, hiding in the foliage. Blue monkeys leapt from branch to branch, eating nuts, calling out to each other, scratching their haunches, and dozing on ruined walls. Kalma clapped her hands.

"You found them!"

It was so wonderful – a painting that yielded its secrets slowly as one explored its details.

"Is this Crete?"

"You should visit one day, Hattie."

"I shall!"

***

Mose stood sadly under the tree. He had not wanted to play, so much as to gain entrance to his sister's room, and ask for a story scroll. But he did not know what stories she held on her shelves. He thought he would know what to ask her for when he got there. Disappointed, he turned back to the harem apartments where he was supposed to be having an afternoon sleep.

A pattering of steps broke his reverie. Prince Dhey waved merrily as he hurried by, clutching his scribe's satchel.

"Hey, Mose! Wish me luck!"

Waving in return, Mose headed sorrowfully back to the harem. Meanwhile, Dhey continued on to Hatshepsut's quarters. There he bustled about, emptying his satchel onto her carpet and setting up his paints. Biting a new reed brush, he carefully emptied a leather pouch of water into a pot and swilled it around to wet the bristles. Still dreaming of Crete, Princess Hatshepsut entered her room.

"What's this?"

"Dad says you're going to teach me."

"It's two hours past midday. The house is asleep!"

"You're not."

"I'm seven. I'm awake all the time."

"Good." Prince Dhey tucked his legs firmly under him. "No time like the present."

Princess Hatshepsut was suddenly curious.

"What level are you at?"

"I don't know."

"You don't know?"

"I can read your hieroglyphs at court."

"What do you mean?"

"'The Keftiu are a colourful people from an island in the Great Green, where they make glass vases for my father's pleasure. It's a fair land, where women dance in the groves and men are not allowed to, in case they get turned into monsters like the Minotaur.'"

Hatshepsut flushed.

"You've been reading my diary. Get out!"

"I just got here. Besides, I would never do such a thing." Dhey looked so offended, the princess relented. He dipped his brush into a soot cake and drew an aleph. It was the first hieroglyph of the Egyptian alphabet, and depicted a vulture. "Nanny Leto let me look at your work when we were at court."

"I've never seen you there, apart from once, when you were queuing for the bathroom."

"We sit at the back because my mother's Queen Mutnofret."

"I know who she is."

"Would you like to see what I wrote?"

With mounting curiosity the girl stretched out her hand.

"'On the mountain above the stars, Isis cries.' What's this?"

"I'm a poet."

"Is this supposed to impress me?"

"You asked me what level I was at."

"The passage is from the Osiris myth. It's a line after Osiris is killed by his wicked brother, Set. Osiris' wife, Isis, grieves for her husband."

"Look who knows a bit about Egyptian poetry!"

"Don't butter me up."

"I also wanted to know your level, Hattie. It's embarrassing to take lessons from a girl."

"You don't have to. I'm quite happy reading by myself."

"Don't be so selfish. You never know, we might work together one day."

***

Dhey and Hatshepsut worked with each other every week. Diligent to a fault, the boy obeyed his teacher, presenting her with perfect homework. At the end of the lessons, Kalma took Cretan sweets to the pair. Later, all three would go outside to play by the Nile riverbank until evening.

Sometimes the friends opted for more civilised pastimes, such as the board game of hounds and jackals, or *senet*. While Kalma dined at home with her parents, Hatshepsut would summon a singer, or small group of musicians to play.

As she pointed out to Dhey, it was educational. He wondered if she simply liked the songs. He noticed their listening pleasure was always arranged according to the princess' tastes.

One day, the king and his bodyguards paid the nursery a visit. After exchanging pleasantries with the staff, he took the pair aside.

"How are the lessons progressing?"

"Hatshepsut is a wonderful teacher."

"Dhey's a good student, Father."

"I hear you get along."

"Oh yes! We do lots of things together."

"Good to hear, Dhey. You are to be man and wife. Consider yourselves engaged."

The children gaped at the king. Hatshepsut was the first to recover.

"But Dhey is younger than me."

"Men die earlier than women. As you get older, you'll appreciate the age difference."

"Why didn't you tell us in a few years?"

"I might not have a few years, Dhey."

The prince's eyes filled.

"Are you going to die, Dad?"

"I'm a warrior king. There's a campaign in a few weeks. I must prepare you both in case I don't return. Don't worry," he added hastily. "I will. The marriage won't take place until you are adults."

"Will I be old?"

"Yes, Dhey. And Hattie will be very old!"

Tuthmosis left the children. He conversed with the staff before leaving the nursery. Then, he took his bodyguards for a walk.

There were always endless royal duties before going to war, he reflected. None, particularly pleasant.

***

Holding hands, the royal couple sat on a wooden garden bench. It was afternoon, and the palace was at rest.

"Have you told the children?"

"This morning. It was a shock for them, Ahmose."

"Did you explain you were going to Syria?"

"It didn't help. Whoever heard of brothers marrying sisters?"

"Gods and kings."

"I was trained for the army. You were a military man's wife. We planned for our children to lead normal lives."

"Things have changed. Who knows the will of the gods? Here we are now, rulers of Egypt. It's a heavy responsibility but at least the kingdom will be safe. You have heirs. Our daughter will be secure in a good marriage."

"I wanted Hattie to be the next Great Wife, but I felt to impose Wadj on her was a punishment she didn't deserve."

Chuckling, Tuthmosis released his wife's hand. He rose from the bench. Smoothing her pleated robe, Ahmose stood up. Wandering through the hibiscus and fruit trees, they made smalltalk in the dying afternoon.

***

Leto consoled the boy. News of his impending marriage could have been delayed, she thought. Giving Dhey a piece of sweetened dry fig slab, she led him to the children's play room.

Filled with board games and toy weapons, it was a place in which Dhey dreamed of becoming a warrior like his father.

"You did well at your lessons with the princess. Now it's time to have fun."

"Can I play with someone, Nanny?"

"What about Mose or Wadj?"

"Oh, no!"

"Kalma?"

Nodding, the boy bit his fruit slab and settled down with a wooden horse. Hitching it to a chariot, he busied himself with assembling an army.

Grabbing her shawl, the boy's governess hurried to the home of Nanny Kitane.

***

14.

Awestruck, Leto stood in a living room. Unlike any other in the palace, its whitewashed walls glistened with Cretan frescoes. Sinuous outlines described women in colourful jackets and long skirts. Some picked saffron flowers. Others danced in the courtyards of Minos' palace. Young men boxed each other for sport, while fishermen carried their catches to busy marketplaces.

Presently, Kitane arrived. Her ankles jingled pleasantly with tiny silver bells shaped like pomegranates. She was clad in a long green dress covered with intricate designs of plants. A manservant of breathtaking beauty served cucumbers and slices of seasoned fish. Leto cast him several glances. Like the men on the walls, his hair was wavy and black.

"Dhey's received some upsetting news. I don't like the idea of him playing alone, Kitane."

"What about Wadj or Mose?"

"He's frightened of them."

"Why am I not surprised?"

Kitane turned to an open door.

"Kalma!" Running from her studio, a dishevelled child with paint splatters in her hair, arrived. "Nanny Leto needs your help. Dhey wants someone to play with."

"Shall I take him some food, Mama?"

"If he likes Cretan food."

"I assure you he does!" Leto laughed. "Your daughter is always bringing him treats."

"Hurry up, child. Leto, bring my daughter back for the evening meal. Dine with us. We have Nile tilapia and fresh goat stew tonight."

Leto took Kitane by the hand. Accidentally bumping into the male servant, she flushed and drew her shawl over her head.

***

15.

The palace was in an uproar. Guards doubled around the nursery. Children abandoned their homework in favour of games, while their schoolmasters whispered in corners. An agitated Ahmose visited her husband in his study.

"Is Wadj being attended to?"

"He's in the nursery hospital, Ahmose. He has a cold. It's the best place for him."

"I heard it was malaria. It's killed half the babes in the Delta."

"Nonsense! You know there are mosquitoes in the north."

"There are mosquitoes here, too."

"Not the same kind." Kissing the top of her curls, Tuthmosis gave her a reassuring hug. "Let's go for a walk."

***

Slipping past the sentries, Mose tiptoed into his brother's room. Squinting in the blue shadows he made out the ebony bed with its legs ending in lion's paws. Linen sheets covered the sleeping figure.

"Wadj, are you awake?"

"I have malaria. Of course, I'm awake, stupid!"

"Mummy thinks you have a cold."

"Dad's trying to protect her, so don't tell! Anyway, what difference does it make?"

"You can die from malaria."

"Why don't you take your bedside manner somewhere else?"

"Sorry. I was worried about you."

Mose was surprised at his brother's ash grey complexion.

"What are you looking at?"

"Your skin blends with the walls, Wadj."

"Make yourself useful and get me a drink."

Mose made a trip to the kitchen. He returned with a glass of honey water and stayed with his brother until the first warm rays of dawn.

***

Bored, Hatshepsut decided on a change of scenery. Putting on her best morning dress, she wrapped a shawl around her shoulders, and slipped on papyrus sandals. Humming a popular tune, she walked briskly down the pathway which led to Kalma's family home. Enjoying the fresh morning air, the princess noticed two birds she had not seen before. Wheeling above her with strident cries, they swooped over the trees, calling out to each other. Try as she might, she could not identify the breed, but they announced her arrival long before she entered her friend's courtyard.

Walking through the spacious area, Hatshepsut was greeted at the door by an elderly lady with white hair. The servant took her into a vestibule where she removed the princess' sandals and washed her feet in a gold bowl reserved for royal guests. Wiping Hatshepsut's feet with a towel, the woman re-shod them. Then she rinsed her hands and offered the princess a welcome drink.

Later, a Cretan butler led the girl to a large living room. Young, with long, oiled black locks, he cut a dashing figure. Having settled the visitor into a chair, he went to summon Kalma. While she waited, the princess examined her surroundings. They changed with each visit. The family of painters was always redecorating. Sometimes Hatshepsut found new scenes. Once, an entire wall was painted over. Red changed to blue, and people were exchanged for animals, which she preferred. This time, however, she could not see any changes.

Hatshepsut's reverie was interrupted by the sound of rapidly moving feet. Her friend stood before her.

"Do you know Wadj is sick, Kalma?"

"I've been painting."

"Is that all you ever do? You won't know anything about the world, cooped up in here all day!"

"I hope you haven't come to ruin my morning."

"Wadj could die."

"Mose said his brother was ordering him about last night."

"Since when did you know what Mose gets up to?"

"I get the news. For instance, I know you and Dhey are to be married."

"That's not news. Everyone knows."

Two young male servants brought drinks with freshwater crabs, onion rolls, and apricot tarts. Devouring the snacks, the girls forgot their exchange.

"Come to my studio. I want you to meet Dad."

Wondering why her friend had not mentioned him earlier, Hatshepsut followed. They reached a heavy wooden door, which Kalma pushed ajar to reveal a pretty garden. Among the feathery fronds of lush foliage, tiny blue and vermillion flowers floated cheerfully in a soft breeze. And there he was. Tall, tanned, and black-haired, like everyone else in the house. *Why are Cretan men so handsome?*

"We take care of ourselves, Princess. We also have a different build from the Egyptians."

Hatshepsut flushed.

"Y-you read minds?"

"We all do, except my daughter. She hasn't attended the grove ceremonies yet. I am Nashuja." He turned to his daughter. "Kalma, it's time you visited your friend's brother."

***

17.

"Water!"

The male nurse poured liquid from a faience water-pot down the prince's throat. It was no use. Wadj could not swallow. Gasping, he lay back. The man wiped the child's mouth. He set the pot on a bedside table. Suddenly, he heard noise in the corridor.

Rushing through the door into her brother's room, Hatshepsut skidded to a halt. Panting some way behind, Kalma finally caught up.

"Can we come in, sir?"

"It is not advised, Princess."

Hatshepsut turned to her friend.

"At least you can see Wadj is alive."

Kalma noticed the prince's face was contorted. Unable to hear or see, he was lying on his bed, visibly in pain.

"Let's go outside and play, Hattie."

***

Another morning's royal court session was at an end. Mose tugged at his father's sleeve.

"Dad, my throat's sore."

Ahmose paled, but her husband picked up their child.

"Open wide!"

"A doctor might be better," Ahmose ventured.

"I do this on campaign with my sick soldiers. Your glands are fine, Mose, but your throat is red. Best to get some medicine, little one."

Summoning the physician, Tuthmosis released his son to the palace's sick bay. Taking his wife's hand, he escorted her back to their apartments.

***

<h1 style="text-align:center">18.</h1>

Dhey played with his spinning top in an empty courtyard. Nanny Leto was supervising. Her face was covered by a veil. She remained at a distance. Guards stood to attention around the perimeter.

"Look, Nanny, I can make it whirl a hundred times!"

"Very good, dear."

"That's worth a hug."

"I can't hug you, Dhey. There's a plague. But I send you one from my heart."

Bored, the child picked up his top and moved to a ball which lay by a mudbrick wall.

"Where are the sticks for stickball, Nanny?"

"Locked up with the equipment."

"But I want to play!"

"You can't play stickball by yourself."

"I must practise. It's not my fault there's a plague. Please, Nanny, I'm so bored!"

Leto beckoned to a guard.

"Send for the gym instructor. My charge needs exercise."

***

In another wing of the palace, the sick bay was occupied. Intrigued, Mose's bodyguards looked on. The chief doctor was making a great show of efficiency. His assistant handed him implements, which he brandished with enthusiasm.

"Stick out your tongue."

Probing with a polished copper spatula, he examined the boy's tonsils.

"Am I alright?"

"You're fine, Prince Mose." The doctor turned to his assistant. "Crocodile claw with hippo horn for this one."

Clutching his potion, the prince retired to his apartment, bodyguards in tow.

***

Manoeuvring a ball of twine and leather with great skill, Dhey whacked it with his curved stick. Ricocheting back and forth across the empty courtyard, it whirled round the stumps of palms, dribbled under benches, and smashed into plants. The gym instructor stood some distance away. His face was covered with a scarf.

"The boy has talent. Look at the way he's handling the ball!"

Leto grimaced under her veil.

"It's tragic."

"To exhibit dexterity, Nanny Leto? Prince Dhey is an athlete!"

"Since the plague, our prince plays games by himself. At night he even takes both sides in *senet*."

"I understand your concern, however –"

"Dhey's not sick!"

"But the other children are, good lady. Don't forget, Dhey's a prince in line to the throne."

***

Putting down her scroll, Hatshepsut felt her neck. One side was swollen. She drank the cup of goat's milk which Nanny Kitane left her every morning. Next to it, there were two perfectly baked onion rolls. For some reason, the princess did not feel hungry.

Slipping on her papyrus sandals, she made her way to her parents' living room.

"What's the matter, petal?"

"Nothing, Daddy."

"Thinking about your homework, dear?"

38

"No, Mummy, I'm ahead of the class. My neck's swollen."

Her father felt the sides of her throat.

"Open your mouth."

Hatshepsut obeyed. Tuthmosis checked her throat, while Ahmose hovered anxiously.

"It's nothing, but maybe you should see the doctor, Hattie."

***

Gasping, Mose opened his eyes. It was black.

"Am I dead?"

Sitting up, he fell out of bed. Trying to rise, he found he could not stand. Crawling to the far side of his bedroom, the child felt for the window shutters. Scrabbling at them with his small fingers, he yanked open the painted cedar. Falling back onto the floor, covered in sweat, he breathed the cool dry air.

***

19.

Stomping off to her pupil's quarters, Princess Hatshepsut was in a towering rage. Once outside Dhey's apartment, she waited to be announced. A guard cleared his throat.

"With respect, Your Majesty, this part of the palace is in quarantine."

"If you don't let me in, I will have you quarantined!"

Reluctantly, the man swung open the door. In the middle of an enormous room, sat her pupil, completely alone.

"Would you like a lesson, Dhey?"

"Oh, Hattie!"

The boy leapt up and ran across the carpet to hug her.

"Let go! I have a sore throat."

"Don't worry, we can recover in the same hospital."

Pulling away the small hands which clung to her waist, Hatshepsut took the prince to his study mat.

"I brought some songs for you, Dhey. You can copy them. We can sing the verses together when you're finished."

He stood on tiptoe and started kissing her cheeks.

"Oh, that's wonderful! You're the first person I've hugged in days and days."

The princess clapped her hands. An elderly man tottered forward.

"We need the resident harpist."

"But Prince Dhey doesn't have one, Your Majesty."

"What about his mother?"

"Lady Mutnofret will be displeased to lose her musician."

"So will I, if you don't bring me one!"

Bowing, the man hurriedly retreated.

***

Outside Mose's room, the guards looked at one another with unease.

"Did you hear something?"

"Let's check."

Pushing open the door, the men were greeted by a gargling noise. Rays of light streamed across the floor from an open curtain.

"I see him!"

One of the guards rushed into the bedroom. The other took a torch from the wall and followed. Sticking it inside an empty bracket, he assisted his comrade with the prince. Pulling Mose up, the men heaved his body onto the bed.

"Is he alive?"

"He's breathing."

"I'll fetch a doctor."

The first guard covered Mose with a blanket, while the other ran out of the room. Eventually, the doctor arrived. Opening his satchel, he took out a falcon's feather and put it under Mose's nostrils. A slight movement in the feather indicated the boy still breathed. Lifting the prince's eyelids, the doctor peered into the pupils.

"The patient does not have long to live."

***

Dhey completed his homework. Carefully placing his papyrus sheets on the mat to dry, he readied himself for bed. A dresser took his kilt away for washing, while a young woman massaged his feet. Drawing the curtains, she turned to blow out the light.

"Please leave the curtains open. I want to see the moon."

Obliging him, the woman drew the drapes ajar, blew out the wick lamps, and left.

Moonbeams streamed through the shutters. Dhey thought of his sister and how pleased she would be to see his perfect homework in the morning.

***

Mose's throat rattled. The palace physician closed his eyes. "Send Osiris' messenger to Pharaoh."

An assistant hurried away to do the doctor's bidding. Two men in white, bearing a stretcher with a gold-and-red coverlet, entered the chamber. Reverentially, they placed Mose on the stretcher, and covered his body. Leading them to the mortuary, the doctor supervised the sealing of the door. There, the corpse would wait until it could be moved to the place of mummification.

***

20.

Palace mourning lasted seventy days. While Moses was mummified in the Beautiful House, his parents kept busy with their palace duties. One afternoon, a messenger presented himself before Tuthmosis. The king was making plans for the Syrian campaign, which was now delayed due to an outbreak of plague.

Making obeisance before the sovereign, the man waited.

"What is it?"

"Prince Wadj has joined his ancestors in the fields of Yaru, Your Highness."

Tuthmosis did not flinch.

"Thank you for the news. You are released."

Visibly relieved, the messenger left the royal presence. Stopping at the kitchens, he received a honey cake for his pains. Then, he returned to the palace physician to make his report.

***

Pharaoh declared three days of national mourning. There was no school. Nanny Kitane decided to visit the princess. It was chilly. Wrapping a long scarf of Cretan wool around her neck, she made her way along the banks of the Nile to the royal quarters. Sentries allowed her to pass. She always thought it strange the residential apartments were so close to the Nile. If she had a boat, it would be possible to bypass the corridors and courtyards bristling with weaponry. Next time she might try it!

Nearing the princess' apartment, Kitane spotted a child on the steps. Recognising Hatshepsut, she hurried towards the forlorn figure, and sat next to her. Opposite them, obscured by trees, was the nursery hospital.

"My brothers are with Osiris."

Throwing protocol to the winds, Kitane placed her arm around the princess. Tears fell as the girl sobbed. Unwinding her scarf, the nanny wiped the child's face and allowed her to blow her nose on its fine wool.

"I'm sorry for your loss, Hattie. You will meet them again."

"I don't believe in the afterlife."

Blowing her nose vigorously, Hatshepsut handed back Kitane's scarf. Then she rose and walked down the steps in the direction of the hospital.

"They're not there, Hattie."

The princess paused. Looking at her feet, she appeared to be struggling with something. Afraid she was going to cry again, Kitane offered Hatshepsut her scarf. The girl shook her head. Slowly, she climbed the steps to her patio and turned indoors. Her nanny followed.

Once inside, Kitane ordered date juice and bread. Fluffing up the cushions, she made the girl rest on a couch.

"Let's order a singer."

"We're not allowed. Dad's orders."

"Soloists are required to sing dirges at present. It's the palace rules. I'll send my daughter to keep you company."

***

44

21.

The king and Great Wife sat sadly together in their sitting room. Saying nothing, they took comfort in each other's presence. The sweltering afternoon cloaked the palace in its oppressive embrace. Towards the second hour past midday, Tuthmosis looked up.

"I hear singing, Ahmose."

"Isn't merriment forbidden?"

"I wouldn't call this merriment."

Ahmose strained to hear. Faint sounds of harp strings floated through the still air.

"It's coming from inside the palace."

"Are you sure, Ahmose? I thought it was from the riverside. Villagers always take the opportunity to feast during their days off work."

"There's singing from our daughter's wing, which means someone is breaking your law within your own home, Tuthmosis."

"I'm going to look into it."

"No execution orders, darling. We've all had enough of death for one year."

Tuthmosis looked out the window. The Nile gleamed, soothing his heart with its tranquil flow as it slid past palms and hibiscus bushes. Kissing his wife on the head, he left the royal chamber.

Following the faint sound, Tuthmosis hurried down the main corridor. His head whirled. To lose one son was heartbreaking, but two was a national disaster. However, the sound of music was unexpectedly cheery, even if it did sound like a funeral rehearsal.

Passing his daughter's apartment, he skidded to a halt. Wailing in a minor key, drifted through the tightly shut doors, which were flanked by sentries. The king beckoned to them, and they pushed open the heavy cedar doors to reveal the sight of Hatshepsut and Kalma.

Eyes closed, the girls sang along with the harpist, who also sang passionately with his eyes tightly shut. On being disturbed, the singers opened their eyes. Their faces were flushed.

"Rehearsing for the funeral?"

"Yes, Dad."

"Good to see you are practising. Carry on."

The doors closed. Tuthmosis thought he heard laughter. He made his way back to his apartments, where he relayed the news to his wife.

***

It was late in the evening. A harpist played soothing melodies. Lying on their stomachs, the girls indulged in a game of *senet*. Kicking her feet in the air, Hatshepsut concentrated on her strategy. Her friend frowned.

"You're winning, Hattie." "I always win, Kalma."

"You don't sound pleased."

"That's because you deliberately lose." "But of course! What are friends for?"

Knocking over the pieces, the pair squealed with laughter.

"May we join you?"

Clad in eveningwear, Hatshepsut's parents stood in the doorway. The harpist stopped playing, and flung himself face down on the floor in obeisance. Kalma sat up. Hatshepsut put the *senet* pieces back into place.

"Do you want to play, Dad?"

"Your mother and I want to listen to your music."

"My harpist isn't as good as yours."

Kalma threw a *senet* piece at the princess' head. She turned to the royal couple.

"Princess Hatshepsut was just saying how she wished her family were here. I must go."

"Stay, Kalma."

Gesturing to the musician to continue playing, Tuthmosis removed his outer garment. Relaxing with his wife on the couch, he squeezed her hand affectionately. Hatshepsut and Kalma returned to playing *senet*.

At first, they were self-conscious, but as the royal couple listened and talked to each other, the girls soon forgot about their guests.

***

In the Beautiful House, an embalmer made the first incision in Mose's corpse. He was immediately chased out of the building, as tradition dictated. Then, the other embalmers got to work. Over seventy days, the preservation of Mose's body, and preparation for his funeral took place. The embalmers removed organs through the initial slit made in the side of the corpse. From these, the liver, intestines, stomach, and lungs were preserved in natron. Afterwards, they were wrapped in bandages and interred within calcite canopic jars. The stomach cavity was washed with palm wine. The prince's heart was removed, cleaned, and put back into his body for its use in the underworld. All the while, priests said prayers and performed the magical rituals which would enable Mose to take his place in the hereafter.

During this time, Wadj joined his younger brother in the adjacent chamber. Incense was perpetually burned to sweeten and cleanse the air. Tomb builders hastily finished the boys' limestone burial chambers. Meanwhile, craftsmen from the workers' village fashioned wooden coffins and stone sarcophagi. Furniture makers constructed gilded wooden shrines. Masks were placed over the boys' mummies. Interred within their wooden coffins, sarcophagi, and shrines, they were finally ready for the slow march to the Valley of the Kings.

On the day of the double funeral, wailing mourners led a cavalcade through the barren hills. Sturdy Nubians supported the litters of Tuthmosis and Ahmose on their shoulders. Propped on horizontal poles, the gilded cedar litters bore the royal couple over rocky desert terrain to the tombs.

Hatshepsut stayed at home on the pretext of looking after Dhey. Nobody forced either child to attend.

***

Part II

22.

A decade later, children played freely in the streets of Egypt. The plague was gone. The palace youngsters from ten years ago were now young adults. Dhey courted women. Hatshepsut and Kalma still played *senet* and visited each other. The major topic of conversation was the Cretan men who visited Kalma's parents.

One morning, at her friend's house, Hatshepsut broached the subject.

"Are all Cretan men handsome?"

"They're my uncles, Hattie!"

"I mean the other men on your island."

"I keep telling you to go there."

Hearing the young women, Kitane appeared. Still pretty, she was no longer Hatshepsut's nanny, although she remained part of the palace staff.

"It's nice to see you both so happy."

"Our princess would like to visit Crete, Mama."

"Have you spoken to your parents, Hattie?"

"They want to marry me off."

"You can still visit."

"It's not possible. I'm a prisoner of rank."

"You could travel with an ambassador before your wedding, Hattie. Tell your father it's for your education as Great Wife. You will need to be involved in the affairs of state. Knowledge of international trade and diplomacy is mandatory for the king's chief wife."

***

Clad in business attire, Ahmose visited her husband's office. It was the right time of day. At the ninth hour, the sun had not yet started to heat the air. Tuthmosis had breakfasted and was in a genial mood. Dressed in a kilt and jacket, he was ready for court.

"Have you come to collect me, Ahmose?"

"Hatshepsut must be married."

"She's still a child."

"She's as old as the pyramids!"

"Dhey is an adult. I'll ask."

"Dhey will be told!"

"He's my heir. I owe him some respect." Tears sprung to Ahmose's eyes.

"My sons were once your heirs." Her husband put his arms around her.

"Don't worry. I'll speak to him today. Our daughter will be the next Great Wife." Sobbing into her husband's jacket, Ahmose felt her heart break.

***

It was the beginning of a migraine. The argument with his daughter had been going on most of the morning.

"I'm not marrying, Dad!"

"You're betrothed."

"I like Cretans."

"You can't marry one."

"Dhey has a million concubines. Why can't I have someone?"

"It's his duty to have a harem. As a king of Egypt, he represents the bull. Your job is different."

"I know, my children must be blue-blooded. Still, it would be nice to find true love."

"I'm sorry, Hattie. I tried to delay the wedding."

Hatshepsut walked to the window, where the Nile coursed past, winking in the afternoon heat. She turned to face her father.

"It's not your fault, Dad. Nobody can change the monarchy. Dhey will be a good husband."

Relieved, Tuthmosis exited his daughter's chambers, and hurried to court.

***

The girls dipped their toes into the river. It was midday. Crocodiles were downstream. Basking on large, grey rocks, they opened their jaws to regulate the heat in their bodies.

"You can still visit Crete, Hattie."

"Dad won't allow it."

"Have you told Dhey? He won't mind. He has a girlfriend."

"Iset-the-Beautiful – bah!"

"The point is, Dhey will let you do what you like."

"My children must be his alone."

"There are things you can do to avoid having children."

"You know a lot for a girl who has never had a boyfriend."

"Mama told me."

"Ah, yes! Your mother knows a lot. But you know, she never told me anything, not even about the change of life when I asked."

"That's because you're a princess. She was only your nanny."

"I hadn't thought of that!" Scrunching up her toes, Hatshepsut let the water flow through them in delicious tickles. A male hippopotamus lumbered into view on the other side of the riverbank. Easing his gigantic body into the shallows, he twitched his tiny ears. Another, smaller in size, joined him, followed by several calves. Soon, the family was sitting in a docile group, enjoying the coolness. "I have a dress fitting this afternoon, Kalma. It's time to go inside."

***

23.

It was the season of Peret. Crops were planted. Palace festivities lasted several days as the future King Djehutymes and Princess Hatshepsut celebrated their formal engagement as adults. After the morning rituals, the princess retired to her own apartment. Most afternoons she slept or played board games with her lady-in-waiting. Dhey usually retired to his harem to put a towel over his throbbing head.

One afternoon, the new bride visited Kalma. With a police escort, Hatshepsut made her way down the winding path of landscaped gardens. Hibiscus flowers were in full bloom. Bright yellow, red, and pink petals peeked out as she took the familiar route.

On arrival, Hatshepsut found it difficult to get through the door. Pushing through a gap between lintel and frame, she finally squeezed into the room. Packed with paint and equipment, Kalma's studio was a hive of industry. With a granite pestle and mortar, the Cretan artist crushed up cobalt and malachite to make her pigments.

An unfinished mosaic took up the centre of the room. Multi-coloured tiles lay in scattered piles across the floor.

"Coming to the parade, Kalma?"

"I'm working."

"Boys will be there."

"I'm marrying a Cretan."

"In Egypt? Good luck!"

"In *Crete*."

"You'll go grey waiting for a ship."

Reluctantly, Kalma put down her pestle. Wiping her hands on an oily rag to remove the dry paint, she pushed back her hair. Twisting it into a knot, she clasped it in place with bands of gold thread which lay on a bench. Clearing the door of excess alabaster statues, and mosaic tiles, the pair extricated themselves from the studio which threatened to bury all who entered it. Outside, Kalma blinked in the sunlight. It had been several days since she had left her work.

Princess Hatshepsut led the way across the palace to the riverbank. Dozens of red, green, and white tents dotted the lawns. Chefs cooked, while servants set out a range of food for the wedding guests. Afterwards, replete diners scattered dreamily across the gardens which sloped down to the Nile. Jugs of water and wine cooled in the shade of palm trees. Attendants poured drinks into glazed pottery cups which were decorated with images of the bride and groom. While many adults dozed under trees, dancers entertained the crowds. Tumblers, clowns, and acrobats performed in groups. Children executed flips across the lawns, often ending up in the Nile. Eating, talking, and laughing, people from all walks of life enjoyed the spring afternoon in which Egypt celebrated the continuity and prosperity of its divine royal family.

Kalma collected a plate of sweetmeats. Hatshepsut picked up a wine jar. They retired to a tent reserved for royals.

"Where's your husband?"

"No idea."

Ordering the servants out, Hatshepsut poured white wine into silver cups. She offered one to her friend. Toasting each other, they made plans for magnificent monuments which Kalma would decorate. After lunch, the princess welcomed back the servants. Thick linen tent sides, embroidered with gold thread, were rolled up, and tied back so they could admire the setting.

Below, a family strolled into view. First, an Egyptian lady with braided plaits walked past. She wore a sparkling beaded dress. Then, her husband appeared. He was slender and elegant, in plain garb, but wearing a gold collar, the sign of royal favour. Several daughters followed, eating and chatting. Finally, a young man brought up the rear. Hatshepsut set down her honey pastry. The newcomer was striking. Tanned, with clear lines marking the sides of his face, he stood out in a way she could not fathom. It was as if he were the only person in the group.

Brushing crumbs off her skirt, Kalma looked about with a disappointed pout. There were boys, but none of them had the slender waists of Minoans. The young man Hatshepsut kept staring at, finally turned to look at them. Kalma waved in his direction. He inclined his head.

"Do you know Lord Senenmut, Hattie?"

"No, but I see you do."

"Your father, King Tuthmosis, honoured his family. He's also single."

"I'm married."

"To your brother, who doesn't even like you! Senenmut's family has risen through the ranks. Now that he's an aristocrat, it's perfectly proper for you to be with him."

"I've never seen his family at court. And my *half* brother does like me. We're husband and wife, as is the custom of a civilised country. Unlike that barbarous isle of yours, where bulls mate with queens who break their marital vows, and Minotaurs crash about, terrifying everybody!"

"The Minotaur is a legend. Whoever heard of bulls mating with humans? Anyway, everyone knows Dhey's in the palace with Iset."

The two returned to spending the afternoon in conversation. Towards sunset, they made their way down to the Nile. Kalma waded in the shallows while the princess looked for the young man who had caught her eye. To her disappointment, she only met people who wanted to congratulate her on her arranged marriage.

***

24

Evening fell. Gazing out of her window at the Nile, the newly married princess was sunk in thought. In the distance, hippopotami bellowed. A large moon rose over Thebes. The sight was a balm to Hatshepsut's emotions, and she never tired of it.

On the other side of the palace, her exhausted husband was in his quarters with an aloe vera compress over his temples. A servant rubbed his feet. Iset retired to her wing of the harem. Dhey was painfully aware of neglecting his chief wife that afternoon, but Hatshepsut did not mind. Watching the river glide by in a slow shimmer of moonlight was a relief to the princess after a week of fanfares and parades.

Suddenly, a striped tom cat leapt onto her windowsill. It landed on the floor. Rubbing Hatshepsut's legs, he purred as her draperies floated over his handsome head. She bent to scratch behind his ears. Where he came from, no one knew, but Hatshepsut suspected her feline friend had followed her one night from a temple mass at Karnak. Kalma even suggested it was an evil priest who changed his shape to spy on the princess.

A saucer of meat sat under the window. Breathing a prayer of thanks for her lady-in-waiting, Hatshepsut placed it in front of her visitor. Searching about for her own favourite snack of coriander bread, she saw it positioned by the same kind hands, on a corner table. Its savoury smell begged her to sample its delicious freshness. A royal taster was on duty. He stood outside with the sentries, ready to be summoned. Tearing off a piece of bread, Hatshepsut ate.

Another group of security staff was below her window. Not the usual guards she had grown up with, but a fresh batch from the Royal Special Forces. Now married to the next king, Hatshepsut's home bristled with protection. It was hard not to feel a prisoner. The princess' thoughts turned to her father. She knew he was resting in the east wing of the palace. Even though he had a harem, old habits were hard to break. For King Tuthmosis preferred the company of one wife, that of his beloved Ahmose.

Suddenly, a rustle outside drew Hatshepsut's attention to a slender figure. Lord Senenmut hurried down the path. His family was staying in the southern rooms of the palace during the festivities. Apparently devoted to his mother, nothing would stop him from keeping an appointment with her before bedtime. Rumour had it, he even read to her. Probably horror stories. As a reader of academic treatises, Hatshepsut smiled. *I wonder what a son of mine would do for me*, she thought.

***

25.

Holidays existed for common Egyptians. There were none for the Queen of the Two Lands. Ahmose was expected to attend all royal public functions. And there were so many of them!

Suddenly, her apartment doors flew open.

"Princess Hatshepsut!" a guard shouted. "I could not refuse her entry, Your Majesty," he explained.

"I can get ready in front of my daughter. What wig should I wear, Hattie?"

"The short one. It's hot."

"Wise choice."

"Speaking of choices, my husband and I need to build our tombs."

"Isn't it a bit early for that?"

"It will take five years to scour the hills for the right one."

"Your father's thrifty. They'll have to be small."

"We want to hire Lord Senenmut."

Ahmose's handmaidens struggled with their mistress' long hair. Tying back the flowing tresses, they bunched them under a linen scarf, and tried to fit a wig over the ensemble. Her head rocked back and forth. She gave her daughter a distracted smile, which Hatshepsut took as royal permission to tomb build.

Leaving the apartment in triumph, the princess went to her office to make plans.

***

26.

Royal tomb building was underway. Boats, carrying cargoes of limestone, slipped through the waters below the palace. Others carried men to work on the west bank of the Nile. There, they laboured under a craggy mountain dubbed Meretseger, or She Who Loves Silence. Resembling a natural pyramid, its mighty peak swung high into a roof of brilliant blue which overlooked an empty, arid valley.

Amber cliffs rose like a barren blessing, ready to guard the homes of eternity for Egypt's future kings. For King Tuthmosis had decided his entire family would be interred in those desert hills. No more grandiose pyramids. No more ostentatious display to tempt robbers. There would only be the modesty of a natural hideaway. Truly, Hatshepsut thought, the king's parsimony was in keeping with his military training!

Dhey stood at the door. His wife was standing on the patio.

"Thinking about our future, Hattie?"

"Watch the boats with me."

Crossing the carpeted floor, Dhey joined his wife. Lawns cascaded to the Nile, which was filled with boats.

"Egypt looks as if it's under construction, Hattie. Do you know there are builders in my quarters?"

"You'll be king one day. Extensions to your apartment are necessary."

"I'd prefer to move in with you."

Taking his hand, Hatshepsut led him outside. They walked across the patio, and down the whitewashed mudbrick steps onto the grass. Barefoot, the princess felt the cold dew. Wet blades of grass thrust through her painted toenails.

"Have you seen the latest palace portraits, Dhey?"

"We sat for them."

"Then you'll know we're officially happy."

Dhey squeezed his wife's hand.

"If you need anything, just ask."

They wandered down the riverbank. Sitting on the grass, the royal couple watched a myriad of boats travelling freely through limpid waters. Their spirits lifted, and their thoughts melded into one.

***

27

Neglecting to put on her sandals, Hatshepsut made her way down the corridor to her father's quarters. The guards let her in without hesitation. At the end of his apartment, Tuthmosis was enjoying his morning grape juice. He glanced at his daughter's bare feet.

"In a hurry?"

"I need to learn about palace administration."

"Have breakfast, first."

"I'd prefer a tour of your office."

"In good time."

Setting his cup down, the king broke bread. He dipped it into a saucer of humus. Breathing deeply to curb her impatience, Hatshepsut took a seat. She suddenly noticed her father was grey at the temples. Taking up a bread cob, she tore it apart. The smell of coriander and spices wafted from the freshly baked interior. Realising she was hungry, the princess followed her father, and dipped her bread into the humus. A manservant ladled hot beans onto their plates, and poured milk into two cups. Diced fruit appeared. Afterwards, the pair washed their hands in gold finger bowls. Attendants dried their hands.

The royal duo was finally ready for work.

***

For weeks, the young princess wondered if she should go back to bed. Every morning, while it was still dark, a guard rapped at her door. Overzealous maids ripped the sheets off her supine body. Hatshepsut would swing her feet off her warm bed onto a cold floor. Half asleep, she met with dressers in an alcove adjacent to her bedroom. Forced to rise earlier than usual, the disgruntled female staff added to the chill of the early hour.

When she was dressed, the princess drank a cup of wine mixed with honey, and made her way to the office. Her spirits always fell the moment she entered the room. It did not matter how prepared she felt, there was always an insurmountable pile of cuneiform tablets and papyri, waiting to be tackled.

One morning, the princess rebelled.

"Why do I have to read this, Dad?"

"Cuneiform is the international script."

"It looks like birds' feet!"

"You wanted to learn."

Hatshepsut looked at the clay tablets in bewilderment. Syrians, Mitannians, even the Canaanites, had their own dialect.

"I can't do it!"

"Your mother attends to the palace correspondence when I'm at war. When the time comes, your husband will also have need of you."

***

It was afternoon. Prince Dhey and Kalma enjoyed drinks on his balcony. A servant stood by a corner pillar, ready to serve. The sun was about to set.

"How many languages does my wife speak now?"

"Twelve, including Hittite."

"Hatshepsut read at an early age."

"And she was your teacher for a time."

"In hieroglyphs, which I find useful these days. Do you find it strange she reads, Kalma?"

"It's not the custom for Cretan girls. But we have customs which would be strange to you."

"Like the Minotaur devouring Minos' guests!"

"That's a legend."

"It should be a reality."

"To feed foreigners to a monster as tribute?"

"It would save bashing their brains out with a mace."

Kalma smiled.

"Hopefully not ours."

"Crete is a valuable trading partner for Egypt."

Dhey drained his white wine and gestured to the servant to refill their cups. Kalma gazed dreamily at the Nile, which shimmered in the last rays of the sun.

***

28.

Hatshepsut and her father enjoyed their mid-morning break over bread and dates. Cuneiform tablets from Mitanni lay strewn across the desk.

"I've been talking to Dhey, Hattie. He wants your assistance."

"Am I to translate?"

"Administration staff translates palace correspondence. However, you should review everything. In that way, you'll be familiar with both domestic and foreign affairs."

"I'm no luckier than the men in your turquoise mines."

"We all have to work. Be grateful it's here and not in the mines. Now, I'm due at a royal hunt."

Finishing his snack, her father excused himself. Hunting was a sport Tuthmosis relished. He hurried to his apartment, where he donned a fresh kilt. Putting on a leather corselet, the king tied its sashes across his chest. Then he slung a wide leather belt over his hips and stuck daggers on each side of his waist.

Tuthmosis' heart beat with an irregular thump. Recently, he noticed there were periods when it sounded faint. At forty, the Crown had sapped his strength. Ironically, pharaohs were required to be young and strong in order to reign. There was even a rule about it. In early dynastic times jubilee festivals were held every thirty years to celebrate the continued rule of an Egyptian king. They also carried the death penalty for monarchs who could not run gruelling foot races.

Stepping into his chariot, Tuthmosis felt a click in his right knee. A doctor had diagnosed arthritis a year ago. It was never a good idea to give a king bad news. However, Tuthmosis did not behead the man, and the condition scarcely bothered him. He put it down to his will and belief in Horus, who was the protector of Pharaoh. Untying his horses' reins, Tuthmosis flicked a whip lightly across their backs. Wheeling out of the palace gate, he headed to the banks of the Nile. A group of

63

retainers and bodyguards followed. Taking the barge across the river, the king drove his chariot into the barren hills. His retainers tried to keep up, but he raced hard over the rocks. Accustomed to battlefields, the horses kept up a gallop until they lost the group.

Pulling up before a scorched hill, Tuthmosis wiped the sweat off his brow. There was no one about, not even a solitary lion. Hot silence weighed heavily on him. Whipping off his corselet, he threw it on the floor of his chariot. Spotting a cool cave covered by tamarisk trees, he decided to take shelter. Tethering his steeds in the shade of the trees, he approached the cave mouth. It was no more than a rock cleft.

Comfortable in the knowledge the shelter was too small for feline residents, he sat in its coolness and looked out. The blue sky would have been beautiful were it not for Ra's blazing heat. Distant shouts from the royal party floated in the still air. Tuthmosis remembered the time when, even as a general, he was allowed to hunt alone. Now, as Pharaoh, all he wanted to do was run away from the relentless attention. No one had prepared him for a career without a moment's peace or privacy.

Soon, a pack of twenty chariots pulled up outside the cave. A worried security chief leapt out of his carriage and headed for the tamarisks.

"You need to move away from there, Your Majesty. It's not safe. I'll unhitch the horses."

"Stop worrying, Maya! As you can see, I'm quite well."

A rustling sound behind him caught Tuthmosis off guard. He turned. The rocky brown wall at the back of the cave started to disintegrate. A sleeping lioness unfurled herself. Before the king had time to think, she swept past like a shadow. Barely touching him, Tuthmosis felt the animal's breath as she bounded out of the cave and leapt on the man approaching her lair. Swiftly, the king picked up his bow. He let fly a volley of arrows which missed the enraged animal. It was too late for Maya, who rolled under the lioness' paws.

"Quick, men – attack!"

Drawing one of his daggers, Tuthmosis moved forward to join his men who were desperately trying to fit arrows to their bows. Suddenly, he heard mewling, and turned in time to see the rest of the wall disintegrating. Four cubs moved towards him. Waddling on stumpy legs, they padded over to the rock where the king had recently sat. Outside, came the thwack of an arrow, a pained roar, and a loud thud. One of the cubs moved towards Tuthmosis and butted its head against his thigh.

Thinking rapidly, the King of Egypt made a decision.

***

Careening up to the palace, Tuthmosis dismounted from his chariot. Picking up handfuls of wriggling felines, he barked orders.

"Baskets! Get a towel, now!"

Guards brought panniers into which Tuthmosis dropped the cubs. They closed the lids. A servant offered him a towel. Snatching it out of mid-air, the king wiped the desert dust off his face. Then he followed the baskets into the royal apartments. Ahmose was waiting.

"Where have you been, dear? It's past sunset."

"I had an encounter with a lioness."

"I wish you wouldn't take such risks. You're King now."

"I'm a hunter, too."

"You're foolhardy."

"You were worried about me."

Tuthmosis took his wife in his arms. Angrily, she shook him off.

"I don't want to be widowed. Your heir isn't ready to take the throne, yet!"

Unclasping his wife, Tuthmosis turned to a nearby fruit bowl. Selecting a bunch of grapes, he devoured them with gusto.

"I must find our daughter."

***

Footsteps sounded outside her study. Hatshepsut stopped reading. A familiar head popped around the door. Tuthmosis placed a tawny lion cub on the ground. It stumped over the polished granite to a rug, and immediately started chewing on it.

65

Eyes wide, the princess walked over to inspect its furry form.

"Is it a cat, Daddy?"

"Baby lion."

Forgetting everything, Hatshepsut knelt down and started playing with the fluffy newcomer. The cub rolled on his back, allowing her to tickle his white tummy. Purring loudly, he splayed his paws and closed his golden eyes.

"Are there more? I'd like to have them all!"

"Four. Your mother isn't happy with me. You could have ours."

"Keep the cub. Mummy will come round."

The princess scooped up the tiny lion, and put his round softness to her face.

"You have to give him a name, Hattie."

"How about Menes?"

"Founder of the pharaohs? That's ambitious!"

"I'm an ambitious girl."

"Now that's settled, I'll take him to the trainer. Maatakhhuef will care for the cub."

"But I want to take care of him!"

"This is not a cat. Menes needs discipline."

"Those trainers are brutes. I've seen them break baboons' arms to tame them."

"Nobody is going to break his bones, but this little man will need feeding through the night. He needs minders."

Reluctantly, Hatshepsut pulled herself away from the cub.

"Can I play with him a bit longer?"

"For a while. I'll send Maatakhhuef to you. He can show you a few things about lion care. Now, a bath is in order. Your mother might change her mood about having a lion for a pet if I'm scented and oiled."

With a mischievous smirk, her father departed. As soon as he closed the door, the young princess joined her new pet while he dragged her rug about in his jaws.

***

Kalma sulked at breakfast. The king was quieter than usual. Sipping fruit juice, he waited for everyone to finish.

"Why did nobody give me a cub, Hattie?"

"We ran out. Eat your breakfast."

"I don't see why everyone should have one and not me. I'm part of this family, too."

Tuthmosis downed his grape juice.

"You can have my cub. I have a headache."

"Drinking after a hunt is never a good idea."

"It was your nagging, Ahmose. I drink on campaign with no side effects."

"I'm not nagging. I don't want you to die before your time. You're a king now. You've given up the right to be frivolous."

Tearing a piece of bread, Tuthmosis poured honey over it. Kalma cleared her throat.

"Can I have a girl?"

"There are no more, Kalma!" Hatshepsut snapped.

"There is a baby lioness," Tuthmosis said. "Hattie, you need to be in the office. Your husband expects an update on the latest correspondence from Mitanni."

Rinsing his fingers in a bowl, the king rose. Everyone followed his lead.

"I haven't had a decent breakfast since I started eating at the royal table," Kalma complained.

"Why don't you have breakfast at home?"

"This is on the way to my appointment with the viziers, Hattie. I'm freelance now. Besides, I want a lioness. Can I come to your office?"

"Why?"

"Your cub keeps you company. I want to learn from you."

"So long as you keep quiet. I'll be working."

***

29.

It was two in the morning. Her lamp was nearly extinguished. Hatshepsut poured oil into the lamp bowl. Lighting a salt wick, she continued reading. She could not make out the route down to Napata. There were so many cataracts.

Sitting back, she checked her irritability, took a breath, and surveyed the office. This space, with its plain whitewashed walls, was so unlike her sumptuously decorated apartment, where heavy curtains kept both mosquitoes and cold out. Here it was cool during the day, just enough to keep one alert. Nothing distracted her academic musings during the normal hours of business. However, now in the early hours of the morning, it was freezing. The silence was so heavy one could almost hear it.

Usually, Hatshepsut enjoyed the office more than her cosy apartment. In this space, with a bathroom, and meals brought to her at regular intervals, she felt self-contained. Her scribe's talent in reading, translating, comprehension, and interpretation were all she required.

It was as if from here she ruled.

***

The knock on the door was light. Hatshepsut checked her correspondence to ensure any state secrets were hidden. A guard stood in the doorway.

"Announcing Lord Senenmut, Your Majesty."

Dressed in white, the courtier swept into the room and bowed low.

"Greetings, Princess. I am honoured to be here."

"Be seated. You should know, my husband normally arrives at this hour."

Pulling his robe about him, the visitor gracefully lowered himself into a chair. *You can't hear him move*, Hatshepsut thought. Senenmut glanced at the shelves, but was careful to avoid any interest in her desk. Hatshepsut rattled her brains for a subject of conversation. A manservant entered with pomegranate wine and two gold cups.

"Mother tells me Your Majesty has some treatises on architecture."

The princess stared. *Don't tell me he reads those to her at bedtime!*

"Let me explain."

"No need. Help yourself."

The princess tried to smile, but felt it resembled a hyena's grin. Speedily helping himself to several papyri, Senenmut left the room with an awkward goodnight.

Dhey entered.

"Was that Lord Senenmut?"

"He wanted scrolls on architecture."

"Makes sense. Sen's an architect."

"I thought he wanted them for his mother. He reads to her at night, I hear."

"Horror stories only. It's a miracle she can sleep afterwards."

"Apologies for the empty jar. My unwelcome visitor drank our wine before I could stop him."

The smallest crinkle appeared in the corner of her husband's eye. Hatshepsut's servant returned with a full wine pitcher. He exchanged the used gold cup for one that was clean. Clearing the remains of the visitor's presence, the man backed away with a low bow. A new moon rose while the royal couple made conversation. Outside, crickets sang. Warm breezes played with palm fronds close to their balcony.

For newlyweds, Dhey thought, life was not so bad.

***

30.

In the following year, Hatshepsut and her husband learned about the country's administration. With Pharaoh's conquests, Egypt was transforming from a kingdom into an empire. It was in these times that Hatshepsut discovered her home was more than a place in which to live. The place where she was born, raised, and wed, it was also an economic hub. The palace was a microcosm of Egypt with goods and services. After several months, Hatshepsut found she was genuinely interested, not only in the contents of the palace warehouses, but also in the jetties where accountants tallied supplies. Boat crews moored their vessels, while supervisors maintained strict discipline. She watched in fascination as men carried jars of oil, wine, and beer on and off the craft.

Meanwhile, at the rear of the palace, honking geese, and flapping ducks arrived every few days. They disappeared into the bowels of the royal kitchens, which were far grander than Hatshepsut ever imagined. The sheer volume of food at the palace was new to her. Thousands of meals were prepared each week. People, like her mother, always changed their minds about what they wanted to eat. It astounded her that whatever people ordered, they received in a timely fashion. Slowly, during many months, the princess learned the workings of the palace.

After midday, Hatshepsut always retired to the certainty of her office with its academic atmosphere. Cuneiform did not appear nearly so arduous after time spent in the royal granary!

***

31

Kalma squinted in the morning sun. Like Crete, it would be unbearably hot before noon. Making an early start was the secret to a productive day. Stirring her paints, she started a bull fresco.

In Crete, only men were artists. Despite this, Kalma's father, Nashuja, had trained her. It was now her job and her greatest delight. She loved swirls of paint. Firm and elegant outlines made her heart soar. Kalma's hand was so controlled it could sketch from the head of a figure, down one side of the body, to the feet, producing a perfectly proportioned outline.

In the seventh hour of the morning no one was around. The air was fresh as she painted outside on the family porch. She sat opposite a fat cat who was grooming himself. He took exercise by wandering about the district, but it did him no good. He must have had ten stomachs! The feline stopped, as if reading her thoughts. He glared.

"I know you're not pregnant, Miau."

The cat returned to his grooming. It was true. Mister Miau-Mau was fat. He belonged to the Chief Vizier Useramen, who spoiled him rotten. There was nothing that man would not do for his pet. The choicest cuts of meat were thoroughly inspected before leaving the butchery for Mister Miau-Mau's bowl. Fish was diced into tiny morsels so the portly feline could digest his repasts more easily. So easily, Kalma reflected, he inhaled his dinners.

Suddenly, the Chief Vizier was there. Standing above her in his white robes, with a gold collarette, and staff of authority, the man was as big as his cat, except that he had twelve stomachs.

"All set to paint frescoes in my home, Kalma?"

"I'm painting for the court. If you want my services, you'll have to wait."

"I – I thought you knew."

"Knew what?"

"I informed Tuthmosis – I mean, His Majesty."

Calmly, the artist stirred dark blue and filled in the lines of a belt for her bull acrobat.

"These are coloured sketches for the Delta palace mosaics. I will leave next week."

"Payment is three talents. Gold."

"The palace is enormous, Vizier. I could be there all year."

"Ten."

"Ten it is."

"I'll be off."

"Invite me to dinner. I must see your home if I'm to paint it."

Useramen made agreeable noises and waddled away. Kalma set down her brush. Taking a piece of roast meat out of her paint bag, she handed it to her feline companion. Purring, Mister Miau-Miau reciprocated by staying close to her while she worked. He even evinced interest in her charcoal stick, which he unfortunately ate. This sped up painting of the compositions which were finished by late afternoon.

***

32

It was sunset. All four owners took their lion cubs for a stroll through the gardens. Hatshepsut and Kalma led the group. Their cubs growled to each other in a rumbling conversation which only they understood.

"Did you know lions hunt at night, Kalma?"

"Ours won't. There are no gazelles in the garden."

"But there are humans!" Hatshepsut tugged on her lead. "I see Dad kept the best- looking one for himself."

Kalma turned to observe the king's cub gambolling in the shrubbery. A delighted Tuthmosis watched it fondly while it chewed its way through a succulent leaf.

"We won't have any aloe left," Hatshepsut noted.

Kalma pulled her own cub along the path. The little girl played with her skirts, making her trip and stumble. The Great Wife, Ahmose passed by, a vision of graceful loveliness. She was followed by a trainer, who led a shy and obedient female cub. Hatshepsut grimaced as she tugged on the strong baby lion which destiny had chosen for her. The path opened up to a grassy hillock. Tethering their cats to a tree trunk, the girls stretched out on the grass and watched the sun go down. The brother and sister cubs sniffed each other and began to wrestle.

Slowly, their leads wound round the trunk and became entangled. To prevent the pair from choking, they were let off their leashes. Behind them, Tuthmosis laughingly extracted his pet from a shredded hibiscus bush. Yellow and red petals fell to the ground. They blew across the grass into the river.

"We got the duds, Kalma!"

"At least they're friends. Where's Dhey?"

"At the harem with Iset."

"When I'm married, I want my husband to myself."

"It's only Dhey. His affairs won't break my heart." Stars emerged in the darkening sky. Hatshepsut lay back and propped her arms behind her head. "Commoners marry for love. Our match is for the continuation of the dynasty."

"You can still have love, Hattie."

Enjoying the cool evening breezes, Hatshepsut sat up to watch her parents. Tuthmosis flashed her a wide smile. Ahmose was sunk in thought. The sun slipped behind the palms. A yellow moon climbed the heavens. Eventually, the royal party made their way indoors, where servants took the tired animals back to their quarters.

***

33.

It was Shemu, the season of harvest. Passing one hand across his glistening brow, the king sat down on a bench. It was time for the afternoon session at court.

"Are you alright?"

"I don't feel well, Ahmose."

"Maybe it's the sun. Would you like some juice?"

"We have work to do."

Ahmose reached out her hand. Tuthmosis squeezed it hard. Shaking, he rose. His legs felt unsteady. They made their way inside, but the king grew more agitated. Sweat poured down him and he clasped his left arm.

In a panic, Ahmose called for the royal physician, who promptly arrived. After checking the king, he gave orders for a stretcher to be brought. Tuthmosis was carried to his royal bedchamber where he was made comfortable.

Drawing Ahmose aside, the doctor chose a corner, away from the guards who threatened to engulf the room.

"King Tuthmosis has suffered a heart attack, Your Highness."

"Is it serious?"

"Pharaoh has a mild heart condition. It will be fatal if he does not cut down on his duties."

The man bowed and made a rapid exit. Ahmose stood motionless in the corner. Everything slowed down. She could no longer hear the guards. Turning to her husband, Ahmose saw he was fast asleep.

*****

34.

Smoke trailed into the air as the lamps sputtered to death. Irritated, Hatshepsut rose from her desk and called for assistance. She had already worked eight hours without a break. A female servant quickly replaced the oil, and added new wicks. Then she retreated quickly. It was well known the princess did not approve of breaks in her workflow. No sooner had Hatshepsut settled back into her chair than the door flew open with a sentry's loud announcement.

"The Great Wife, Ahmose!"

Hatshepsut rose again, this time in deference to her mother's rank. Ahmose took the seat opposite her. The princess clapped her hands, and a servant appeared with wine and dates. The Great Wife sampled the beverage.

"This is from Crete, Hattie!"

"Kalma placed an order with the butler."

"It's very good. I'm so glad your father replaced that dreadful nanny, Aya with your friend's mother."

Hatshepsut allowed Ahmose to eat a few dates in silence. Then they chatted about the day, making inconsequential remarks about the weather, their footmen, and the slowness of service at a recent palace banquet.

"Hattie, I want you to start training to be the God's Wife of Amun."

"What does Father have to say about it?"

"Your father is not well."

Ahmose's words wafted through the office like a dry rustle of wind. Hatshepsut tensed.

"Is it his war wounds?"

"He suffers no pain from his injuries. I have made an appointment for you at the temple in two days' time."

Ahmose drained her cup. Rising, she said goodnight to her daughter and vanished into the darkened hallways of the palace.

***

35

Thousands of cicadas chirped their evening song. A gold moon hid behind the palm trees of Kalma's apartment. For once, the artist's studio was tidy. Hatshepsut put her feet up on a fleece- lined stool. A Keftiu servant poured mead from a tall glass ewer.

"I'm to be God's Wife."

"Ooh! Do tell!"

"It involves a lot of chanting and early mornings."

"A powerful position for a woman. I wonder why your mother is making you do this now."

"Dad's dying, Kalma."

"My father's had dozens of heart attacks. He's still here."

"Talking to my mother was strange. It was as if she expected me to step up instead of Dhey."

"Don't be silly. When your father dies, you will rule by your husband's side. But your father won't die. Now tell me all about being the God's Wife of Amun."

Hatshepsut settled in for a long chat. In the distance, a lone jackal howled.

***

36.

It was the middle of the night. A timid messenger stood at the princess' office door.

"His Majesty, living forever and ever, has departed for the fields of Yaru."

"Did you inform my husband?"

"No one can find him, Ma'am."

Allowing the man to scuttle away, Hatshepsut pushed her chair back and drained a cup of red wine. Picking up a handful of dates, she left the office and realised she had a crick in her neck.

*****

Dhey looked bleakly out at the Nile. Palms around him swayed in the night breeze. His wife emerged from behind a large hibiscus bush.

"Why aren't you in your bedroom, my dear? It's not safe here."

"I should have been prepared, Hattie."

Walking up to her husband, Hatshepsut hugged him. Dhey's slim body felt frail in her arms. Pulling him back from the riverbank, Hatshepsut chose an acacia bench for their seat. It was a warm night, and the stars hung like apples in the sky. Dhey pressed her hand. A heron called melodiously as it swooped over the shimmering water.

"I'm not ready to be a king."

"I'm not ready to be a queen, let alone Great Wife, but here we are."

"You were always older and wiser than me."

"That's a great compliment for your ex-teacher, Dhey, but never mention age to your wife. Women don't like it."

A sliver of light illuminated the horizon. Palms waved their prickly fronds in the evening breeze. On her right, Hatshepsut saw a guard standing under a portico. It jutted into the Nile. Unease set in. She thought of the nursery which he protected. It was too close to the river. Boats sailed by all the time. It would be easy for an assassin to gain access. A royal nursery should be transferred to the back, she thought. Blocked by several rooms and corridors, it would be as strong as a Nubian fort.

"What are you thinking, Hattie?"

"Food. Let's get you something to eat."

Turning indoors, Hatshepsut reflected on the architectural turn of her thoughts. Lately, she thought of nothing but buildings. Perhaps she should volunteer her services to the Crown. Smiling to herself, she suddenly broke off her ruminations. A slim man dressed in white, approached them. Dhey was the first to speak.

"Can't sleep, Lord Senenmut?"

"Your Majesty, King of Upper and Lower Egypt –"

"Yes, yes!" the prince laughed pleasantly. "But wait until after the coronation."

Hatshepsut itched to ask the courtier his opinion on the nursery's location.

"Do you have my architecture books, Lord Senenmut?"

"I do, Your Highness."

"Bring them to me at noon tomorrow."

Passing him, the royal couple headed for the dining hall.

"Is it necessary to be so curt with the man, Hattie?"

"He should have returned my scrolls months ago."

"You're making a fuss over nothing. What are *you* going to do with boring building codes and the angles of obelisks?"

***

37.

The future Great Wife was annoyed. It was nearly time for her meeting at Karnak. Her husband's coronation was imminent, and nothing was ready. Chief Steward Nefer stood before her.

"I know you ordered flour last week, Nefer. We should have bread and pastries ready a day before they are needed. Where are they?"

"The boats were late, Your Majesty."

"Don't lie! Flour is provided by our estate."

"I will have the baking completed by tonight."

"Don't disappoint me."

Nefer hurried off. No one could have the baked goods ready for the coronation unless a hundred men worked straight through the night. Hatshepsut looked up at the sun dial and cursed. Nothing was going right, and now she had a meeting at the temple.

***

Priestesses rattled their sacred bronze sistrums in the gloom. Incense rose up the wooden columns and formed a cloud. Singing hymns, the women proceeded down the long corridor to the house of the god. A priest opened the gilded doors of Amun's shrine. Levers at the back of the god's house propelled a small statue of solid gold into the open.

Acolytes placed offerings of fruit and bread before the figure. Hatshepsut rattled her sistrum louder, trying to focus. With the strain of preparations for her husband's coronation, she had forgotten to eat.

An hour later, the god was fed, dressed, and put in place for the day. Hatshepsut could go home. Relieved, she exited the building where her royal litter waited.

At the palace, Dhey waited impatiently.

"Where have you been?"

"At the temple. I'm God's Wife, remember."

"The bread for the people isn't ready. As for the pastries, forget about it!"

"The staff will work through the night."

"I hope so. In the meantime, an emergency meeting has been called. You're late!"

Inside the audience hall, hundreds of courtiers huddled in groups. They talked heatedly, and made wild gesticulations. Finally, the royal couple entered. A hush fell over the gathering. Dhey took his father's throne while Hatshepsut took a seat on his right. Chief Vizier Useramen stepped forward.

"Welcome to your first audience, my king."

"It's not my first audience and I'm not your king, yet."

Momentarily put out, Useramen bowed his head to gain time.

"The floor is open, Your Majesty."

Hatshepsut leaned over and whispered in her husband's ear. Clearing his throat, he began.

"In seventy days my father will be ready to take his place with the gods." Pious murmurings followed. "Only afterwards shall I be crowned King of Upper and Lower Egypt."

A young courtier stood up.

"Your Majesty intends to follow the policies of his father. Does this mean we will retain our posts, or should we wait for the new Horus to declare the appointments?"

Useramen was on his feet.

"His Majesty will not answer such a question!" Hatshepsut whispered in her husband's ear.

"The list of courtiers will not be changed," Dhey said.

The tension in the room lifted. The royal couple looked at each other and tried not to smile.

***

In his dim office, the High Priest of Amun peeled a pomegranate. The morning's fruit platter offered to the god, sat at his elbow. A striped cat purred in one corner. Hapuseneb had already thoughtfully provided it with a fish's tail. He noted its girth and wondered if it travelled elsewhere at night. A junior priest stood before him, waiting for his response.

"What does our future king mean by keeping the list of courtiers unchanged?"

"Most noble High Priest, he intends to follow in his father's footsteps."

Popping a piece of fruit between his lips, Hapuseneb rolled it around. Sweet spurts of juice from plump granules filled his mouth.

"Was the future Great Wife in attendance?"

"The royal couple was at the meeting."

"It's a clever idea. Hers, no doubt."

The junior priest offered his superior a gold water bowl, and a towel. Hapuseneb rinsed and dried his hands. In the corner of the room, the cat's purr grew louder.

***

82

38.

It was breakfast time. Dhey grumbled about the food. Kalma chose bean curd from an array of tables. She had an appointment, and was once again taking her first meal of the day at the palace. Hatshepsut joined them. The princess frowned with concentration as she selected plain yoghurt and a glass of goat's milk.

Finally, Dhey slammed his fly whisk against the windowsill.

"Nothing's ready for the coronation, Hattie!"

"Some things are. Clearly, one of them isn't your temper."

"I'm to be a king in two days and my royal regalia is still being made."

"If it isn't ready, you can wear your father's."

"By Amun's beard, you know I'm not the same size as Dad! At least tell me there's enough beer for the crowds."

"It's being made."

"Like my regalia, I suppose."

Kalma joined the conversation.

"It's not as though there was no warning. The mummification period alone took seventy days."

"Kalma's right, Hattie. Why wasn't anyone looking out for Egypt's future king? Death is always followed by a coronation."

Hatshepsut bristled.

"I've always looked out for you, Dhey! You will be coronated."

Kalma finished her bean curd and picked up her paints.

"I have work to do."

The royals were too preoccupied with their gripes for a farewell. Kalma slipped away. Her skirts rustled as she stepped across the threshold which led to the patio and gardens. Breathing the fresh air of freedom, she hurried past the shrubs and flowers. Eager to put as much space between herself and her grumpy friends, the artist plunged into the garden.

Enjoying the scents of jasmine, and ripe grapes wafting from the arbours, she slowed her pace. Fat fish played and clopped in the palace pools. A large bumblebee flew out of the nearest hibiscus trumpet. Sitting on a petal, legs covered in pollen, it rested briefly. Then it was off to a neighbouring flower.

At the end of the royal gardens, Kalma turned and wandered happily through the long palace corridors. It was on the way to her job at Useramen's house. Columns decorated with lotus and papyrus designs loomed above her. They held no resemblance to the paintings she had just completed for the vizier's living room. Useramen might be shocked at first, but Kalma was confident he would come round to the idea of swords and axes hanging from the walls. She could balance the design with a couple of women picking lotuses. There were such motifs in Cretan homes, and even those as far off as Thera, a lovely place where women with long hair picked saffron, instead of the stiff Egyptian water lily.

Kalma had plans. One of the vizier's friends might select her for a future commission. Extra work could prove lucrative. How many stately homes could she paint in a decade? With gold, she could marry well. And maybe even to someone younger. After all, women outlived men. You only had to see the palace harem for evidence!

"Going somewhere, Kalma?"

"I have a private commission, Lord Senenmut. Where are you off to this morning?"

"To offer condolences."

"Be warned, Hattie is with her husband."

With a cheeky swing of her plaited head, Kalma passed on. She continued her pleasant thoughts. What about pavements? Tiles? Walls? The possibilities of selling art were endless. There was a manufactured substance made entirely of sand, called faience. Resembling the blue of turquoise and lapis lazuli, it was made cheaply, with a bit of copper oxide thrown in. Could she perhaps get involved in the manufacture of faience by buying her own factory?

With these thoughts, Kalma arrived at Useramen's home. Surrounded by trees and lush gardens, it sat directly opposite the southern part of the palace. Received warmly, she spent a happy afternoon plying her trade. The Great Mother Earth Goddess knew to guide her to a better house, away from the palace in which mourning was becoming a habit. The king was dead, long live the king! It was time to get on with the art of life.

***

39

Dhey fiddled with his sashes which billowed out from his ceremonial apron. The blue-and- red pattern depicted the feathers of Horus, the falcon representative of Egyptian kingship. Hatshepsut wore a finely pleated robe. Dressers offered the couple choices of matching outer robes and headgear.

"Anyone would think we were gods, Dhey."

"We are."

"We're *people*. I'm not saying I don't believe in the gods, of course."

"But you don't, Hattie."

"I didn't *say* it."

"You should be hired as a lawyer in the Hall of Judgment. I've never met anyone so preoccupied with the meaning of words."

"Welcome to the world of politics."

Relieving a dresser of her crown, Hatshepsut crammed it on her head. Dhey felt fatigued. All his clothes were stiff. He could barely move. Now, they had to proceed down the road to Karnak, past worshippers and crowds. All those dreadful subjects, who were half drunk on their three days off.

Suddenly, he spotted the red-and-white Double Crown in his wife's hands.

"Why do you have my crown?"

"The original was too heavy. Temple designers produced a lighter weight."

"But how did you get it?"

"I'm God's Wife. The sceptres are alright, even for a lightly built man –"

"You tried out my sceptres?"

"I checked all the regalia with Hapuseneb. After all, he oversees Karnak."

As she chatted bossily, Dhey tried on the headdress. It was as light as a feather. The sceptres fitted snugly in his hands. They would not chafe, even with the lengthy ceremony. Only the jewellery posed a problem. It was light, but there was so much of it. His wife directed the dresser to remove several bejewelled medallions. The result was those with the greatest religious significance were kept, while others were set aside.

Finally, the pair made their way to the courtyard. Two gilded litters, fashioned of cedar wood, with long carrying poles, lay on the ground. Teams of Nubians waited patiently in the sunshine. Dhey took his position in the front litter, while Hatshepsut took the smaller one behind her husband. They were hoisted onto the shoulders of their bearers, and carried to the main jetty.

There, they boarded a royal barge. Gilded from prow to stern, the vessel sailed upstream to the temple complex at Karnak.

"You know, Hattie, we should erect a couple of obelisks, like Dad."

Hatshepsut's eyes gleamed as she dutifully murmured her approval. Approaching the temple, Dhey felt the heat. Common Egyptians, who thronged the sidewalks, were accustomed to it. For an aristocrat, it was different. Dhey was used to the indoors. Now, the sun god had put on the fullness of his splendour for the event. The new king wondered if he was up to the challenge.

****

40.

By evening, the coronation was over. Sipping red wine on a porch overlooking the Nile, the new sovereign and his chief consort were silent. Content to relax, they listened to the river lapping on the shore below them. Night birds whistled. A jackal and her cubs trotted out of the bushes.

Silhouetted against the sky, they made their way south.

"Off to the palace kitchens."

"It's odd to see them on this side of the river, Dhey."

"I hope it's not inauspicious."

"They're hungry animals, that's all."

"Jackals are connected with Anubis, lord of embalming."

"I know who Anubis is."

"I wasn't sure, as you don't believe in the gods."

"Don't tease. I am the God's Wife, after all."

"For the power, I suspect."

"Naturally." Stretching her legs out, Hatshepsut closed her eyes. "All we need now is an heir."

***

41

Dawn broke above the palace with a shout. It was summer. In a buoyant mood, Hatshepsut visited her husband's office, on the way to breakfast. When she arrived, she noticed Dhey's eyes were frozen on a clay tablet.

"What's wrong?"

"The Nubians are playing up. I don't understand it. Father crushed Nubia."

"You're the new king."

"What has that got to do with it?"

"They want to find out what you're made of."

"But I'm a scholar, not a warrior."

"You're a Tuthmoside, which means you belong to the military family of Tuthmosis. We are all warriors."

Dhey lifted one eyebrow.

"Perhaps you should go into battle."

"Many women in our family have supported their husbands." Hatshepsut gave him a swift peck on the cheek. "You will be a splendid general, dear. The Golden Hawk of Egypt will devour his prey as he crushes our enemies."

"Propaganda speech used whenever we rob people of their gold."

"Put down the rebels and take gold as payment for the trouble they cause you. It's not robbery. As Egypt's monarch, you're entitled to bring vassals into submission."

Dhey set aside the tablet. Rising from his desk, he picked up a gilded staff. Leading Hatshepsut to breakfast was his first duty of the day. Once in the dining hall, they found themselves almost alone. A few courtiers were dotted about the place. Useramen and his family ate quietly in one corner. After their meal, the vizier's children left to attend the palace school. His wife would stay until the end of the morning session at court. Afterwards, she always returned home to instruct the family cooks to prepare a meal, while she bathed and beautified herself. Then, she waited until late afternoon when her husband returned with their children.

Lord Senenmut was also in the dining hall. Seated alone, dressed in white, he ate slowly and sparingly. Paying attention to every grain of his loaf, he drank his milk as though it was part of a ceremony. Hatshepsut nudged her husband.

"What do you think our great architect is thinking about, Dhey?"

"Sen is responsible for my obelisks project."

"So soon after your coronation?"

"I'm obliged to follow our father in everything."

Hatshepsut detected a faint cadence of sarcasm. Deciding not to answer, she ate her yoghurt. Now and then, she peeked at Senenmut, but he kept his eyes firmly on his food.

****

42.

Generals marched briskly to and from the royal quarters. Throwing charts of papyrus across ebony tables, they discussed battle strategies. Staff installed sand circles. Dhey and his officers used sticks to draw Nubian villages, military manoeuvres, and routes of attack in the sand.

For weeks, masculine voices carried through the corridors as war preparations gained momentum.

*****

One afternoon, an angry Hatshepsut stomped down the path to Kalma's house. There, breathing fiery impatience, she ordered the sentry to announce her presence.

When the hostess appeared, she took the queen's elbow and led her to a summer pavilion.

"You look wonderful, Hattie."

"I'm fat, Kalma."

"Pregnancy isn't being fat."

"It is when you're circular."

Puffing, the Great Wife sat down on a nearby chair. Fresh goat's milk was served to her by a Cretan maid.

"I'm sure your husband is pleased."

"All he thinks about is war."

"But he must be happy you're about to give him an heir."

Hatshepsut sipped her milk.

"I don't think it's a boy."

"Then next time. Girls are just as good."

"No, girls are better, Kalma."

Hatshepsut permitted herself a smile.

"When is the campaign?"

"In a month. Dhey will be back in time for the birth." An awkward pause ensued.

"We'll celebrate his return, Hattie."

***

The Great Wife stood at the king's door. Her husband was in a corner, assembling his bow and quiver.

"When do you leave, Dhey?"

"The generals leave in three days."

"How many troops?"

"Twenty thousand."

"You haven't packed."

"As I said, the generals are leaving."

Hatshepsut's heart leapt.

"It must be for your safety!"

"I knew you would be happy."

She composed herself.

"It makes sense, that's all. We don't have a son yet."

***

43.

Evening fell. Royal navy ships were readied for Nubia. Men sweated under loads by torchlight. Dried fruit, nuts, and legumes joined sacks of barley. Dismantled chariots were stacked neatly alongside pottery jars of wine, olive oil, and dried meat.

At dawn, the troops marched out of the palace and past their king. Dhey sat immobile on his throne, his face a mask. Finally, several generals climbed aboard the packed vessels. Ropes were flung off, and the ships made their watery journey south.

When Dhey finally rose, his knees buckled. Taking a moment to stretch, he made his way back on foot to the palace, trailing a group of bodyguards, courtiers, and priests. As they approached the main gate, a messenger ran out and flung himself in the dust at the king's feet.

"It's a girl, Your Majesty."

Congratulatory shouts pierced the air. Composing himself, Dhey separated from the group. Taking his bodyguards, he made his way along the path behind the main palace to the nursery. Recently, Hatshepsut had convinced Senenemut to transfer the children's quarters from the banks of the Nile to a more secure section of the palace. Hemmed in by walls, it had only one path leading to it from the main courtyard. Dhey turned his mind to his child. He knew the courtiers were already gossiping about the lack of a male heir. By sundown, all of Egypt would know.

Reaching the birthing chamber, he straightened his posture and took a deep breath. Inside, Hatshepsut was sitting up in bed. Her long hair was brushed over her shoulders. In her arms lay a tiny bundle. As if in a dream, Dhey walked across the soft carpets to her side. Taking his daughter in his arms, he kissed her forehead. She opened her eyes, and he gazed into the dark depths. Instantly, he felt a bond. He held his daughter for several moments until the nurse took the baby from him. Gently placing it on Hatshepsut's breast, the woman then left the couple to talk.

"Well done, my darling. Shall we call her Neferure?"

"A lovely name."

The king looked around. The walls were covered in hues of blue and white.

"Has Kalma redecorated?"

"Blue and white is used in Crete to calm children."

Dhey kissed his wife's cheek and departed. He was careful to close the door quietly behind him. Hatshepsut ordered a bath. Normally Egyptians showered or washed, but Kalma had recently introduced her to the Cretan bathtub.

Luxuriating in a mixture of natron and scented oils, the Great Wife of Upper and Lower Egypt felt her body heal.

***

44.

The harem was abuzz. Women ran frantically about, carrying warm water and linen towels. Dhey paced up and down in the outer courtyard. Servants brought him refreshments, but he did not eat or drink all day.

Night fell, torches were lit. In the dusk, a woman with flowing hair and the green robe of a midwife approached the king. Her face was forlorn. Trying to swallow, Dhey realised his spittle had dried up.

"I have news, Your Highness."

"Are baby and mother well?"

Hearing himself croaking, Dhey stopped. The midwife prostrated herself.

"Your Majesty, living forever and ever, has a son. His mother has returned to the stars."

She rose and disappeared swiftly into the shadows.

***

Servants lit oil lamps in the Great Wife's apartments. Kalma was in a corner, sketching the striped cat who visited her friend in the middle of the night. She was certain it was the same one she had seen around the temple complex at Karnak. No doubt some priest was shape changing in order to spy.

Finally, a palace messenger arrived. He shifted from one foot to the other. Hatshepsut pursed her lips.

"A son to the king?"

"This evening, Your Majesty."

The Great Wife's eyes flitted to a large hibiscus bush outside her window. Bathed in a golden sunset only moments ago, it was now lit by torchlight.

"You must be hungry. Join the staff in the kitchen. They will give you a meal. And convey my best wishes to Lady Iset."

The messenger prostrated himself several times.

"P-pardon me, Your M-Majesty, I th-thought you knew. The Lady Iset joined her parents in the blessed fields of Yaru when the child was born."

Kalma's charcoal pencil snapped. Startled, the cat jumped on a windowsill and out into the bushes. Hatshepsut did not move.

"You must be very tired. Go now."

Bowing, the messenger retreated. Kalma rose from her corner.

"At least the palace has a boy."

"And now my husband is free to indulge his death wish by going to the front."

Wiping a tear with one hand, Hatshepsut looked about. Kalma extracted a linen handkerchief from her bodice and offered it to her friend.

"Don't be sad. Your competition has gone."

"She was only a concubine."

"Iset could have caused problems."

"It's a good thing I value honesty from friends. I could have you executed."

"I'm your only friend. Besides, you can't execute me. What would you do for an artist?"

***

45.

Hatshepsut stood at her husband's office door. Light pink robes billowed around her slim figure.

"I want to see my nephew."

Dhey rose from his chair to greet her. His eyes were ringed from lack of sleep.

"His mother's dead, Hattie."

"Please accept my condolences. May I see the baby?"

Overcome with emotion, her husband waved one hand. He hid his face in his robe. Having received the king's permission, Hatshepsut departed. With a purposeful stride she made her way to the harem, where she was admitted to the inner rooms.

A wave of sadness greeted her at Iset's apartment. In the doorway, a harpist played a mournful dirge. Ladies-in-waiting moped. In the corner of the main bedroom, a small bundle lay in a cot on a mattress. The whole place smelled of incense and faecal matter. Heading straight for the cot, Hatshepsut picked up the baby. Eyes closed, his head wobbled in the Great Wife's hand. The infant smacked his lips and her heart melted. Suddenly, a wave of anger swept over Hatshepsut.

"My nephew's swaddling clothes are wet. Change him at once! Then have him brought to my rooms." Marching out, she glared at the harpist sitting in the doorway. "And play something cheery before I have you beheaded! A son has been born to the king."

***

46.

Dhey shuffled awkwardly. He dreaded confronting the Great Wife, his beloved Queen Hatshepsut, on a good day. Now that his world was falling apart and he craved tenderness, she appeared as fierce as the lioness goddess, Sekhmet. She was even drinking goat's milk like a thirsty cat.

"You can't simply go around threatening people."

"You should have seen those quarters."

"My dear, I am the monarch. I own the harem."

"And I am the Great Wife. I administer the harem you inherited from our father."

Dhey changed the subject.

"Do you like the name 'Tutty'?"

"I hope it's not his real one."

"He was named 'Thutmose' by me."

"Fitting for a future pharaoh. And it leaves you free to fight Egypt's enemies instead of sitting at home."

Dhey laughed nervously.

"You sound as though you would like to see me dead at the front!"

Hatshepsut drained her cup of milk.

"Do what you like. The child stays with me."

***

47

Leafing through his papyrus scroll, Dhey tried to concentrate. The story of Bata was a favourite. Ever since childhood, he enjoyed its vigorous prose and twists of storyline. Tonight, however, his mind was a jumbled mess. Trying to concentrate was a nightmare. He was thinking of calling a harpist to play for him when Kalma appeared.

"To what do I owe this pleasure?"

"I need a drink, Dhey."

"Cretan red?"

"Egyptian will do."

Rolling up his scroll, Dhey placed it on a shelf. He clapped his hands. A servant appeared. Wine was despatched from the royal cellars. Quail eggs, bread, and imported Greek olives arrived from the kitchens.

Realising they were hungry, the two ate and drank in silence. At last Kalma sat back, replete. Dhey swept his last piece of bread through the remaining olive oil. Servants appeared with bowls and towels. They rinsed and dried their hands.

"Are you attending Iset's funeral, Kalma?"

"I didn't know if it was appropriate."

"The harem, including Hattie, will be there."

"She didn't tell me."

"She expects you to attend."

"I'd hate to put a foot wrong with her."

"This isn't Crete. Iset was not competition for your friend. Her death is a blow for me. I loved her and we have a son. But Hattie and I will care for him. We are a *family*."

"Are you going to war?"

"According to Egyptian custom a king is required to lead his army at least once in his reign."

"And now you have a son."

"I have a son and daughter, and a brilliantly capable Great Wife. You could say I was blessed."

***

48.

Pharaoh raged against his generals.

"You deprive me of a glorious battle in Nubia with a skirmish against Bedouins in Sinai!"

A general stabbed the map with his forefinger.

"Sinai is on the way to Syria, Your Majesty."

"Syria?"

"Where your father hunted elephants."

"Are we're fighting a nation, after all, General Ahmose?"

"We thought you would be pleased."

"I'm surprised."

"You're older now, sire."

"And with a son," General Paneb added.

"An heir, no less!" General Senefer chimed in.

The men beamed at their king.

"I must tell the Great Wife," he said.

***

49.

Hatshepsut scratched her lion's mane. Turning on his back he stretched out his chin for a deeper tickle. Dhey moved out of the way of the sturdy hindquarters and spiked tail.

"Syria?"

"In ten days."

"I thought you said it was Sinai, Dhey. Did I hear wrong?"

"Sinai is on the way to Syria."

"And you expect me to believe the generals just made this decision?"

"I thought you would be pleased."

"I would be if I wanted my husband chopped into tiny pieces and strewn across foreign lands!"

"I won't die, Hattie."

"How do you know?"

Hatshepsut's voice rose. Her lion put up his head. Dhey stared into a pair of fearless gold eyes.

"I do wish you would put a harness over that thing."

"My lion has a name, Ra. It's about time you used it."

"It's about time Ra had a collar. There's more likelihood of me being killed by that beast than by any Syrian."

Rolling onto his stomach, the lion licked Hatshepsut's hand.

"Maat, take Ra to his quarters!"

Immediately, the royal trainer appeared. With a gentle command, he led the young lion to his enclosure where he could rest and eat. Dhey tried not to show his relief.

"I'll write to you every day, Hattie."

"Send me letters about our neighbours' customs. I'm interested in different cultures."

"I shall. Now if you will excuse me, I have a meeting with my archery instructor."

After Dhey's departure, Hatshepsut sat in silence. It was a beautiful afternoon. She called for the manicurist, and sat by the Nile as it eased its way past the palace.

*****

50.

Packing his favourite dagger, Dhey looked around his apartment for the last time. Clean and swept, it would remain untouched until his return. Alive, or in a shroud, he reflected. He stepped onto the patio. A night bird called as it swept across the Nile. Waters lapped in soothing repetition on the banks below.

Lights went out in the Great Wife's apartment. Sentries laughed under the palms. It was the tenth hour of the evening. Food was brought to the men. After eating, they stayed for another hour. Then, they exchanged places with the new guards, and returned home.

Dhey turned indoors. Hatshepsut was in his living room.

"I'm here to wish my husband well on his campaign."

"You are seeing me off, now?"

"I wanted to say goodnight."

The king crossed the floor and took his wife in his arms. Kissing her gently, he held her close.

"You will do a wonderful job while I'm away, Hattie."

"I know you will come back."

"Of course, I will. Amun won't let me leave you with two brats to raise on your own!"

*****

51

Sunrise was perfect. Papyri thickets rustled as birds flew up into the sky. Balmy breezes blew across the river. Hatshepsut splashed in the cool water with her companions. It was better to bathe at the foot of her apartment, than to stand under a bucket of water poured by attendants whose mouths were so tight they looked sewn up.

After a while, several of the companions made their way back to shore. Guards enjoyed the view of the women as they emerged, naked and glistening, from the Nile. Dropping themselves on the grassy sedge, they dried off. All except Hatshepsut and Kalma.

With swift, strong strokes, the queen swam to the middle of the river, towards a sand bank.

"Careful, Hattie!"

"Stop fussing, Kalma! There're no crocs in the morning."

"I wouldn't be so sure."

Nervously treading water, Kalma stayed in one place, a little way offshore. Hatshepsut swam to the bank and hauled herself out onto a boulder. Swinging round, she placed her feet on the sand. Tiny grains clung coyly to her inner soles.

Humming to herself, she twisted her hair and wrung out the fresh, cold water. Over the hump of the bank, sliding downwards on the other side, reeds shifted and swayed. Hatshepsut froze. Peering down, she saw a shape bobbing in the water. Its ridges were a giveaway.

"Everything alright, Hattie?"

Hatshepsut did not answer for fear of the creature. If she opened her mouth, it might come lumbering towards her. Then, she saw the object more clearly and relaxed.

"I'm fine. Stay where you are."

Kalma continued to tread water and tried not to think. Hippos often bathed in these waters at sunset. Meandering downstream, they chose this spot for their nocturnal splashing. It was always comforting to hear them snorting and bellowing as they tumbled through the waters, a short distance from the palace apartments. Fenced off, they rarely approached the royal side of the river. Being with them in the water was another matter. A sudden plop next to her made Kalma hold her breath.

Several friends waved to her.

"Where's Hattie?" one of them called out.

"On the other side of the bank."

"Is that safe?"

Some of the girls slipped back into the water. A few of the sentries edged closer to the shoreline.

"Everything's fine," Kalma called brightly. "Call of nature."

The sentries moved back. The women who had got into the water returned to shore and resumed chatting as they dried off. On the other side of the sand bank, Hatshepsut drew near to the odd shape. Trapped in papyrus plants, it bobbed in one place. Squatting down, the Great Wife reached out and drew it towards her. When it touched the shore, she pulled at the rim. It was surprisingly heavy. She put her back into hauling it up the sand bank. Then, taking a breath, she opened the lid.

"Kalma!"

There was no time for fear. The artist swam furiously across the crocodile-infested river. Lithe as a water snake, she pulled herself up onto the large boulders and ran to the sand bank.

"It's a baby!"

Jolting upright, Hatshepsut breathed heavily. It was suffocatingly dark. The faint smell of incense reminded her that she was in her own bedchamber. A partially drawn curtain revealed a full Theban moon overhead. Trembling, she arose. Slipping a gown over her sweating body, she stumbled across the rug to the window and peered out.

A gold moon hung over the palms, its beams cascading across the water. The familiar sand bank, seen since childhood, rose in stark white curves. Bellowing, a hippo raised its head, twitched tiny ears, and grumbled gently to itself as it splashed back into the depths.

With a shaking hand, Hatshepsut closed the drapes.

***

106

52.

It was breakfast. The Great Wife sipped her goat's milk. Kalma scoffed fresh bread rolls which were coated in spices and honey.

"You're quiet this morning, Hattie."

"Tell me I only have one daughter."

"Last time I checked."

"No sons adopted by accident?"

"You're the mother of one unruly daughter."

Hatshepsut stood up to indicate the end of the meal. They left the dining room, Kalma chatting brightly about her new painting. As usual, they walked down the long corridor. Normally, they adhered to a routine. One turned in the direction of her studio, while the other made her way to her office. Today Hatshepsut hesitated.

"Do you mind if I see it, Kalma?"

"The painting? I haven't started." Noting her friend's unease, Kalma took her arm. "But of course, you're always welcome to see my work. Just don't correct me with the Egyptian canon of proportion!"

Her tinkling laughter reminded Hatshepsut of Kitane, mother to Kalma, and nurse to her so long ago. Goose bumps travelled across her skin.

****

53

The High Priest scratched his ear.

"Was the baby in your dream a boy or girl?"

"A boy."

"It means you want a son."

"I already have a child."

"Every Great Wife is obliged to bear a son to her lord."

"Which I will do."

"Indeed! Her Majesty is still young."

Hatshepsut hesitated, as if she was mulling something over.

"I was the Great Wife in my dream, but I don't think the child was Dhey's."

Stoking the incense burner, the priest placed several lumps in the brazier. Dipping a cloth into holy water, he wiped his palms.

"Tell me, Your Highness, was the boy normal?"

"Why wouldn't he be?" Hatshepsut's mind raced. "Wait! There was something. It was the cloth which lined the basket."

"Did it have an insignia? The emblem of Horus as a falcon, for example?"

"Yes."

"An auspicious dream. You will give birth to a boy within the year."

Hatshepsut rose. Hapuseneb bowed as she left his Karnak office.

***

Announced by a guard, the Great Wife, Queen Hatshepsut took her seat on a cushioned stool. Gilded, with duck legs, it was Kalma's special chair for royal visitors. Next to it was a table laden with flowers, white wine, and a dish of nuts.

"What do you think, Hattie? I'm painting a wall design for your northern capital."

"It looks Cretan."

"It is."

"Egyptian designs are appropriate for a war palace, Kalma."

"Your husband requested art for a pleasure palace."

"In that case, it's perfect."

"It'd better be!" Kalma laughed. She draped a large papyrus sheet over her drawing table. "What's the matter?"

"I'm thinking about the child in the dream."

"The priest said you want a son. That makes sense."

"The child's cloth was Canaanite."

"Can you recall the design?"

Hatshepsut rose from her gilded chair and searched the artist's desk for colour sticks. Small chunks of yellow and red oxide, white gypsum, blue cobalt, and malachite lay in separate dishes. She found a papyrus scrap. Taking several chunks, Hatshepsut drew the first lines of a colourful robe. Kalma twisted the paper up to the light.

"This is the style of our immigrant shepherd folk, but are you sure about the colours?"

"I'm sure. It was *my* dream."

***

54.

Aaron was quiet. A priest of the Apiru, he had never received a call to the Egyptian palace. Now, the most important wife of King Tuthmosis, living forever and ever, had summoned him. There had been no arrests of his people, no persecution, and no recruitment of families for Sinai's turquoise mines. However, Aaron was on guard. He noticed the Great Wife was slender and petite, but had an aura of authority. After she had finished speaking, he remained silent.

"Have you nothing to say, Aaron? Don't worry, no harm will befall you."

"Speak up!" one of her guards interjected.

A look from Hatshepsut silenced him.

"My understanding is that Your Majesty will give birth to a boy in the next year."

"If you believe the priest of Amun."

"And you don't?"

"Don't be impertinent!" the same security officer barked.

"Forgive me if I have offended," Aaron continued, steadfastly addressing the Great Wife. "It was just a question."

"Questions are fine. So, you think it's nothing?"

"Dreams are sometimes only dreams."

"But you're a priest. Is that all you have to say?"

"I am not a Canaanite, although I am from that region." It was Aaron's turn to smile.

"The cloth is of interest because I cannot understand its origin."

"Maybe because it only appeared in my dream."

"I do have an opinion, Great Wife, but I would ask that we be alone. Your security men may check me. I am not armed."

Hatshepsut clapped her hands. Her guards departed with alacrity.

"I know you're not armed. Besides, I have military training."

"I have heard Egyptian royal women are skilled in the arts of war."

"What is your opinion?"

"Please give me your word that you will not be offended."

"Granted."

"The child is not yours."

"I don't understand."

"He will be adopted into the royal house of Egypt."

"By me?"

"No."

"Is the child a king?"

"Not an Egyptian king."

"How could he be adopted by us and not be treated as an Egyptian royal?"

"He will be an Egyptian prince."

"That's more understandable."

"He will deliver his people from persecution."

"Here?"

"His tribe only has one god."

"One god?"

"The Creator."

"We also worship the Creator."

"His people have no other gods."

"The only people who believe in a sole deity are Egypt's mudbrick workers. But I treat them well." Hatshepsut mulled over Aaron's words. "If you allow my security staff to escort you to my dining room for guests, you may bathe and eat before going home."

The man assumed full prostration. It was never wise to test an Egyptian queen's patience.

***

Hatshepsut reflected she was visiting Kalma more than usual, but the artist did not seem to mind. They sat quietly in the studio, while Kalma worked, and the troubled royal mulled over her life. At last Kalma spoke.

"Did you find out what the baby in the dream meant?" "It was just a dream, Kalma."

"Is that what the priest of the Apiru said?"

"Either that, or we're going into eternity together with our baby!"

Kalma roared with laughter. Picking up a stick of carbon, she drew on a papyrus sheet. With quick deft strokes, she brought out the lines of several male dancers, a large bull, and women dancing in olive groves.

Hatshepsut peered at the scene.

"Is everyone who experiences a divine revelation in your culture, drugged?"

"Always."

Hatshepsut chuckled. Outside, the Nile glimmered with a swiftly setting sun. Water rolled along like molten lava before fading into pitch-black night.

***

55

Searing sky hung over the troops. Desert sand burned underfoot. Egypt was hot, but Sinai was scorching. The Egyptian army marched in silence. At noon, it pitched camp.

"We should move at night," Dhey suggested to his generals.

"It's not safe."

"We don't have enough water for the men, Ahmose!"

"They're soldiers. They're used to thirst."

"How do you expect them to fight? Syria is still up ahead. I want a healthy army."

Ahmose turned to the other generals.

"What do you think?"

Paneb cleared his throat.

"Sinai's terrain is rocky. Horses could stumble in the dark."

Senefer, stroked his grey stubble.

"True, Paneb, but there is a major trade route which is easy to navigate."

"We'll be caught out at night," said Paneb.

Dhey's brow furrowed.

"This is not a matter for discussion! We travel at night."

"Are we going to camp now and travel this evening, Your Majesty? Our troops are exhausted. Even if we rest until dark, I doubt whether the men can do a full night's march."

"We can march tomorrow night, General Ahmose. In the meantime, set up camp at the back of the mountain where we won't be seen."

Bowing to their sovereign, the generals made their way out of the tent.

***

A Sinai dawn was different from anything Dhey had ever experienced. Cold winds buffeted the side of the mountain behind which they sheltered. Pale yellow light crept slowly up purple crags. There was no warmth at this time. Soldiers wrapped blankets close about their shivering bodies and tried to sleep.

Dhey stood outside his tent, drinking warm milk, while watching the sun rise. Everything looked blue and orange. Ahmose, covered in a sheepskin for extra warmth, approached him.

"Can't sleep, General?"

"Do you still think it's a good idea to travel at night, Your Majesty? I have no doubt my men perished of cold in their beds this morning!"

"Have a beer with me, Ahmose. It'll warm you up."

Passing under the royal tent flap, they went inside. General Ahmose took a chair which was sensibly covered in sheepskin. He accepted a gold cup filled with sweet date and barley beer. Most Egyptians drank beer at breakfast, and the king was no different. A manservant left linen napkins with a jug for each man.

"How are the generals this morning, Ahmose?"

"Most of them slept well, Your Majesty."

"Cold will do that."

"By the way, this beer is good."

"The barley is fresh."

"And dates last well on a campaign. To Your Majesty's health!"

Downing the drink, Ahmose wiped his lips on a fresh napkin. Dhey reached behind him and pulled out a *senet* board. Pushing aside his beer, he made room for it on the table between them. Then, opening a drawer at the end of his board, he emptied out a set of white pawns, and four ebony throwing sticks.

"A game before breakfast?"

Ahmose opened the drawer on his side and took out black pieces. Shaped like the spinning tops of his youth, they filled him with nostalgia.

Picking up the sticks, Dhey threw them onto the table and made his move.

***

56.

Three days' march led the Egyptian army to the reed huts of the Shasu tribe. Pitching their tents out of range, high up on an escarpment, the generals met in the royal tent to discuss their strategy. Manservants deposited food and drinks on large trestles. Due to the secrecy of their talks, most of the serving staff were then dismissed.

Ahmose opened the meeting.

"How do the enemy feed their livestock? I see nothing but sand!"

Paneb crunched a pastry.

"The problem for us is that the nomads hide in those dunes."

Dhey sipped pomegranate juice.

"You're right. We have to be careful. Our strategy is to attack the visible houses."

"Provided we can reach them, Your Majesty."

"We outnumber the Shasu, General Paneb."

"Your Majesty, with respect, my esteemed comrade is right. We don't know the terrain."

"Then, I will send scouts, General Ahmose. We attack before dawn."

"Why not at the usual ninth hour of the morning, Your Majesty?"

"They're shepherds. They'll be awake at dawn."

Paneb frowned.

"General Ahmose might be right, Your Highness. During the day, they will be outside grazing their flocks. It will make it easier to attack their homes."

"And raze them to the ground," Ahmose added.

"We need to kill a few," Senefer chuckled.

"A great idea!"

Taking a fat olive, he popped it between his thick lips. Dhey glared at him.

"We fight at dawn. Take prisoners and sheep. We'll need fresh meat for Syria."

"Pardon me, Your Majesty. Do we really want to be loaded down with prisoners?"

"When we attack, aim for the chieftain, General Paneb. Take him prisoner. Don't burn the huts. Capture half a dozen shepherds and their flocks. Leave the rest."

"I don't like it."

"Why, General Senefer?"

"Hostage shepherds can be a danger. If they make a deal with the Syrians, it could go badly for us."

Dhey was amused.

"Do you think we will lose, Senefer? If they defect, we'll recapture them when we thrash Syria."

Breaking up the meeting, the generals retired to their tents. There they whiled away the daylight hours with their colleagues. Towards dusk, they met with their soldiers. Campfires were lit to cook food, and doused immediately afterwards. Positioned behind a wall of shields, which acted as a fence, the Egyptian army was invisible to the enemy.

After dinner, the men went to bed. Watchmen sat outside. Wrapped in blankets, they tried not to fall asleep in the cold.

***

57

Mere awoke earlier than usual. Everything was eerily still. He thought he heard voices in the mountains. It was not the first time that week. Going outside, he milked the goats. Putting one pail on his kitchen bench, he left the rest outside for the villagers in exchange for onions, dried meat, and fish.

Inside his kitchen, Mere poured the milk into a wooden cup. After his drink, he placed the cup in his satchel with his lunch, which consisted of a loaf of bread and cheese. He paused for a moment. Then he decided to pack a slab of dried meat and several onions. Draping the satchel over his neck and shoulders, the shepherd guided his flock out of the gates in the opposite direction of the voices.

***

In the Egyptian camp, Dhey's dressers armed their king for combat. It was morning and still dark. Outside, swords and shields clanked as men prepared for battle. Infantry, archers, and spearmen were organised into groups.

Dhey climbed into a waiting chariot.

"It's a wonder they haven't heard us," he said to his charioteer.

Flicking the reins, his driver steered the way down a rocky hillside to the lines of silent troops. The sun rose. Dhey's chariot trundled out from behind the mountain, where they were stationed, and moved to an escarpment. He raised one hand to give the signal.

"Stop, Your Majesty!"

General Senefer stood before the king.

"What's wrong?"

"I wish the Hawk of Ra victory."

He knelt in front of the chariot.

"I'd rather you got out of my way, General."

"As a representative of the king's elite corps, I have been asked to remind His Majesty that only his men will make the descent today."

"I'm not going to fight?"

"You will inspire your men from above as the divine Horus of Upper and Lower Egypt."

Dhey flushed purple.

"You might have told me that last night!"

Senefer put one hand to his chest and bowed his head. Backing away in deference to his monarch, he turned on his heel to join his battalion. Dhey raised his arm. On seeing the signal, Egyptian troops raced down the mountainside. Uttering bloodcurdling battle cries, they poured into the valley below.

In furious silence, Dhey stood in his chariot, next to his driver. Holding the gilded wooden rails, his knuckles turned white.

***

58.

Mere heard a commotion in the valley. He responded by driving his herds further into the hills. At midday, he milked a goat and drank from his wooden cup. Opening his satchel, he took out his bread and cheese. Carefully pulling off a quarter of the loaf, he then broke the cheese into crumbly portions so it would go further. He chose the shade of a boulder which lay behind a row of wild acacia trees. Then he settled down for a nap.

Meanwhile, in front of Mere's empty house, a horde of Egyptian soldiers ran past. Screaming women picked up their children, and fled inside their homes. The soldiers did not follow. Instead, they rushed in the direction of reed walls which surrounded the Shasu chieftain's hut. It was situated in a compound with a group of smaller huts for his wives. Tribal guards tried to resist the Egyptian army but were hacked to pieces.

Ahmose and Paneb leapt down from their chariots and advanced towards the chief's hut. An arrow whizzed through the air. Ahmose ducked behind a tree. Several more arrows flew. One grazed Paneb's shoulder, and he fell to the ground. Suddenly, he was surrounded by his men, who pulled him to safety. Then they rushed into the hut. In a few moments, the chieftain was pulled off his ornate chair and dragged into the compound.

Senefer now approached the grizzled, middle-aged leader. He motioned to the Egyptian soldiers.

"Leave him!" Immediately, his men unhanded the chieftain. "As you can see, the divine ruler of Egypt has heard of your rebellion."

"We are a small village, General."

"Sand dwellers have many homes, most of which are not seen."

"I assure you, Great One, our influence is limited."

Mollified by the man's manner, Senefer twisted round to see Ahmose and the bandaged Paneb moving towards them. He raised his hand to halt their progress and turned back to the chief.

"Come with me. Pharaoh requests your audience. You will not be harmed."

***

It was dusk. Goats bleated, knowing it was time to return home. The sheep continued to graze. Mere scouted the land for water. He noticed a cleft in the hills where a stream ran through. Barely a trickle, he followed its path. Clambering over a rocky incline, he came to a pond in a ravine where his goats and sheep could drink. Mere returned to the animals and herded them down into the ravine towards the water. Building a fire, he kept vigil over his flock.

From his hilltop, Dhey espied some of his army returning to base. He recognised Ahmose and Paneb. A chariot containing a man in a long robe, trundled between the two. His arms were bound. Dhey guessed it was the captured chieftain. Eventually, they drew up to him. Ahmose was the first to speak.

"The Chief of Shasu bows before you."

The captive was placed on his knees. Soldiers tipped him forward to bow on the rocks.

"Untie him, General Ahmose," said Dhey. He focussed on the foreign leader. "Fortunately for you, I am in a benevolent mood. No one will be harmed so long as you promise there will be no more rebellion. We also demand annual tribute from the Shasu."

"Pardon me, Your Majesty, but we are a poor people."

"Can you believe this dog's rudeness?" Paneb snapped. He turned to the foreign chieftain. "You will be whipped for your impertinence."

Dhey ignored his general and continued to speak with the tribal leader.

"You are famed for your colourful woollen cloth and musical instruments. A contribution of such wares would be appreciated by my country."

"Not to mention turquoise," Ahmose added.

120

"Sinai is full of turquoise, Your Majesty," the chieftain said. "But it is already mined by Egypt."

Senefer pulled up in his chariot. His face was red with rage.

"I requested the chieftain come with me, Your Majesty. Instead, these two ruffians trussed him up like a villain and took him away."

"I've asked him to be untied." Dhey turned to the Shasu chief. "We also require ten shepherds and fifty sheep for the foray into Syria. We will replace your sheep and return your shepherds when we come back this way."

The man bowed his head.

"Do we take him back, Your Majesty?" Paneb asked.

"You are not going to take him anywhere! Senefer will ensure our guest is bathed and brought to my tent to dine with me. Return to the village with a detachment of soldiers. Bring back this man's wife and children, and leave the soldiers to guard the village. The Shasu will be less likely to counter-attack while we have their leader."

***

Dawn broke under the eastern cliffs where Mere and his flock hid. It was the third day, and he had run out of provisions. Instinctively, he knew it was time to return home.

Meanwhile, in his tent, Dhey awoke bleary-eyed from a bad dream. His foot soldiers had been giving advice! Dressing quickly, he made his way to the communal tent. Several generals prostrated themselves. Ahmose was the first to rise.

"Where are the chief and his family?"

"Still in bed, Your Highness."

"Awaken them. It is time for our guests to return home."

Dhey left the communal tent. Outside, he met General Paneb.

"You have accomplished a great victory, Your Majesty."

"No thanks to you, the chieftain will be a strong ally of Egypt."

Putting his nose in the air, Dhey walked back to his tent.

***

Taking a deep breath, Mere rounded the hill through which he had first led his flock. Below, in the valley, the huts of his village still stood intact. Women pounded millet and cooked bread in the ovens. Children played in the surrounding sand dunes. He hurried his flock down the hillside. When he was at the main fence, he slowed down, and drove his sheep and goats through with an air of nonchalance. People waved to him from their doorways, and continued with their work.

A tavern owner emptied slops into a gutter.

"Where have you been, Mere?"

"Grazing. There's good pasture in the hills."

"You missed the Egyptians."

"When?"

"Three nights ago. They took our chief prisoner but released him when he promised tribute. Took a few flocks and shepherds, too."

Mere hurried home where he fed and watered his flock. After breakfast, he baked a barley cake and offered it to the gods.

***

Trekking down the steep mountain, Dhey gripped the rails of his chariot. His driver trundled over baking rocks as slowly as possible to avoid an accident. In front, two battalions of troops marched. Behind, there were two more, including the baggage train.

Ahmose, who was riding in the first battalion, cocked his head to the left. He turned to an adjutant.

"Do you hear that?"

"I *see* it, sir."

A dust ball billowed towards them from a great distance.

"Stop the troops!"

The adjutant scurried away to do Ahmose's bidding. Soon, the Egyptian army halted under the blazing midday sun. A hot wind blew into Dhey's face. He picked up his composite bow. Light in weight, it was made of wood, horn, and layers of sinew. It was also superior to any bow in the world.

"Proceed to the front," Dhey ordered his charioteer.

Immediately, the man picked up the reins and urged the horses forward. They shook their manes, grateful for a slight breeze as they jogged along. Filing past the troops had the desired effect. Dhey felt the men's hearts lift. At the front, General Paneb was watching, grim-faced. Dhey noticed the approaching dust storm.

"I hear voices, General."

"I see horses, Your Majesty."

"What do you suggest?"

"We have the advantage of high ground. I suggest we wait until they get nearer. Then we can assess the situation."

"A good idea."

Ahmose walked up to the pair.

"Are we attacking, Your Majesty?"

"I want to assess the numbers first."

"Our king should return to the middle of the cavalry."

Dhey gripped his bow.

"I'm not going anywhere."

Squinting in the searing sunlight, Pharaoh watched the approaching dust ball. Soon, the nebulous ball grew arms and legs. Fierce foot soldiers rushed across the open plain, followed by chariots.

Calculating the distance, Dhey raised his bow to his shoulder. Before the generals could say anything, he let fly three arrows in quick succession. Enemies fell. The Egyptian infantry cheered.

Urging on his charioteer, the king charged into the valley below. His army followed suit.

So, this is what it's like!

The wind blew Dhey's hair back. He was alone, galloping across the plain, with no one in front, and the enemy still a distance away. Now he felt like Pharaoh. Like his ancestors before him, the wind of victory blew wildly under his sweat-filled helmet. Finally, Dhey could join the ranks of Sekenre-Tao, Ahmose, and his own father, the great Tuthmosis. Raising his mighty bow, the king let fly a volley. To his surprise, men fell. Emptying his quiver, he felt his chariot wheels spin through dust and blood.

Driving his chariot as hard as he could, General Paneb finally caught up with the lone king.

"Truly, Your Majesty fights like Horus," he gasped.

Part of the army broke away from the main group to protect their sovereign from the enemy's front line. Choking in the dust, Dhey motioned to his driver.

"Slow down!"

Patiently, the pair waited for the army to catch up. Hundreds of soldiers and chariots passed them and closed ranks. Stacking his bow carefully in one corner, Dhey drew a short sword. The Egyptian army formed a protective buffer around him.

Once their king was protected, several Egyptian military units fanned out to surround the Syrians. Occasionally, enemy soldiers broke the Egyptian ranks to attack. Distinguished by their beards and coiffed black hair, they were easy to target.

A chariot charged the king's right. Its rider catapulted out of the carriage, over the heads of the Egyptians. Dhey lifted his sword in readiness, but the man crashed to the ground, where he was immediately set upon by Egyptian soldiers.

The battle lasted until late afternoon, with the enemy warriors routed or taken prisoner. Dhey sheathed his sword. While he had not used it, his ability with the bow had shown a power, which his men interpreted as divine. He was now in a position of respect. The story would be told around campfires for generations to come.

***

61

Weighed down with prisoners and booty, the Egyptian army progressed along the same route it had come a few weeks ago. Riding jauntily along, without his charioteer, Dhey led his troops.

At the water stops dotting the route, soldiers dug up jars which had been strategically placed by their countrymen in anticipation of their return. It was a common tactic of the Egyptians to ensure supplies of water were available for their army on desert routes where there were few wells. Along the way, the generals also decided to take the opportunity to consult with one another.

One morning, General Ahmose confronted the king.

"Your Highness, why don't you head your battalion instead of the entire army? You would be safe in the middle, with your Amun division."

"Then I would not be Pharaoh."

"It's not a title you can lose. But you risk your life at the front, sire."

"My father led from the front."

"But –"

"Tuthmosis was a great general, is what you want to say. However, I am his legitimate son."

"What you need to know, Your Highness, is that there is another Syrian army waiting for us, up ahead."

"How is that possible?"

"We're still on their territory, mighty Pharaoh."

"Are they stupid enough to encounter us after our horses are fed and watered?"

Soldiers in earshot snickered. The king's comments were relayed down the ranks. Cheering began, sporadically at first, before turning into waves. Soon, the camp was filled with noise. Ahmose paled.

Making a shallow bow, he retreated to the group of generals.

Following the example of his father, Dhey headed the Amun unit. However, it was positioned at the front of the army. Not seeing any other units before them, his steeds started to baulk. One stallion reared. The king jerked the reins back. His horse's forelegs returned to earth.

"Good boy, Geb!"

The other stallion nibbled his brother's ear. Both were bred from Syrian steeds which were imported during the campaigns of Tuthmosis. Now, they were on their home soil for the first time. It was a good omen.

A silver-plated chariot trotted up to the team. Halting before Dhey's nervous steeds, a man leapt out of his cart and bowed before him.

"Hail, Your Majesty! We are about to descend into the valley below."

"My understanding is that I will be leading from the front."

"Your *battalion* will be, sire."

Without waiting for a reply, the messenger turned his chariot around and headed back to his own battalion.

"The generals are sending messengers to do their dirty work," Dhey muttered.

A citadel lay below. The king's heart sank. It was a fort not recorded on Egyptian maps. Ranks of Syrians were amassed on the battlefield in the morning light. He would be dead in minutes.

Dhey pulled back on the reins. He took a deep breath.

***

A flood of Pharaoh's chariots appeared to fall from the sky as they swept down the hills. Tufts of green flew from the horses' hooves. Dust swirled up, choking and blinding the charioteers. In the valley, they clashed with the Syrians. Horses whinnied in terror. Chariot wheels broke off their carts, and flew in all directions, causing injuries. Vultures circled lazily overhead.

Bearded men in long Syrian robes fought Egyptian foot soldiers in short kilts. Locked in hand- to-hand combat, the Egyptians had the advantage through weaponry. Short kilts meant there was more leg on which to inflict wounds, but the speed and slice of the Egyptian sword usually meant their Syrian opponents had no time in which to disable the enemy. Dhey stayed on his hilltop in his chariot, inspiring his troops as the incarnation of the god Horus.

In an hour, it was over. Defeated, the Syrians fled towards their city, which was blocked by Egyptians. At the gates, they were hacked to pieces or taken prisoner.

A general from the Horus battalion approached the king. It was Dhey's cue. Descending into the valley, he made his way at an even pace to give his horses time to negotiate rocks and spare them from injury.

On the valley floor, the carnage was complete. Carrion birds pulled at carcasses, feasting on gory entrails. The smell was indescribable. Trying not to choke, Dhey made his way to where the prisoners stood.

Presenting him with the chief of the citadel, General Ahmose made the latter prostrate before Dhey seven times, his face in the dust. When the man rose, his beard was white.

"The King of Egypt accepts your surrender."

Shouts of joy erupted from the Egyptian troops. Deafened, Dhey stood still. He displayed the appropriate amount of haughty grandeur, expected of a mighty king and warrior.

Finally, the city gates opened, and the Syrian chief accompanied his Egyptian captors inside to collect war booty. For safety reasons, Dhey remained outside. His men set up a makeshift camp while they kept a watchful eye out for potential Syrian armies.

Vultures hopped past, their feathers covered in blood.

***

62.

Waiting in the cold dawn for her husband, Hatshepsut tried not to shiver. Hundreds of eyes were fixed on her. Wearing the formal attire of Egypt's Great Wife, she was stiff and self-conscious. Her crown felt crooked. So did the pendant on her breast. Surrounded by palace security, she discreetly checked her regalia. Everything was in place.

Idly glancing at the courtiers, Hatshepsut's eyes picked out Lord Senenmut. Standing with the others, he was lost in thought. One of the few not gazing at the beautiful consort of Tuthmosis- the-Second, Djehutymes, Lord of Upper and Lower Egypt, he must have been thinking about his work. Irritated, she turned away.

Suddenly, the crowds in the street started to cheer. Horses clopped along the pavements. Taking a breath, Hatshepsut straightened her back. At a sign from the Royal Fanbearer, she rose. Now the cheering was deafening. It soared into the blue where hawks circled. The significance was not lost on the superstitious masses, who cheered more loudly. Musicians struck up their lyres and beat drums. Dancers whirled through the streets. Butchers hurried to the open-air ovens with haunches of beef. Vegetables and fruit were piled onto tables extending from the main Karnak temple to the palace. The smell of warm bread filled the air as thousands of loaves were baked.

At last, she saw him. Clad in armour, confidently leading his troops, Dhey drove his chariot down the main street. His horses wore feathers in their headgear. Their saddles were embroidered with red thread. New harnesses jangled pleasantly with their solid gold rosettes. The king rode up to the dais where Hatshepsut waited. They rubbed noses in an affectionate greeting. The crowd roared. It was time to go inside the palace.

***

The royal couple retired to Dhey's apartment for a rest before lunch. In the bathroom, a dresser removed the king's parade clothes. He

129

stepped into a cubicle. Servants poured water over his body, after which he was lightly scrubbed. Then, the royal limbs were oiled and scented. Afterwards, a linen robe was draped around him by his dresser.

Finally, Dhey entered the living room where his wife waited with a cup of beer, specially brewed for her husband's homecoming.

"You look different, my husband."

"And you are beautiful."

"How was the front?"

"Exhilarating."

"Which means you're going to ply the trade of a warrior king."

"I've proved a point."

"No more battles?"

"Only if necessary. It was hard to lead the army. The generals took convincing."

"Egypt is ruled by the army, Dhey."

"You make a good point." The king downed his beer, and pushed open the door that led to the patio. A fresh breeze blew in from the river. "I missed our garden."

"And me, I hope."

"Every day."

Putting his arm around Hatshepsut's waist, Dhey kissed her.

"I find that hard to believe."

"Why?"

"Your heart belongs to Iset."

"She's dead."

"It makes no difference in matters of the heart."

Unwinding his arm from Hatshepsut's waist, Dhey led her into the garden, along one of the tree-lined paths. They sat on a wooden bench. He drew her down next to him. Positioned in an arbour covered with grape vines, the seat gave shelter from the sun, while it also caught the Nile breezes. Dhey pressed his back into a painted mud-brick wall.

"Is there someone, Hattie?"

"As Great Wife, it is my duty to be faithful."

"I want you to be happy. If you change your mind, let me know."

"It's nearly time to join the celebrations."

Hatshepsut rose. Her husband followed her lead. Taking her hand, Dhey led her out of the garden. They made their way back to the palace, and to the banqueting hall.

***

63.

Pouring hot beans from a cooking pot into two bowls, Kitane pushed one towards her daughter. Her husband, Nashuja, was already at work in his studio.

"Is Dhey back, Kalma?"

"You mean our Pharaoh."

"I was his wife's nanny. Allow me a little familiarity, darling."

"But we're not their family, are we?"

"We're part of the royal household of Egypt."

"As servants."

"What's got into you? Hattie is your childhood friend."

"I'd like to get married and start my own family."

"If there's someone at the royal court, please let your father and me know. Or would you prefer an arranged marriage in Crete?"

"I'll never go back to that place."

"Why not?"

"I hate that island!"

"You're always babbling about it to Hattie."

"I feel obliged to impress her. Egyptians think they're the only civilised beings on earth."

"Is there anyone at court?"

"Not yet."

"Then I shall pray to the great Mother Earth goddess."

"I attend the grove ceremonies."

"Boyfriends aren't husbands."

"What boyfriends? I like to dance!"

Clearing the bowls, Kitane put out fish soup. Afterwards, she cleaned the dishes in a ceramic basin. Kalma joined her father in his studio. Outside, Egypt's street festival continued for several days. Plentiful food from an excellent harvest boded well for the king who had brought Egypt's victorious army home.

***

64.

Kalma threw herself into the comfort of Hatshepsut's settee. The queen was playing with her daughter.

"You must be pleased Dhey is safe at home again."

"I'm happy about the successful military campaign. My husband's reign is secure."

Dandling Neferure on her knee, Hatshepsut kissed her plump, red cheeks. The child gurgled and tugged at her mother's gold necklace.

"I saw Lord Senenmut, Hattie."

"When?"

"Yesterday, at Useramen's house."

"How is Mister Miau-Miau?"

"Fat as ever."

"I've always liked that cat. He shows the greatest contempt for his master."

"I don't know why. Useramen gives him the best meat and fish. Pays me well, too. By the way, Lord Senenmut is designing a new wing of their house."

"But he's our royal architect!"

"Surely, it's not forbidden to engage in extra work?"

"It's not against the law," Hatshepsut sniffed. "But it's highly irregular."

"Any extra work with the courtiers bonds our favourite architect with them. It could be useful for palace intelligence. Anyway, he speaks very highly of you."

Hatshepsut's cheeks became as red as her daughter's.

"Is that a fact?"

"He expounds on your virtues. It's all I can do to get away! Fortunately, your architect is building at the opposite end of Useramen's house to me, otherwise I'd never get any work done."

"It's appropriate for a servant to extol his mistress' virtues. Canny, too."

"What do you mean?"

"He knows we're friends."

"His praises are genuine, Hattie. He likes you."

Hatshepsut rose.

"Help me walk Nef to the nursery. I have court this afternoon. You may join me if you like."

"I have a dance rehearsal. Mother is cooking goat stew tonight. You should come."

Hatshepsut bit back a hasty reply. It was no longer appropriate to dine with commoners. The last time was a disaster. Kitane dropped the main dish on the kitchen tiles. Her husband barely spoke a word. Shuddering at the memory, Hatshepsut farewelled her daughter at the nursery. Then she turned to Kalma.

"Drop in for a cup of wine after your rehearsal."

***

65.

Dhey stared out of his office window. His harem was now stocked with Syrian brides. Two more were arriving at the palace from Mitanni next month.

Hatshepsut stood at his door.

"Do you mind if I join you?"

"You're always welcome."

The Great Wife allowed herself to be seated by an attendant.

"I visited Thutmose."

"How is the little chap?"

"Speaking his first words. Have you heard him talk, yet?"

"Since my return, I see him every night."

"That would be why his words are 'Daddy' and 'love'."

"It's 'Kalma' and 'miau' when I'm there!"

"Our friend still paints frescoes for Mister Miau-Miau's master."

"I've heard our vizier's house resembles a Cretan villa more than an Egyptian home."

"Useramen married a girl from Crete last summer. His second wife."

"I didn't know."

"Which reminds me, the Mitannians arrive soon."

"Wedding preparations are under way."

Dhey drummed his fingers on his desk.

"Is there something wrong?"

"Don't you ever wish we led normal lives, Hattie?"

"We *are* leading normal lives. Please, at least make a show of happiness on your wedding day. You know what the Mitannian ambassadors are like."

"I'll try. Now, if you'll excuse me, I need to rest."

Hatshepsut left the office. Her husband was tiring more easily of late than she remembered.

***

66.

The temple of Karnak was home. As a child, Hatshepsut remembered her father taking her by the hand to visit the inner sanctum. Its darkness housed a tiny statue of the god. It had always filled her with reassurance that Amun was as small as one of her dolls. Now, she was the God's Wife and High Priestess of Amun.

Taking a deep breath, she crossed the threshold guarded by gilded doors. Hatshepsut remembered watching her father make the first brick for his section of the temple. Straw and mud in a mould was all it took. It looked like the wonderful mud sculptures she and her brothers made in the back garden by the fishpond. Her deep desire then had been to confiscate a brick mould and take it home, where they could dig the rich black earth of Egypt, and mix in a little Nile water. To Hatshepsut, the gods were intrinsic to her life. Dhey said she was a non-believer, but to her Amun was part of the family.

An acolyte approached and prostrated himself.

"The Chief Priest is waiting, Your Majesty."

Hapuseneb had just finished dinner. It was obvious from a piece of shredded duck stuck between his upper teeth. On seeing her, he beckoned with hands covered in gold rings.

"Come in, Your Majesty! I just ate. First thing since breakfast. You know how it is."

"One's day can be full."

"You don't feel the strain, do you, my child?"

"As our king's chief wife, I'm expected to be at our nation's helm."

"Nautical terms suit you. Shall we go stargazing?"

Hapuseneb bustled about. An acolyte fetched his cape and staff. Then, he and his visitor climbed the narrow staircase to the temple roof. From there they viewed the vast lands of Karnak sprawled below. Over sixty acres of land, with livestock and produce, belonged to the priests.

Hatshepsut turned to her host.

136

"One day this will be filled with hundreds of kings' temples."

"Glory be to Amun," he intoned piously.

"I wonder where the cattle and fields will go."

"We'll get more land." Hapuseneb found the North Star. "Look, Your Majesty, you can see the heavens predict the harvest season of Shemu in a few days!"

They gazed into the inky vault, dotted by trillions of stars.

"My husband and I intend to rule Egypt for many years. In the last few weeks, he has not been well."

"War wounds?"

"Malaria."

"The temple will redouble its prayers."

For some time, the priest and royal watched the stars in silence. Then, they picked out their favourites, naming them with ease. Afterwards, they recited a prayer and burned incense.

Finishing a small flagon of berry juice together, they praised Amun for his grace and benefits, after which the Great Wife departed the hallowed precincts for her home.

***

67.

Hatshepsut watched the gasping man writhing on sodden bedsheets. He was sallow, and it took several moments for him to recognise her.

"Is it time for court?"

"You have a fever, Dhey. I'll make an appearance. Stay here and get well."

Attendants struggled to keep the king in bed. Flailing his arms about, he tried to get up but was gently pushed back. Hatshepsut made her way to the Great Hall, where she took her throne. Whispering a few words to Useramen, she listened to a request from the first ambassador.

At noon, she retired to her apartments. Drinking a cup of pomegranate juice, Hatshepsut watched the Nile. Deciding she needed a change of scenery, she went outside to the fishpond. It was where Dhey loved to spend his leisure time. Set among trees and flower beds, it was filled with fat fish. On the pool floor were decorations of aquatic life and plants. It was easy to see to the bottom, and even easier to catch the fish as they darted through strands of algae and rocks.

When she arrived, Hatshepsut was surprised to see a man. He rose from the polished granite bench by the pond. Dressed in courtly robes, he bowed low.

"Lord Senenmut?"

"I trust Your Majesty does not mind. I come here after court to refresh my mind."

"You've chosen the right place. I often come here to think."

They watched a fat perch gulp water. It surveyed them for a moment and then slipped between two rocks.

"Is the king resting today, Your Majesty?"

"He's ill."

"Soldiers always have malaria after a campaign."

"My husband's a king, not a common soldier."

"You may remember your father, the mighty Tuthmosis, often returned from war with malaria. It was common for him to take a week off."

"I don't recall him ever being sick after a campaign."

"Probably because you were a child. My father told me about it." Senenmut gathered his white robes around him. "I trust you will be encouraged. It's time I left. There is work to do."

Sun gleamed on the royal architect's plaited wig, and his immaculate robes seemed to glow as he walked the lonely footpath to his office.

***

Puffing, Kalma paused at Hatshepsut's door. Taking a few deep breaths, she calmed herself.

Once composed, she allowed a sentry to announce her arrival.

"I came as quick as I could. How's Dhey?"

"I've been attending to the affairs of state, Kalma."

"Has he malaria?"

"He was delirious this morning."

"Is there anything I can do?"

"It's the normal result of military campaigns. There's nothing to do but wait."

"My mother told me your late father always contracted it after campaigning in Nubia."

"So I hear."

An ebony gaming board sat by the window. Kalma coiled her hair into a business-like bun.

"Let's play *senet*."

"An excellent idea. Winning always puts me in a good frame of mind."

"Be warned, Hattie, I've been practising!"

***

68.

In the Great Audience Hall, international envoys stated their business. Viziers weighed their words carefully before advising Hatshepsut. Scribes wrote screeds of notes. It was as if the court was accustomed to a lone queen acting on behalf of Egypt. Ambassadors from Mitanni waited patiently until late morning. At noon, they retired to their visitors' quarters.

There was no afternoon court session while the king was ill. His weary consort ate in a room set aside for her personal dining. Consuming a mash of cooked vegetables, followed by fruit, she replenished her energy lost during the morning.

While most palace staff enjoyed a nap, Hatshepsut summoned Kalma to play board games.

"I hear the Mitannian brides arrived, Hattie."

"Their ambassadors came this morning."

"Isn't Dhey supposed to marry the women next week?"

Hatshepsut moved her piece onto a water square. Swiping it, Kalma placed it neatly in a row, forming to her right.

"You realise, Kalma, you are obliged to lose to a queen of Egypt? I am also Great Wife which makes me chief queen."

"Not today!"

"Before I call for the executioner, explain yourself."

"You're King at present."

"Even more reason to lose to me!"

"At court you are the sole sovereign, but here we are simply friends."

Hatshepsut sipped her wine. A gleeful Kalma picked another piece for her collection. Outside the window, Senenmut appeared, walking down the winding path to the river. He was deep in thought. Hatshepsut put down her drink.

"You win, Kalma. It's time I did something else."

***

140

Twelve days passed. One morning, Hatshepsut applied thick makeup to her face to conceal her eyes, which were ringed by lack of sleep and worry. Up before the servants, she donned a simple shift, and slipped out of her apartment. At a discreet distance, a guard trailed her to ensure her safety.

Hurrying to her husband's bedchamber, she pushed past the royal physician. Dhey's face was waxen. Eyes closed, he barely breathed.

"Is he dead?"

"Soon Horus will reunite with his father, Your Majesty."

"I finish court at the second hour of the afternoon. Update me afterwards."

***

Seated on a low wall, the solitary figure gazed into space. She spotted him immediately.

"I find you in the gardens again, Lord Senenmut."

"My work is done for the day, Your Highness."

"So is mine."

"May I ask how the king is faring?"

"You may ask."

The queen joined her courtier on the wall. Aware of the guards rustling in the bushes, she ensured there was an appropriate space between them. Senenmut waited for the answer, which did not come.

"I enjoy the garden at this time, Your Majesty. It gives me peace."

"Dhey is already dead."

Senenmut froze. He collected himself quickly.

"My deepest condolences."

"I asked our doctor to delay his report until after the second court session. There is no such session, of course. I wanted time alone."

Palms undulated gently in the afternoon breeze. A loud sigh of a hippopotamus in the shallows broke the stillness.

***

70

A leaden pall enveloped Hatshepsut. Since childhood, she had been groomed to be a royal wife. Now she was suddenly the Dowager Queen of Egypt, after being the Great Royal Wife of the Living Horus. Many kings died before their consorts. It was expected. Still, the end had come too soon. Light knocking broke her reverie. A guard stood in the doorway with Kalma.

"I thought a personal visit was in order, Hattie. If it's not appropriate, I can leave."

"Don't be silly. I'm pleased you're here."

Offering her a seat, Hatshepsut nodded to her maidservant. Figs, apricots, and macadamia nuts soon accompanied a pitcher of fruit-flavoured beer, silver tongs, and two cups.

"I don't know what to do, Kalma."

"Surely, your advisers know the next step."

"There is only one royal male left."

"Your nephew, Thutmose."

"Aged three!"

"At least there is a male heir."

"The gods were sparing in their gift."

"Be thankful, Hattie."

Hatshepsut banged a macadamia nut on her side table. It would not break. Kalma picked up the silver tongs. Skilfully enclosing the nut in its jaws, she crushed it with ease.

Hatshepsut grunted thanks. She chewed in silence for some moments.

"I couldn't give my husband a son, but a concubine did."

"You are feeling sorry for yourself!"

"It's not that. I have guardianship of the new king, but I'm not his mother. I can't be co-regent and step aside when Thutmose grows up."

"You're not only Dowager Queen, but the God's Wife. Order the priests to lean on the courtiers if they give you trouble."

"Kalma, you're brilliant!"

"I know! I won the first set. Another game?"

***

71

An orange sun smote the western hills of Thebes. Flocks of ibis flew up from the marshes. Silhouetted against the pale sky, they flapped away on black wings. After seventy days at the House of Eternity, the King of Upper and Lower Egypt, Djehutymes was laid to rest in a tomb on the western bank of the Nile.

Spending time with close friends eased the worry of the monarchy for Hatshepsut. Time with Neferure took her away from her troubles. Kalma accompanied her on daily walks.

One afternoon, as the women went barefoot through the garden, a lithe cat flitted past. Darting in and out of the shrubs, he upset several bird families. Finally tiring of his antics, the birds roosted in the highest trees while the playful cat went to watch fish at the Nile's edge.

The women found two garden seats in an arbour.

"Have you eaten, Hattie?"

"At the funeral."

"That was days ago!"

"I'll eat when I'm hungry."

They stared across the water. Hatshepsut never tired of the Nile. Glinting at the end of the day, it rose and fell like the sigh of her soul. The responsibility of Egypt had fallen squarely at her feet. Deep panic was interspersed with moments of strength, and all against a background of profound grief.

"Did you love him?"

"Who?"

"Dhey."

"We had to marry."

"And Lord Sen?"

"You go too far!"

"Someone has to point out the obvious."

"Which is?"

"It's time you shared your life with someone you love."

"I'm a widow in mourning."

"You're a woman who is going to rule."

"Don't frighten me."

"You were born for this role. Your father groomed you."

Kalma picked up a stone and threw it in the Nile. It splashed loudly, scattering drops in the heat-laden air.

"Stop that!"

"Don't be vexed. You've lost your sense of humour, of late."

"I'm drenched!"

"You need to lighten up. It's a long road ahead."

"The Chief Priest said something strange this afternoon."

"Do tell."

"It was more what he did not say."

"You'll be in charge of our country for at least a decade. You're still young. The only way you'll survive is to have a bit of fun. I would have a drink with Lord Senenmut."

Hatshepsut gazed at the sun melting over the palm trees. Soon their trunks would become walls of shadows.

The striped cat trotted up to sit at their feet.

***

72.

Night enveloped Thebes. Slipping past the kitchens, Hatshepsut hurried through the palace gardens. Up ahead lay a fork in the path. She took the lane leading to Kalma's house. Rapping on a door, she was let through the servants' quarters. An unruffled butler admitted her into Kalma's studio.

The artist paused in her brushwork.

"Any progress with the fate of the throne?"

"There will be. Why are you working so late?"

"I have a commission."

"Don't we pay you enough?"

"Not ten talents for a single job!"

"Are you designing murals for a house?"

Kalma returned to the painting.

"For a nobleman's villa. Let's face it, you couldn't afford me."

"I arranged work for you at the Delta palace."

"Things change. I did the preliminary sketches. What does Thutmose think?"

"I – we – haven't seen them, yet. I do speak for the both of us."

"You are co-regent?"

"Adviser."

"You must know I paint in the Cretan style, which does not include depicting royal personages."

"I – we – hadn't thought of that."

"If you and Thutmose are happy with bull leapers and designs, I'm happy to accept a commission. The sketches were filed with the palace studio last week. You may review them."

"They're approved. I'll buy him a rattle."

Hatshepsut poured herself a cup of wine from a jug sitting on the studio bench. Kalma shot her a peculiar look.

"Apart from you, who is speaking for Thutmose, Hattie?"

"It would be better to ask who is not speaking for him."

"You should have a word with the High Priest."

"I did."

"Is that why you're sneaking past my window at the dead of night?"

"I don't want palace officials to know I've consulted with Karnak."

"Karnak isn't the Crown. Its power is limited."

"I assure you, Kalma, the power of the priests knows no limits."

The artist wrapped an embroidered shawl around her shoulders.

"A poppy dance in the groves wouldn't hurt."

"How is that supposed to solve my worries?"

Kalma walked to an alcove where she opened a chest. Rummaging about, she produced a solid gold vial which contained the poppy mixture reserved for sacred Cretan rituals.

"Do you feel like a dance?"

***

73

The sun dial struck noon in the courtyard. Below, peasant children rowed skiffs down the Nile, their sunburned backs splashed with gleaming water drops. High up the riverbank, palace children squealed with delight in courtyard pools. There, they dived for fish, which slid into the safety of lotuses and landscaped papyrus thickets.

Little Tutty waded ankle deep through lotus lilies. His face was scrunched up as he studied the mosaic patterns under his stubby feet. Recognising much of the aquatic life from his fishing forays, he counted the painted fins and scales. Kneeling in the water, he traced a pudgy finger over the black outline of a Nile perch. Then, shading his eyes, he stared up at the sun. Odd, how everyone worshipped the sun, the boy thought. It could blind and kill. His nanny barked a warning from the pool's edge. Tutty stopped staring at the glowing orb. Further out in the Nile, he could hear peasant boys as they splashed and played. He wished he could join them.

In the shallows, laundrymen gossiped while they beat soiled linen into glistening white. Women carried water up from the river to their homes. Everyone watched for stray crocodiles. Sometimes an errant hippo blundered onto the muddy banks, causing blind panic. However, most of the time, the larger life forms lived further down from any human settlement.

Several marshy islands devoid of humans, had large populations of hippopotami. Crocodiles with open mouths, basked on the banks. Sometimes, when they spotted prey, they moved remarkably fast, their ancient dinosaur bodies slithering at high speed down the slippery embankments. It was rare for anything to make an escape from a crocodile. The hippopotamus was the prince's favourite wild animal, but hippos could also be dangerous and took fierce exception to humans who dared interfere with their supremacy. While they stayed downstream, it was always a good idea to check. Laundrymen had been lost, together with an occasional child.

As much as Tutty loved hippos, he attended the Royal Junior Military School, where no cadet was encouraged to look like one. Boys were trained out of their puppy fat from an early age. Meat was almost non-existent in the school dining hall. However, Tutty proved himself an adept lawyer. One day, when he was served vegetables for lunch, he argued for meat rations. With the brilliance of desperation, the prince pointed out that hippopotami, with their enormous size, were vegetarian. With his chubby cheeks and wide girth, he maintained, patting his belly, he could use a strict diet. From that time on, he was always allowed his own food, which included meat and the odd sweet, tucked into his snack box by his doting nanny.

Now, as the child climbed out of the pool, he reflected that as much as he liked animals, and was fascinated by the variety of their forms, he enjoyed the pleasure of the hunt. He had already accompanied his father on one such foray. It had involved a crocodile, a huge behemoth with flashing yellow ivory incisors. Deciding to stop the hunt, it tried to overthrow their boat. His father flung a spear and missed its huge frame. Emboldened, the raging animal charged. Tutty did not remember much after that.

Only the steak cooked to perfection, and his father's smile for him in the banqueting hall.

***

74.

Hatshepsut arrived at the nursery, carrying a wooden toy cat. A nurse was folding linen.

"Where is my nephew?"

"In bed, Your Majesty."

"I won't disturb him."

She turned to leave.

"He's awake. Would you like me to take him the toy?"

"No need. I'll take it to him myself."

The boy's bedroom was dark, but one window was open for ventilation.

"Aunty, is that you?"

"I brought you a gift."

Thutmose sat up. Hatshepsut placed the wooden cat on the boy's coverlet. Its wide mouth smiled at him. Laughing, Thutmose tugged at the rope around its neck. The jaw opened, revealing ivory teeth.

"It's wonderful, Aunty! It looks like your lion."

"He moves, too."

Taking the toy off the bedcover, Hatshepsut put it on the floor. The cat was attached to rollers. Tugging the rope, she pulled it across the polished floorboards. Thutmose clapped his hands.

"Look, he's running!"

Scrambling out of bed, the prince rushed to take the toy from his aunt. He started pulling it across the room.

"Kalma had it made for you. It's Mister Miau-Miau. Do you like him?"

"I love him! He's so round!"

"Is he going to have a name?"

"Hub-chub, Aunty."

"Not Mister Miau-Miau?"

The boy shook his head.

151

"I visit Useramen with Kalma. Mister Miau-Miau might get jealous."

"I understand. Hub-chub is a very good name. You're best friends now."

"Are you here because of tomorrow?"

"I wanted to wish you well. You're the new king, after all."

Thutmose was quiet. He played with his cat's detachable ears.

"I don't want to be king."

"Why not?"

"They all die."

"You won't die."

"How do you know that?"

"I'll be with you. You will grow up to be a strong, courageous monarch." Hatshepsut picked up her nephew. Taking a seat near the bed, she put him on her lap.

"I guess if you promise, Aunty."

"I promise, Tutty."

The queen kissed the top of his head. Relaxing, Thutmose cuddled into her soft, warm body. In minutes, he was asleep. His nurse, who was hovering outside, moved swiftly to Hatshepsut. Skilfully, she slipped the child out of the royal arms and laid him in his bed.

***

In her office, the dowager queen sat above her papyrus memorandum, mulling over state matters. So serious was her meditation that even her butler was not allowed to enter with refreshments. Her strategy had to be as clear as the water flowing through the palace pools, where young Tutty played. Finally, she rose, blew out the oil lamps, and left for the throne room.

***

75

Crowning was an arduous business, and the headgear was heavy. Sitting still with the packing around his head, Thutmose was exhausted. His head hurt, and his fingers were stiff from holding his father's sceptres. Aunty Hatshepsut kept trying to pacify him with her smiles and baby talk.

Everyone was nice to the boy until his aunt left him alone with the priests. They conducted him on a circuit of Karnak's main temple, where he felt manhandled. Their faces were stern. Any softness they had shown in Hatshepsut's presence was gone.

Walking around the columns through various halls, it was cold and dark. Thutmose shivered while they chanted. He could hardly see for the clouds of smoky frankincense.

The child began to choke.

"Buck up!"

An elderly priest glared at him. Looking like the devil god, Set himself, the man had bloodshot eyes and flourishing eyebrows. Suddenly, Thutmose wanted to laugh. With difficulty, he controlled himself and bit the inside of his cheek. When it was over, he was escorted back to the palace to undress and get ready for the evening's festivities.

His aunt rushed to his room as soon as she could see him.

"You have to bow, Aunty. I'm King now."

"How's your head?"

"Sore."

Hatshepsut picked up her nephew and caressed his head. He started to cry. Cooing, she cradled him until he fell asleep. Then she gave him to his nanny and left the chamber. She made her way to her office, where she slammed the door shut.

Sitting at her desk, Hatshepsut slumped forward. Head in her hands, the angry queen breathed deeply. There was sorrow for the little boy, for her dead father, brothers, and late husband. But her overwhelming emotion was rage.

"Menwi! Wine!" Her maidservant appeared with a gold carafe and cup. "And get Kalma."

***

76.

The dreary days turned into weeks and months. Thutmose was woken at dawn, and taken to the king's robing room. He ate breakfast when it was barely light, and was seated on his throne before the ninth hour. Mornings were taken up with administration and the hearing of cases.

Noon was a favourite time for the boy. He vacated his throne for lunch and a nap. However, all too often, there was a second court session. He could not understand a thing. The Grand Vizier Useramen spoke for him. Other officials made decisions.

It was the most boring job on earth.

***

Hatshepsut paced her study in a fury. Kalma sipped wine, and kept still in her corner.

"What am I going to do? The boy can't sit through an audience!"

"Be his co-regent, Hattie."

"I'm his aunt Kalma, not his mother."

"But his mother's dead. You need to step up."

"I don't have the right to be co-regent. It's the reason he's being puppeted by a group of self-interested courtiers."

"I told you before, you're God's Wife."

The distressed queen stopped pacing. Staring at her friend, Hatshepsut said nothing for a while. Time stopped.

"Kalma, you're a genius."

***

77.

In his quarters, Hapuseneb, High Priest of Karnak, entertained his royal guest. Wine and figs were served from gold dinnerware. Several kittens rolled about on carpets. They gambolled and squeaked while he considered the dowager queen's proposal.

"Who ever heard of a woman becoming a king of Egypt?"

"It's happened several times already. It's bound to happen again."

"Nonsense! Most women have acted for young kings until the boys were adults."

"What about Merneith?"

"First dynasty. Not the same situation."

"It's exactly the same."

The priest fussed with the hem of his robe.

"And you can find no other way?"

"Thutmose is a pawn in the hands of the advisers and the army. Amun will miss out if this continues."

The two crunched figs and sipped cold white wine.

"You don't want the throne to satisfy your personal ambition, Your Highness?"

"I have no designs on the throne."

"But you want it for life!"

"I serve my country. I can't be co-regent and step back, once Thutmose is of age."

"Why not?"

"I'm not his mother." *Really, were people becoming thicker every day?*

While Hapuseneb digested this piece of information, Hatshepsut bent down to pat the kittens, who were now squeaking. At two months old, their eyes were vivid blue. After a vigorous playtime, they were starting to tire, and wobbled about. Hapuseneb stroked his upper lip.

"Thutmose has been on the throne for a while. He is fit and healthy. The viziers cannot oppose the will of Amun."

"Apart from my nephew, all the males in my family are dead. Who is to say the same thing won't happen again?"

"Thutmose is as healthy as a horse. The future is nothing to worry about. He'll havechildren."

"In ten years from now. At the moment, his parentage is an issue. Thutmose's mother was a concubine, not a minor queen, or the Great Wife."

"In other words, not you."

"The throne is in danger, Hapu. If courtiers are saying my nephew's blood is not pure, anything could happen. If his mother was the Great Wife, she would be co-regent until the boy reached maturity. But I'm his aunt. If I ascend the Horus throne, it will be as sole monarch, and for life. My nephew must be protected."

"I have heard you correctly, then. You would be King of Egypt."

"If I take the throne as Egypt's sovereign, rather than as an adviser, my nephew will succeed as a legitimate king after my death. His descent from a concubine will not be questioned. For now, he needs to be educated. Did you know Thutmose is too tired to study? He has no time for military training. Last month he was sick."

"Children are always sick."

"Not from exhaustion." Hatshepsut leaned forward. "Remember, I am God's Wife. I visited you tonight out of courtesy."

"And hopefully, for my advice. I need to think about it. There could be dangers up ahead. Now, please excuse me, I have another appointment."

Bowing awkwardly, the Chief Priest of Amun left the audience room. Hatshepsut gently stroked a grey kitten's head.

"Don't worry, little one. I don't need his permission."

Sweeping the kitten up in triumph, she walked out of Karnak and into the balmy Egyptian night.

***

78.

A group of courtiers huddled in the cramped audience chamber. The High Priest of Amun was present. An empty ebony throne sat on its gold platform. Chatting in subdued tones, the men waited for their king. At the ninth hour of the morning, the Grand Chancellor arrived and thumped his staff on the granite floor.

"All rise for Her Majesty."

Useramen turned to Senenmut.

"Where's Thutmose?"

"I'm as ignorant as you, Chief Vizier."

Entering the chamber, Hatshepsut took the single chair. In haste to comply with protocol, the courtiers prostrated themselves on the cold floor.

"You have been gathered here because we have Egypt's business to discuss."

"Are we receiving foreign delegations, Your Highness?"

"Not today, Vizier Useramen."

"What about domestic matters?"

"Tomorrow, Vizier Ptah-hotep."

"Why is Thutmose not here?"

"My nephew is at his lessons, General Paneb."

"But, with respect, should he not attend Egypt's state business?"

"He's a child."

"He is also Chief Commander of the Army."

"My good General Ahmose, if Egypt's Chief Commander of the Army was a toddler, the King of Hatti might be well pleased."

Low laughter rippled through the group. Ahmose paled.

"King Thutmose is our monarch."

"He was, is, and will be again in the future. I have called you today to clarify matters."

Ptah-hotep looked at Senenmut, who appeared to be as baffled as the rest.

"I do hope this isn't a coup," he jested awkwardly.

Hatshepsut was already speaking.

"It is good of you to assemble at short notice. All of you are loyal to Egypt. And for you, the security of Egypt is paramount in your hearts. It is therefore important our country be strong. To be strong, it needs good government. Our allies are loyal, but what of our enemies? What of Syria, Mitanni, and Hatti? It is imperative Egypt sends a signal. We have an extraordinary army and navy. We have talent, and the force of numbers, and discipline. What Egypt needs now is a strong ruler. Therefore, after careful deliberation, it has been decided I shall be sovereign of Egypt."

Stunned silence fell on the gathering.

"With all due respect, Your Highness, Thutmose is Egypt's divine sovereign."

"I am Thutmose's stepmother and his aunt, General Ahmose. He is my flesh and blood."

The Chief Vizier patted his brow with a linen handkerchief. He was perspiring and clearly under strain. Ptah-hotep was also jittery, and kept stealing furtive glances about the room, as if expecting armed conspirators to leap out from behind the wall hangings.

"Then why the need for such a step?"

"I care about my nephew, Vizier Useramen."

"You are completely at liberty to help the boy, but –"

"But what, Vizier Ptah-hotep?"

"He has advisers."

"Too many."

"But surely it is necessary for any king, Your Majesty?"

Hatshepsut rose to her full height, blood drumming in her ears.

"Thutmose cannot make decisions for himself, let alone a nation, until he is an adult. Meanwhile, he needs to study. He needs military training."

"But he is being educated! He has tutors."

"General Ahmose, my nephew sleeps after a day at court. He's exhausted. Thutmose can barely stay awake during the audiences. He can't study or function as Egypt's monarch. It's unfair on a little boy, and embarrassing for Egypt."

General Paneb cleared his throat.

"Why can't Your Majesty be co-regent instead of king?"

"Thutmose is not my son."

It was Ptah-hotep's turn to speak.

"But, Your Highness, with your wisdom and our help, all will be well."

"It's not well, Ptah-hotep! We have enemies gathering like hyenas at our borders. Egypt is being disrespected because there is no adult monarch at its helm."

"Pardon me, but can we be more respected with a woman in that position?"

"You will soon see, General Ahmose. I intend to keep the throne for my nephew until my death."

"Do you intend to be – King?"

"No," Hatshepsut smiled. "I intend to be a *great* king. You are dismissed." The courtiers filed out. Only the High Priest remained.

"Excuse my boldness, Your Majesty, but do you think that was wise?"

"Having multiple advisers, including army generals, is untenable."

"Egypt has always been a bureaucracy. On many an occasion it has functioned successfully under martial law."

"There was only one architect in charge of Khufu's pyramid."

"But Khufu's court had advisers, too."

"There was no kingdom beyond Egypt's borders in his day. It takes ten men to decide whether Thutmose's seal goes on a piece of papyrus! Meanwhile, we have enemies itching to invade our borders."

"Pharaoh is always victorious in battle."

"And who would fight as Pharaoh? Thutmose?"

"I imagine General Ahmose, Your Majesty."

"And his victories will give him reason one day to usurp the throne."

"But being an adult king means –"

"I can go to battle. It's been done before. Now, if you don't mind, Priest Hapuseneb, I have work to do."

***

Hatshepsut retired to her apartments, where she changed. It was already afternoon. Her face in the mirror looked pale and drawn. Deciding to clear her head, she walked outside. After a period of time spent in peace, she paid a visit to Kalma's house. When she arrived, the artist chose to sit in the garden. Tables and chairs sat under an arbour. It was where Kalma's family dined in summer. Cretan wine and olive jars were stashed against the garden wall, surrounded by plants and clumps of fresh herbs.

The friends enjoyed a light meal, washed down with pomegranate juice. Hatshepsut felt relaxed. Colour returned to her cheeks.

"How did they receive the news, Hattie?"

"The courtiers had to agree with me. I left them very little choice."

"So long as you think it's the right path."

"People are short-sighted. What would happen if Thutmose died before adulthood?"

"You could still have children."

"With whom? General Ahmose?"

Kalma laughed.

"He's too ambitious!"

"We have enemies at our border, Kalma. Most of the cabinet don't know, not even the generals."

"I'm worried about you. What if there's an assassination attempt?"

"Unlikely, with Amun's backing."

"Then you've secured the throne for your family."

"Maybe all those *senet* games taught me strategy."

"You inherited your abilities from your father. Now, there is a new wine from Crete I think we should try."

Selecting a pottery jar from the collection, which stood propped against her garden walls, Kalma poured out two cups. Hatshepsut spotted a heron. To her, the appearance of the bird was always auspicious. Picking nonchalantly at the lawn, it gathered its food.

Feeling at peace, the future monarch drank her dark Cretan red.

***

79.

It was the fourth hour of the morning. Quaffing her usual honey water tonic, Hatshepsut made her way to the dining hall. The place was empty. Not even Kalma was there at this hour. Selecting bean porridge for stamina, Hatshepsut ended her first meal of the day with a cup of goat's milk.

At the fifth hour, dressed in a simple robe of white, she was in the palace courtyard, which bristled with armed guards. She climbed into a royal litter. The shortest route to Karnak was selected. Hatshepsut was aware extra police guarded the streets. The litter was chilly, and she was thankful for the warm blanket stowed on the seat next to her.

At Karnak, soldiers stood around the wall enclosing Amun's sanctuary. General Ahmose waited at the main gate. Alighting from her litter, Hatshepsut was escorted from the main entrance into the temple courtyard by soldiers. Before the sixth hour, she was inside the inner sanctum where she made obeisance before the god and sought his blessing.

She then moved to the main hall where Chief Priest Hapuseneb waited. Dressed in pleated linen robes, with a cheetah skin cloak, he held up a censer filled with frankincense. Dispensing clouds of aromatic smoke as Hatshepsut approached, he began chanting. A group of acolytes repeated holy words after him.

Ptah-hotep and the main cabinet, including Useramen, filed into a chamber which looked like a replica of the palace courtroom. It was now the eighth hour of the day. Wearing the Double Crown, Hatshepsut was presented as King of Upper and Lower Egypt. After a brief ceremony, she was taken to the inner chambers of the temple.

The courtiers left the sanctuary.

"That's our task finished, Ptah-hotep. Shall we visit a tavern?"

"A tavern is a sensible suggestion, Useramen. I must say, it's odd there are no public ceremonies."

"We have two kings. It would confuse the masses."

"Hatshepsut is supposed to be presented to the people with the Double Crown before her cabinet. That didn't happen."

"Never fear, my friend, the standard ceremony will be shown on her monuments."

"That woman is a consummate politician. Still, this could be good for Egypt and forus."

Spilling out into the bright sunshine, they shaded their eyes. Several attendants, who were waiting under an awning, stepped forward with ostrich feather fans for their masters.

Lord Senenmut slid up silently behind them.

"Greetings, royal viziers! Ptah-hotep, I hear congratulations are in order. You're to be promoted to the title of Vizier of Lower Egypt."

"I'm already Vizier for our northern territory, Lord Senenmut, a fact you would be wise to remember."

"But now you have tenure because of our new sovereign."

"As does our architect."

"Chief Architect, in charge of the new king's monuments, a fact *you* would be wise to remember."

Senenmut headed for his chariot, which was parked under a group of trees with his driver.

"The cheek! Did you hear that, User?"

"I did."

"Who does he think he is?"

"The king's lover."

Ptah-hotep tripped over a temple flagstone. His wig fell forward.

"Be careful, that's treason!"

"Not if it's true."

Righting his wig, Ptah-hotep glared at his colleague.

"You take things too far."

"It's common knowledge that Hatshepsut and Senenmut have been together since her husband's death."

"You know I hate to gossip."

"But you don't mind hearing it."

"I don't know what's got into you, User."

"We're off to a tavern. I'm feeling jolly. Our new sovereign, Hatshepsut, has just put her life into servitude to build an empire for her nephew. It's time to celebrate!"

Still grumbling, Ptah-hotep followed the courtiers as they walked a short distance to the tavern. There they spent the remainder of the afternoon, drinking to the health of Egypt's two kings.

***

Moving through the main hall, wearing a red crown, Hatshepsut visited the gods of Lower Egypt.

When she had finished, the new sovereign of Egypt retired to her dressing room. Sitting on a gilt chair, she drank a cup of pomegranate juice mixed with liquid yoghurt. An attendant rubbed her legs with myrrh oil. New sandals were placed on her feet.

Swapping the red crown for the conical white one of Upper Egypt, Hatshepsut continued to visit the gods of that region, including her home of Thebes. Offerings of water, wine, and milk were made with incantations and rituals she had spent months rehearsing.

***

80

The coronation was finally over. His regalia exchanged for a green linen robe, Hapuseneb drank a cup of beer. Two officiating priests joined him. The acolytes had long gone.

"Are you going to the tavern, High Priest?"

"Whatever for?"

"Egypt's most powerful courtiers are celebrating. It might be wise to attend."

"I'm not a politician. I serve the god. Besides, I want to go home."

Hapuseneb drained his cup. Throwing a cape over his aching shoulders, he grasped his walking stick. Two guards joined him as he left for home on foot. It was a pleasant time of evening for a stroll. He headed down the lanes behind the temple. The sun had set, but there was still light. Birds called to each other from the trees and the eaves of shops.

The priest's mansion, positioned on the Nile, was complete with gardens, stables, and homes for staff. At the entrance, he removed his sandals. A servant bathed and dried his feet. Walking barefoot across the neatly swept floor to an antechamber, Hapuseneb spent some time in prayer.

Later, he repaired to a cubicle where servants showered him by pouring vessels of water over his body. Scrubbed with soap made of natron and animal fat, he was rinsed off, and dried with linen towels. Perfumed oil was rubbed into his skin. A robe of blue was thrown over his head, and the master of the house was ready to join his family for a leisurely evening meal.

***

81.

Posing for statues was intended to be a single session. Without the kilt or artificial beard of a king, Hatshepsut instead wore a loose-fitting robe, and striped *nemes* headdress. Commonly depicted in portraits of Egyptian monarchs, the *nemes* was a cloth headdress with lappets, which covered the head and neck. It was best to be comfortable, she thought, especially for a sitting which could take all morning.

What dismayed and annoyed her was the artist thought he was in charge. As he came from Syria, it was possible he did not know the protocol, but the man barely bowed! *Perhaps I should take an army to Syria.* Frowning slightly, she adjusted her cape.

"It would be better if Her Majesty removed her cape and crown."

"This is the uniform of the mighty ruler of Egypt. I am not removing my regalia."

"I need to do a preliminary sketch. Sculptors will use it as their reference. You need never sit for an artist again."

Sighing, Hatshepsut requested her headdress be removed.

"I suppose you'll be wanting my hair down?"

"I only require the contours of Your Majesty's head."

With a steady hand, the artist sketched what he required. At the session's end, he prostrated himself and left. Hatshepsut consulted her secretary for the next appointment. The entire day was consumed with sign offs for the latest monuments.

It would take a month, but new monarch was on her way to putting her stamp on Egypt.

***

Part III

82.

Removing his scribe's palette required for hieroglyphic practice, Thutmose fastened his satchel. Lining up with the boys at the Royal Military Cadet School, he did not to speak to anyone. Once inside, he hid his bag behind a pillar on the mudbrick floor. He knew thieves existed and did not want to lose his lunch after the morning swim.

The classroom floor was lined with a thin layer of painted gypsum. Grills high up in the wall let in streams of white light. The army's idea of interior decorating, he thought. Moving to a spare mat, Thutmose folded his legs under him and sat up straight. The teacher fixed him with a glassy stare.

"Where's your scroll?"

"I-I thought we used o-ostraca, sir."

"You thought wrong."

"But students don't supply writing materials. The school does."

"You're right."

The teacher smiled. Thutmose noticed several teeth were missing.

"Are there any scrolls left?"

"Oh yes – at the school gate."

Snickering from the students in the class turned to sneers. The man picked up a cane and tapped one end against his palm as if testing it.

"I'd better get a piece, sir."

"You should have picked one up at the gate."

It was the first caning of his life. Thutmose did not even cry out. Afterwards, he visited the sentry at the gate, only to find out there were no papyrus sheets left.

"Caned you, did he?"

"My fault. I forgot."

"It's illegal, you know."

"I didn't know I had to bring my own writing sheets."

The man stared at the child.

"Caning a prince is illegal."

"But I'm not supposed to pull rank."

"I am."

***

Later that morning, the prince found himself sitting in a cool room with a glass of fig juice next to his elbow. Dusman, a moon-faced teacher with a kindly demeanour, sat at the head of the class, humming to himself. His students worked diligently. Occasionally, he checked their work and pointed out where their hieroglyphs could improve.

A boy next to the prince cleared his throat.

"My name's Itaja."

"Thutmose. My friends call me Tut."

"You mean 'Tutty'."

"That's only for my nanny."

"How old are you?"

"Seven."

"I didn't need a nanny. My parents loved me."

"What, by Ra's beard, is that supposed to mean?"

Hearing raised voices, their teacher looked up.

"They cared for me themselves. However, I know a bit about royalty. Your nannies stop their services at a child's fourth birthday."

"You're looking for a drubbing."

"Boxing."

"What?"

"I box. Meet me in the gym at lunchtime."

With a smug look on his face, Itaja returned to work. Dusman loomed above the prince. His smile was pleasant.

"Everything alright?"

"Er – yes, sir. The bird's wing on my hieroglyph is a bit crooked."

"Let me see." Dusman picked up his pupil's papyrus. "It looks fine to me. See you in the gym at midday."

Humming, the teacher returned to the front of the room before the prince had time to close his mouth.

***

83

Whacks resounded throughout the gymnasium. Every time the boys scored a point, their audience cheered. Dusman was jumping up and down, which for one so fat, was a feat. Thutmose could not help feeling set up. The place was packed. Everyone knew Itaja had recruited a sparring partner. However, Thutmose held his own. At the end of the break, the vexed prince delivered a resounding cuff on his opponent's right ear. Itaja fell to the floor. Immediately, Dusman was over him, armed with a damp cloth and aloe vera.

"You did well, Prince Thutmose."

"Why didn't you stop it, sir?"

"Boxing is part of the curriculum. Itaja needed a sparring partner for today's session." The teacher stood up and clapped his hands. "Back to class, boys!"

Chatting excitedly about the match and their bets, the students headed out of the gym into the broiling afternoon sunshine.

At their classroom door, Itaja caught the prince's elbow.

"Where are you going, Tutty?"

"To eat."

"We always bathe after exercise."

He pulled Thutmose into an alcove where most of the boys' satchels lay on limestone benches. Pushing open a door obscured by cloaks and capes, Itaja led the way into a room which was filled with clean robes, water pitchers, towels, and a gold basin.

After they washed themselves, he threw his new friend a robe.

"Green is for your win, Thutmose."

"The colours have meaning?"

"Everything here has meaning!"

Back in the classroom, the prince noticed their teacher had draped a cloth over his table. On it rested a soup tureen, bread, and pottery bowls. Beaming widely, Dusman ladled broth into the bowls.

Boys lined up to collect their soup and fresh bread cobs. Then they retired to the back of the class, where they sat on their study mats to eat their meal.

Thutmose lined up with the rest.

"I'm glad I came to this class, sir."

"It's for boys like you."

"I was in a different one this morning."

"You're in the right one now."

Dusman handed his pupil a bowl and spoon.

***

84

After school, Hatshepsut summoned her nephew to her office.

"Did you know Dusman was my teacher, Tutty?"

"He's very nice."

"I heard you were caned."

"I forgot to bring my writing material to class."

"But you still like your teacher?"

"I was caned by a different teacher, Aunty. They took me out of the first classroom and put me in another. Dusman doesn't hit anyone."

"No, he doesn't. Thank you for clearing that up. I was told you didn't make a sound when you were punished. That's a sign of a true warrior. You may go now."

Closing the door behind him, the boy returned to his room. Tomorrow was weapons training. Picking up his child's dagger, he whipped it through the air. Flipping it back into his scabbard, he addressed the rest of his kit. The first thing to pack was a leather corselet. He set an archer's bow and quiver of arrows beside the main box of equipment. When he had finished packing, Thutmose picked up a list and ticked off all the items in red.

"My, what an arsenal! Expecting burglars?"

Dressed for dinner in a dazzling beaded gown, Hatshepsut stood in the doorway. Entering the prince's apartment, she chose a padded stool with a leopard skin throw. Her eyes were drawn to the corner stacked with military equipment.

"We have weapons training tomorrow, Aunty."

"Tell me about today's boxing."

"I won."

"I want you to be careful."

"But I'm in the army!"

"You're in Cadet School."

"Soldiers get killed."

"Not in training. I want you to stay in one piece, Tutty. You're going to be King one day."

"I am King."

"Come here."

His aunt held out her arms. Thutmose trotted towards her, and she lifted him onto her lap.

"Are you wearing lotus perfume, Aunty?"

"For this evening." Thutmose dangled his legs as the fragrance of his aunt enveloped him. Kissing her warm cheek, he leaned against her. "Tutty, do you know why I'm acting as Egypt's sovereign instead of you?"

"So, I can go to school?"

"To protect you, so that you can enjoy your childhood. Aren't you happier now?"

"Oh yes, I can sleep at night!"

"I'm sorry I'm not your mother, otherwise I'd be co-regent."

"What's a co-regent?"

"A parent who helps a young king with his work until he becomes an adult."

"I don't have any parents."

Hatshepsut hugged the boy close. Brushing back his hair, she kissed his forehead.

"You have me, but I'm your aunt. The only way I can protect you is by being Egypt's monarch. But kings can't abdicate."

"What does that mean?"

"I can't step back for you like a co-regent."

"So, you must die first?"

"Yes, like your Dad … and my husband."

Thutmose rested his head against his aunt's breast. He put his small arms around her.

"You lost him, too."

***

175

It was time for a drink, but a visit from friends was becoming complicated. Kalma appeared at the sovereign's chambers, holding trays of Cretan delicacies, surrounded by security officers. Hatshepsut angrily dismissed the men.

Setting down platters of seafood and sweets on a table, her friend surveyed the room. Filled with flowers, it smelled of the garden. Delicate draperies hung over the windows.

"You've spruced up the place. How's your nephew?"

"Like all the males in my family, he has a death wish."

"That's nothing new. They're warriors."

"Do you know Tutty has weapons training tomorrow?"

"Good. He's in a military school. That's more than he would have had as a child-king. I always felt sorry for him wearing that heavy crown."

Hatshepsut helped herself to a piece of Kalma's baked squid.

"The coronation crown weighs as much as an obelisk. As chance would have it, both Tutty and I have weapons training tomorrow."

"But surely, you will sit on top of a hill overlooking any battle in Nubia?"

"I may have to fight."

Hatshepsut ordered three different beverages from the cellar. A white-haired wine steward brought three jugs on a gold tray. His long caftan was of Syrian origin.

"Which one would you like him to pour first, Kalma?"

"White."

With great ceremony, the wine steward filled two cups.

"The priests are going to make life easier for me as God's Wife, but there is pushback from the court and military."

"Surely you can handle courtiers and generals!"

"They could be dangerous."

"Then you should have them executed."

"I'd have no one to run the country."

Hatshepsut motioned to her steward to pour red wine.

"You shouldn't mix your wine, Hattie, unless you want a hangover."

"Ceremonial drinking is different. Each wine represents a separate facet of the gods."

"White for the moon, red for sunrise, and a fortified beverage for getting through the darkest passage of horrible demons."

"Correct!"

"But that is for after death, surely?"

"I feel dead." Hatshepsut cradled her wine cup in moody silence.

"They want a warrior, Kalma."

"Nonsense! Dhey only fought once."

"But he fought."

"No one will remember him for his battles."

"Our father's campaigns cast a long shadow, it's true."

"You can't risk your life. Tutty is still a child. He'll be a puppet in the hands of those courtiers if you die."

"Assuming I die."

"You will," Kalma said darkly.

"Not if I'm trained."

"Dear Ra, can you hear yourself?"

"I intend to go on the offensive."

"Don't lead from the front, even if your generals advise it. If you die, Tutty will go back to being a puppet. After a few years, a vizier will kill him, and put himself on the throne."

"You seem awfully sure of things."

"Unlike you, I've only had one cup of weak white wine."

"Why do you think I started with the strong stuff? I need courage."

Before her hostess could reach for the pitcher, Kalma poured herself a full cup of fortified wine.

"What weapons training are you doing?"

"Archery."

"Good! You won't need to be at the front."

"That's what the generals hope, but I've been practising hand-to-hand combat."

"Why on earth would you jeopardise your life in that way? The whole idea of being our ruler is to protect your nephew until adulthood."

"If I go to war, keeping the throne will be an easier job for me. Nobody will be able to say I'm unworthy to rule Egypt."

"You won't be alive to rule! It's suicide, Hattie."

"Life's full of risks."

"Fighting Nubians is certain death. Their archers shoot arrows hundreds of yards with perfect aim."

"Which is why I am taking Nubian archers. Recruited from the prisoners of war during my father's time, they will be useful."

Kalma looked through the open doors. Across the emerald lawn, the Nile sparkled in the afternoon sun. Coursing swiftly past the palace apartments, it had no knowledge that its ruler was about to die.

"Now I know why I paint. The brushes don't talk back!"

"In case I don't return, Thutmose is yours. If his life is in danger, take him on the first boat to Crete."

"He's in military school. I can't exactly knock on the door and ask them to return one prince."

"I'll brief Senenmut and Hapuseneb."

"If those two are involved, I want nothing to do with it."

"They're loyal subjects. Don't worry, I'll be back from the campaign before the end of next month."

"Make sure it's not in a coffin."

Hatshepsut's brows drew together. As an Egyptian king, she needed a successful military campaign to secure her legitimacy. Her army would leave Egypt for Nubia with great fanfare, just as it had in the days of her father. Setting her cup down, she scooped up a handful of Cretan sweets.

"Now, I'd like to see your drawings for the Delta mosaics."

Kalma pressed down her skirts. She was just beginning to enjoy the mellowing effects of the fortified beverage. Guaranteed to slay demons in a pharaoh's afterlife, she found her body reluctant to move from its comfortable chair. However, she managed, and together, the friends made their way to her studio.

***

The classroom was full. Itaja was painting red hieroglyphs with his brush. Thutmose dumped his bag down.

"Still on the 'ABCs'?"

"We all need to learn the basics, Tutty."

"I can string sentences into paragraphs."

"So what? Put your bag in the alcove."

Unwrapping his writing palette, Thutmose dribbled liquid from a water pot onto a cake of lamp soot. A vase suddenly caught his eye.

"What's that container for?"

"Teacher's flowers."

"How come there are no paintings on it?"

Itaja put down his brush.

"Why don't you ask him?"

At that moment, Dusman appeared. His face was as jovial as ever. Laying his scrolls on his table, he puttered about, filling water jugs, and laying out reed pens for those who had forgotten their writing materials. Thutmose cleared his throat.

"Ah, our champion boxer! Help me with this, will you?"

Dusman pulled off a cover from a large object which stood in the room. A gleaming wooden statue, inlaid with gold filigree, was revealed. Thutmose assisted his teacher in moving the piece.

Together, they put their shoulders into the task of dragging it across the classroom. Itaja gazed at it with curiosity.

"What is it, sir?"

"A replica of a *ka* statue. Real *ka* statues contain the life force of a person after death. Can you see the hieroglyphic sign on top of its head?"

Murmurs floated across the classroom.

"Two arms up denote the sign for *ka*."

"That's right, Itaja."

"What's it for?"

"Hieroglyphic practice, Itaja. Everyone must copy it."

The class quietened down. For the next hour, all that could be heard was the sound of breathing, and the dabbing of reed brushes as students set about the task of replicating the statue on papyrus. At the end of the morning, the children's work was heartily commended by their teacher, who heaped praise on the most basic of efforts.

At the end of the day, Thutmose waited until everyone had gone home. Dusman packed his satchel, and prepared to lock the classroom.

"Goodnight, Prince."

"I was wondering – um – why your vase has no paintings on it, sir."

"I made it myself." Dusman looked at his pupil. "Would you like to paint it?"

Before Thutmose could answer, his teacher picked up the vase. He placed it in the boy's hands. Locking the classroom, Dusman waved a cheery farewell, and walked the short distance to his home. Thutmose stood in the courtyard, and waited for his carriage ride back to the palace.

***

Senenmut was outside Hatshepsut's apartment. Thutmose took a deep breath and walked past him.

"What have you there, young man?"

"School stuff."

"Did you make that pot?"

"No, I stole it."

Wondering at his own cheek, Thutmose kept walking. Once in his room, he lowered his satchel next to his bedside, where his clothes and toys lay in a heap. Sitting on the edge of his bed, he examined the pot. It was a pale bluish green. Turning it around in his hands, he felt its smooth exterior. Its spacious round belly was practical. Its neck was not too narrow, and soared up to a strong lip, which would not break.

Reaching out to his chair, on which several spinning tops lay, Thutmose scooped them up and placed them in the pot. Clanking around the clay interior, they rattled into comfortable quiet. Satisfied with the way his pot served as a container, the child placed it carefully on the table next to his bed and stared at it.

An angry Senenmut was in his doorway.

"Don't walk off like that!"

"You're not my father."

Again, Thutmose wondered at himself. Was it the school? The boxing?

"I'm the most important courtier in the land."

Until you're replaced. "I'm sorry. I just got carried away with my new present."

"The pot?"

"My teacher gave it to me."

"You must be doing very well. I heard you excel at sports, too."

So, the slime ball was spying on him.

"You honour me with your words, Lord Senenmut. And you're right. It was a swimming prize."

Disarmed by the boy's change of attitude, Senenmut vanished as quickly as he had appeared. The prince closed his door and slid the bolt into place.

***

Only his aunt attended supper. Most of the courtiers were at their homes. Thutmose was on his best behaviour. Hatshepsut turned her duck wing thoughtfully between her long fingers.

"It's a bit tough, Aunty. Try the beef."

"I heard you were rude to Lord Senenmut."

"I apologised."

Hatshepsut put the wing down. Passing over the beef, she selected a goat dish cooked with coriander and cumin. Tearing a piece of flat bread, she dipped it into the stew.

"Try it, Tutty."

The boy picked up his spoon and ladled some of the mixture onto his plate. Tearing a piece of bread, he imitated his aunt. Tender morsels, mixed with herbs, and vegetables, slid down easily. The two ate the remainder of their meal in peace.

***

87

A strong wind swept across the river. Palace garden paths were strewn with leaves and petals. Obeying the royal summons, Kalma made her way to the prince's quarters. Arriving at Thutmose's apartment, she noted it was clean and neat, with hardly any furniture. It was as if at this age the boy was learning how to keep a tidy army tent.

"I hear you're quite the diplomat, Tutty. Did you really say sorry to Sen?"

"Rudeness does not befit a prince and warrior."

"Wise words. What can I help you with?"

"I want to paint this vase. Maybe you could tell me something about it, too."

Kalma picked up the pot and turned it around in her hands.

"It's produced with a blue slip from Kharga Oasis."

"Do I need special paints?"

"It's glazed."

"Is that a problem?"

"I paint papyrus and make mosaics, so I'm not an expert."

"You paint walls, too."

"A pot is different. Ideally, it needs to be painted before firing, but I think we could use paints."

"Do you have any?"

"We could get some from Hopta, the image-maker. He paints statues. You'll need raw materials to make paint, and gum to make it stick. Is this a school project?"

"I just wanted to paint a vase."

Placing the pot carefully on the table, Kalma tossed her long, curled locks. Patting him on the shoulder, she left the prince. Thutmose watched her elegant form swaying gracefully out the door.

***

<h1 style="text-align:center">88.</h1>

Hatshepsut missed her aim on the archery field.

"He's doing what?"

"Painting vases. You could have hit that target."

"Stop giving me surprises, Kalma! My nephew is training to be a general, not an artist."

Stringing her bow, she let fly again. An arrow whizzed through the cold morning air and hit the copper target.

"When do you leave, Hattie?"

"Two weeks."

Another arrow circulated through the hot air.

"Do you fight battles in the morning or afternoon?"

"Midday."

"I wouldn't be able to stand the heat, let alone fight."

"You would if your life depended on it."

Tilting her head skywards, Kalma watched a falcon skim the air overhead. Floating above them, the bird stretched its wings lazily as it hovered, waiting for its prey to appear.

"I just remembered, Hattie, your nephew needs paints."

Bidding her friend a hasty farewell, Kalma hurried back to the shade of the palace. Twanging her bow deftly, Hatshepsut let fly a volley of arrows.

***

"Oh, there you are! I've been waiting ever so long."

Rising from his custom-made chair, the prince pushed his hair back and stood to attention.

Kalma noticed he was wearing his best kilt and linen shirt.

"I brought paints, Thutmose." Tipping out several blocks onto a table, she separated them. "Carbon makes black, orpiment turns to yellow, iron oxide gives you red – I had to get that from the desert. And azurite and malachite are for blue."

"You have pretty hair."

"Are you listening?"

"Oh yes – intently! Would you like a drink?"

Kalma turned to see her host gesturing towards a shelf next to the bronze mirror on his dresser. Pomegranates, grapes, figs, and dates spilled out of a gold bowl. Several wine and juice pitchers crowded the small space. But it was the Cretan ewer which drew Kalma's attention.

"I'll have some wine, please."

With alacrity, Thutmose poured a cup, and offered it to her. She drank and suddenly remembered an additional ingredient to the child's toolkit. Pulling out a phial, Kalma placed it on the table.

"Here's gum to mix with your paints. Now, you're all set with materials. Hopta will send a student over to show you how to apply them to the vase. Do you have a drawing of the design you want?"

"I was thinking of painting straight onto the vase."

"I would suggest a sketch first, even if it's applied directly to the object. You're not a master, yet." She smiled at the child. "The wine is particularly good. Did you steal it?"

"Er – no. Borrowed it from Cookie."

"Do you have to pay it back?"

"That's when I'll steal it."

"From your aunt's cellars? I don't recommend it. Come to my home. There's some stored in large jars. It won't be missed."

Thutmose straightened his back. He suddenly felt very grown-up.

***

90.

A fire crackled merrily in one corner of the sitting room. Hatshepsut fussed over the hearth, pushing back embers with a poker. Kalma warmed her hands by its rosy glow. An amused expression trailed the corners of her mouth.

"That nephew of yours already has an eye for the ladies."

"He's seven."

"Tutty was staring at me the other day, Hattie."

"It's his eyes. They're round, like mine."

"Despite your statues, he looks nothing like you."

"Trust me, he wasn't ogling."

"Why are you being so defensive?"

"He's a child!"

"He offered me wine."

"Are you sure?"

"Pomegranate, no less."

"The love fruit? I'll have him caned!"

"Don't be silly. It was very sweet. He needs a proper drinks cabinet."

Her eyes trailed to Hatshepsut's three-tiered affair.

"Out of the question. Tutty's a child."

"He's practising to be a soldier. He may as well practise being a pharaoh."

"That's my job and that of the priests."

"I wouldn't leave them to educate your heir in the ways of women."

"They wouldn't dare corrupt him."

"All I'm saying, is the boy needs more furniture."

Kalma left her friend to sit by the fire alone. Throwing the poker to one side, the monarch reflected she had less than a week to prepare for war.

***

91

The field filled with boys warming up in the cold grey of morning. Mist blew in from the Nile, obscuring their vision. Itaja did stretches while Thutmose twanged his bow.

"It's our toughest day at Cadet School, Tutty."

"I hope you're ready, Itaja. I'm about to win the Golden Fly." Thutmose looked down the sight line of his acacia bow. "Don't you wish we had the real thing?"

"We'd fly backwards if we used adult bows. They're heavy."

"It's frustrating. I want to be on a real battlefield."

"You will be. For now, you're a child, like me."

Itaja put an arrow in his bow and let it fly. It hit the wooden target and clunked to the ground. He fired several more. They all hit the target, only to fall uselessly into the grass. Grunting, he checked his arrows.

"Look, Tutty, they've given us blanks! No wonder the arrows aren't sticking into the target."

Thutmose grinned.

"You're more like me than I thought. I wanted bronze-tipped arrows to impress my girlfriend."

Unholy glee lit Itaja's eyes.

"Girlfriend? Do tell!"

"She's older."

"That's always good."

"What's always good?"

Dusman stood beside the boys, a jovial expression on his round face.

"Our prince here has a girlfriend."

Thutmose flushed violently. He cast a furious glance at Itaja.

"Good! He's going to be Pharaoh someday."

The teacher left the pair to check on the welfare of his other students while they awaited their archery instructors.

"Why did you have to open your big mouth, Itaja?"

"It's wonderful to have a girlfriend. I wish I had one."

"You embarrassed me!"

"Why? Is it because you really don't have one?"

"Don't be stupid! I served her drinks at my apartment."

"Is she pretty?"

"Very. She asked me back to hers."

"Ooh, you *do* have a girlfriend!" Itaja strung his bow. "Does she have any sisters?"

"I'll ask."

The boys sat on a grassy hillock. Their classmates milled about, yawning in the early dawn. Itaja reflected that even if he spent his childhood training for war, there was always love.

***

92

Setting a gift on his teacher's desk, Thutmose waited. Dusman looked at the object. Wrapped in papyrus, it was entwined with a red ribbon. A gob of dried mud, stamped with the cartouche of King Thutmose, sealed the package.

"You have your own seal, Tutty. How lovely!"

Carefully picking apart the royal seal, to preserve it as much as possible, Dusman unravelled the ribbon. Spellbound, the boys watched their teacher, who resembled a happy child at a birthday party. Finally, he pulled away the wrapping paper. Brown eyes sparkled.

"It's my pot! Oh, it's beautiful! Did you get a designer to do this?"

"I – er – painted it."

"These hieroglyphs are perfect. Boys, come over here, and look."

Thutmose breathed sharply. The last thing he needed was jealousy from his classmates. As the children crowded round their teacher, Dusman pointed out the hieroglyphs.

"Did you use azurite or malachite, Tutty?"

"Both, sir. Azurite on the rim and malachite below it."

"Gives it colour gradation. Do you see how he did that?"

The children moved in to get a better view.

"Can we start painting vases?" asked one.

"Only if Tutty would like to teach."

"Me?"

"You will?" Dusman clapped his hands with delight. "He's agreed!"

Realising he had agreed to teach, Thutmose cleared his head and started to think.

"First, we need paints."

"Yes, yes." Dusman picked up a reed pen to prepare a list.

"Red ochre, yellow ochre, carbon, orpiment." Thutmose ticked off the colours with his fingers. "And pots which are not glazed. We need to apply the paint to dry clay."

Eventually, the class returned to normal. Dusman arranged with the school kitchen for a morning snack to be served. Pastries arrived as the sun dial marked the tenth hour of the morning. It was time for target practice. Grabbing their pastries, the boys hurried out of the classroom to the school fields.

Itaja took his place next to the prince.

"Since when did you become an artist, Tutty? I thought you wanted to be a soldier."

"I do," Thutmose said between swift bites of his pastry. He was already itching to get onto the field for their combat practice. "Maybe I can do art in my spare time."

"They say generals have a lot of time."

"General? I'm going to be King of Upper and Lower Egypt!"

"You are now. Your aunt is helping you to get an education. She has you in military school for a reason."

"While she's fighting real enemies in Nubia."

"Don't be jealous. When you're older, you can go, too."

The prince finished his pastry and swigged his water canteen.

"Come on, let's go outside and do our exercises."

***

Thutmose put on his best gown for a visit to Kalma's home. Embroidered, with hundreds of beads stitched into the fabric, it glimmered like a sea of orange and blue. Trying to concentrate, Kalma found her artist's eye distracted by the shimmering sea of colour.

"Do you think you could teach me how to make pots?"

"Why on earth do you want to be a potter, Tutty?"

"I don't."

"Then why ask me? There's a lot to the art of ceramics. I don't want you wasting my time."

"I need to know more, like the firing process, for instance."

"Pottery-making is for the lower classes."

"But you're not lower class! You know all about it. And you have friends who can help."

"I'm a Cretan artist who knows other artists, but you're the next king."

Kalma put out gold plates, which she kept for special occasions. Serving the child pieces of fried goat's cheese and salad, she poured him grape juice into a silver cup.

"I really want to be a general."

"You will be in charge of Egypt's army one day."

"Aunty is Chief Commander of our troops now."

"That's right – for now."

"I *was* Chief Commander."

"Don't you want to be a child and have fun?"

A beautiful girl with black hair and kohl-laden eyes entered the room. She waited in a corner until it was time to clear the dishes. Thutmose glanced at her. Kalma offered him a tray of hot duck slices with warm rolls. Stuffed with sesame seeds and garlic, they smelled delicious, but the prince accepted only one roll with two duck slices.

"I don't have any fun. I'm always studying or exercising. Now, Dusman wants me to teach. All I wanted to do was paint vases in my spare time."

"Do you have any friends?"

"Itaja."

"Whose son is he?"

"Vizier Ptah-hotep is his dad."

"That's good. Ptah-hotep is a member of your aunt's cabinet."

Thutmose grew thoughtful.

"Do we always have to be mixing with the right sort?"

"You don't want to be associating with the rubbish collector's brat, do you?"

"I read a text at the temple the other day, which said we are all equal before the gods."

"Are you sure you were reading an Egyptian scroll? There's a religion which says we are all equal, but it belongs to one of the Canaanite tribes."

"How am I going to lead ordinary soldiers, if I don't know the first thing about them?"

"Kings have always led commoners. And the Egyptian king has the god's ear. That means Amun listens to him alone. You'll find out that everything's strictly hierarchical."

"There are some older texts that say differently."

Kalma changed the subject.

"Do you go to parties?"

"I attend lots of ceremonies."

"But with other children? Watch for invitations. And go! You need to enjoy yourself."

"You're the first person to ever say that to me." Thutmose smiled at Kalma. His eyes wandered down her layered skirt. "You're wearing a different kind of dress today."

"It's a special morning skirt for receiving distinguished guests."

Thutmose knew better than to pursue the conversation. He could already see Kalma tense, as though she meant to say something. *Please don't tell me I'm just a child.* His eyes scanned the room.

"Did you have an interior designer, Kalma?"

"I designed my home."

"I like the frescoes."

"They're Cretan."

"From Knossos."

"That's right. How did you know?"

"Aunty told me."

"I can teach you pottery, but if you just want to paint vases, you should ask Dusman to supply you with the pots. Then you can paint them and get them fired in the palace kilns. The boys will like it better. It will look like magic to them."

The prince brightened.

"That will give me more time to practise my archery."

***

94

Floating down the Nile in a palace skiff was not the ideal way to relax. Kalma fluffed up her blue-and-gold cushions, while Hatshepsut rowed with one paddle. Even now she was building up muscle.

"I heard Tutty enjoys painting vases all day, Kalma."

"It's not my fault."

"I didn't say it was, but he should be training."

"He wants to be a soldier. Painting vases relaxes him, that's all."

"And who is Itaja's father?"

"Ptah-hotep's son. You should know that."

"Ptah-hotep has three wives and ten children. I gave up remembering the names of his brats long ago. I am pleased my nephew is mixing with the right sort."

"Thutmose needs a break, Hattie. Let him go to parties, where there will be girls of his own age. In a few years, he'll be ready to inherit his harem and start a family. In the meantime, Thutmose needs to know how to interact with girls, not simply be able to shoot a bow and arrow."

"That's not a bad idea. You give sound advice."

"It's why you keep me as your friend."

Directing their skiff towards the shore, Hatshepsut floated up to the riverbank below the palace. Guards, who were keeping a discreet distance in their own barque, followed. Anchoring their boats at a berth reserved for security personnel, they disembarked and waited. Two policemen from the palace in regulation white, blue, and gold uniforms approached. They helped Kalma out of the boat, but Hatshepsut refused assistance.

"Join me for combat practice, Kalma."

The friends made their way to the palace compound, where they mounted a chariot. A roan stallion whinnied and bucked, while its black companion munched grass. After coaxing the unruly pair, Hatshepsut gathered the reins and headed for the barracks. Holding onto the rails,

Kalma felt the wind ruffle her long hair. At the barracks, a field was cordoned off for the monarch.

It was noon and the sun was a fiery ball in the sky. Why the sovereign had to practise at midday was a mystery. Dismounting, Kalma found a shady spot under a tree. Hatshepsut strode out into the middle of the field where the instructor waited. Bowing from the waist, he stood back. They conversed for some time before he handed her a *khepesh*. Its curved blade made it the most dangerous weapon on the battlefield.

Then the swordplay began. Kalma suddenly realised the blades were real. Hacking as hard as she could, Hatshepsut advanced, and then retreated under the furious blows. The instructor was not holding back. Worry drew Kalma's facial muscles into taut lines. She followed the pair duelling under the blinding sun. Their swords flashed, then it was all over. Hatshepsut's right arm fell by her side. Running towards them, Kalma noticed blood running down her friend's arm.

"Are you hurt?"

"Stay away, Kalma!"

"Who is this?" the instructor asked.

"A spectator."

"I'm her friend. Are you trying to kill Pharaoh?"

"I'm her trainer."

"Just go away, Kalma!"

Confused, the artist looked into her friend's eyes. They were orbs of concentrated fury. Sheepishly, she made her way back to the safety of the shaded area.

***

Outside the training field, Hatshepsut waited for Kalma to climb into the chariot. The horses were skittish, and she pulled hard on the reins. Her arm started to throb.

"What were you doing, Kalma?"

"I could ask you the same question. Real swords? Are you out of your mind? And why were you so angry?"

"Don't approach me when I'm in battle mode."

"Your men will try to protect you. I hope you don't turn on them like that."

"Discipline helps soldiers remember their place."

"Is that what you think I need to do? Remember my place? I thought we were friends."

"We are friends."

"I'm not some lackey you can dismiss when you feel like it!"

Pulling up the horses, Hatshepsut took a deep breath to control herself.

"Look, I have a different role now. It was my mistake to bring you, but I thought you would understand."

Flicking the reins, Hatshepsut urged the horses into the shimmering mirage of the midday heat, back to the palace.

***

95.

"On your marks! Get set! GO!"

As the gong rang, ten boys tore down the racing track on foot. Chariots waited at the north end. Leaping into his cab, Thutmose took the reins of two steeds and galloped down the rest of the track. Itaja lost some time in seizing the reins, and gaining control of his horses. Eating Thutmose's dust was the best he could manage.

At the end of the race, the school principal presented the prince with a green ribbon. The boy tied it round his waist. Itaja took his yellow sash for second place, and looped it about his belt.

It looks good in the sun. Even nicer than the green.

Thutmose turned to accept congratulations from the boys as they parked their chariots. Sweetmeats were served. A house master tapped Itaja on the shoulder.

"Congratulations, my boy! You were fitter than you were last month."

"I trained, sir. Even so, I failed to win."

"You don't need to compete with the prince. You handled the horses. In battle, it pays to hang back a bit." The house master chuckled and handed Itaja a sweet cake. "Anyway, I prefer the yellow colour of your sash to the green."

Itaja flushed with pleasure. Their house master was a famous charioteer who had fought under King Tuthmosis. Biting into his sweet, the child realised he was hungry. Then he thought about Kalma.

***

In the middle of her studio, Kalma mixed her paints from mineral compounds. Itaja clumped into her studio, wearing sandals which were slightly too big for him. The artist remembered Vizier Ptah-hotep had several wives and believed in saving money.

199

"I like your sash."

"I won a prize at school."

"You won?"

"Second place in the chariot driving."

"Who was first?"

"Prince Thutmose."

"Good. You always have to come second to him."

"Do I?"

"You must never beat a royal, but you knew that."

Itaja shuffled in his oversize sandals.

"The house master talked to me afterwards."

"That's because you're the real winner and not the prince. It teaches you to hold back in battle, too. Egypt's king must always reap the glory."

"That's what my house master said!"

"Thutmose will lead from the front. Remember, you don't have to get yourself killed."

Kalma carefully packed her paints away. Offering Itaja a plate of sweets, she gave him her best smile. The boy drank in the loveliness of her eyes, black hair, and perfect red lips. Truly, there was no more beautiful lady in the world.

***

96

It was morning, and they had practice with real arrows. The Golden Fly trials were two weeks away. Thutmose carried his bow and quiver with the air of a professional archer. Itaja glanced at his friend's arrow heads, peeping out of their quiver. It was his birthday, and he was shivering outside on a wet field with a haughty prince, instead of eating breakfast with his family.

"How is Kalma?"

Itaja flushed crimson.

"Still painting, Tutty."

"Do you paint too?"

"Yes."

"Thought so."

The boys stood next to each other, several paces apart. Itaja took a breath.

"Let's shoot together, Tutty."

A volley of arrows sped across the field into copper targets. Several of Thutmose's bounced off, but Itaja's kept smashing through the metal. At the end, the boys walked over to collect their arrows. Thutmose flicked his feathered arrow heads thoughtfully.

"Who makes your arrows, Itaja?"

"Maherpa. He's been making them since your grandfather's time. I asked Dad to get him to make me some. They're cheap, too. Dad hates spending!"

"Mine are manufactured at the palace. The arrows are made of bronze. Some are thinner than others. Show me yours." Itaja obliged. The prince checked the length, weight, and feathers. "See? Yours are consistently thicker than mine. Maherpa must use the same mould for all of them."

"Are you going to get him to manufacture yours, too?"

"I'm going to ask the palace to hire him. Thank you for beating me today. It taught me something."

***

Itaja hovered at Kalma's door. He understood she did not wish to be interrupted in the middle of her work, but it was his special day. He also had a gift for her.

"Ah, the birthday boy is here!"

Welcoming him across the threshold, Kalma kissed her guest on the cheek. Offering him a parcel tied with gold string, she watched him unwrap it.

"It's an arrow quiver!" "Do you like it?"

Itaja turned it round in his hands. It was decorated in the Minoan style. Male hunters chased lions, who in turn, chased gazelles through lily motifs. Their golden shields and daggers glinted from the leather background.

"Is it embossed with real gold?"

"It is."

"I have a gift, too, Kalma."

Solemnly, Itaja handed her a plate covered with a cloth.

"Dates. Lovely!"

"That's not all."

Kalma looked at the bowl. It appeared irregular and chunky. She tipped out the dates. Examining the gift, she noticed it was handmade. A Cretan bull dancer stood upright with his arms in the air. Painted lilies surrounded him. A large bull, in a child's wobbly hand, lowered its horns.

Painted on its pink bottom was an orange flower.

Kalma squealed with laughter.

"Did you do this?"

"Tutty helped me find a kiln in the palace studio. He's always in the pottery wing."

"Hatshepsut was wondering at the odd products manufactured there!"

"Please say nothing."

"This is the best present anyone's ever given me! Lunch?"

Two servants emerged from a corner with gold tureens. A Cretan meal of fish, salad, cheese, and warm bread was followed by delicious honey-laced pastries. Itaja could not remember feeling so happy in his life.

***

97

Below the palace, the two boys practised throwing their spears. Stockier than his friend, Thutmose threw faster and further than Itaja. After half an hour, they sat down.

"How's your girlfriend, Itaja?"

"Kalma's not my girlfriend!"

Thutmose grinned.

"Did I mention her name?"

"Stop trying to catch me out. It's mean."

"I think you made a good choice."

"Are you serious, Tutty? Or just making fun of me? Prepare to have your ears boxed!"

"Kalma will still be beautiful in ten years. Then you can marry her. In the meantime, you need to develop your upper body. You were a good boxer, but now you're too skinny."

"I've grown two inches since the month of Peret, but I can't put on muscle."

"Carrots don't build muscle."

"It's all very well to judge if you have plenty of meat. My Dad is always saving for new wives."

"I'll get the palace to send you some steaks."

"Dad's a vizier. He'll be offended."

"I'll stamp it with the royal seal. Tell your parents we're pals. They'll be impressed. Parents are always happy if you mix in the right circles. Now that's settled, let's go for a swim."

Doffing his kilt, the prince ran down to the Nile and threw himself into the cool water. Itaja followed suit. Laughing and playing, they rolled around in the shallows. Above the bank, Hatshepsut and Kalma sampled the latest palace wines while they chatted.

"My nephew looks happy."

"Itaja is a good influence."

"You said Ptah-hotep was his father, but his mother is Cretan, isn't she?"

"From my city. Our families know each other. His older sister also married my cousin."

Hatshepsut sipped her honeyed wine, digesting this information. Below them, the boys climbed out of the Nile's cool waters and lay on the bank to dry. Feeling playful, Kalma threw a pebble in their direction. It hit the grassy sides of bank and tumbled down. Thutmose picked it up and chucked it at a passing heron. The bird, which was trying to extract lunch from the mud flats, flew up and glided soundlessly away above the trees.

"I visited the Chief Priest for a blessing before the battle in Nubia. Karnak wants my nephew back on the throne."

"What did you say?"

"That I wanted Tutty to live a normal life until he's ready, which means after my death."

"And what did Hapuseneb say?"

"Nothing, but I've been thinking about changing my portraits." "I don't understand."

"Egypt needs to feel its sovereign is male."

"Everyone knows you're a woman. It's fine with Egypt."

"It's not. Why do you think I'm going to Nubia?"

It was winter, and the sun was going down earlier than usual. Kalma called out to the boys. Then, she drained her strong Cretan wine.

"I'm ready for dancing."

***

In a grove of hibiscus and incense trees, Kalma twirled in perfectly executed moves. Two snakes writhed in coils around her white arms. She closed her eyes and saw the deep oily blue of Crete's waters. Her dancer's feet moved lightly across the soft grass, but in Kalma's mind, she was in the wilds of her favourite mountain, twirling on a painted gypsum floor, overlooking the sea.

Hatshepsut was the only foreigner Kalma allowed to view the rites of the snake goddess. The closeness of the grove kept them warm as the moon rose. The divine monarch sat at the edge of the tree line and tried not to get in the way. Her friend's eyes were closed. Occasionally, the whites rolled up from under her fluttering eyelids. The dance grew wilder and faster. Kalma threw off the snakes. They slithered away to hide in the rocky garden beyond the grove.

She threw up her arms. Gold bracelets rattled, her anklets tinkled with pomegranate bells, and her layered skirts swirled in a flurry of colour. Blue, cerise, white, and yellow produced the effect of a spinning top. Hatshepsut watched, entranced. The vortex of colours spun her memory back to a palace chamber. Its golden warmth surrounded a child she recognised. Writing on his papyrus, royal forelock plaited on one side, she recognised her nephew.

The rattling of Kalma's bracelets grew louder.

***

98

The boys collected their arrows from around the copper target. It was late afternoon and the sun's heat was abating.

"Do you know the mud workers want a week off, Tutty?"

"Aunty told me it was only a day."

"Someone needs to put those Jewish mud brats in their place – big noses and all."

"I have a big nose, Itaja. Does that mean I'm Jewish?"

"You have a huge honk, Tutty!"

Thutmose laughed. The boys wiped the mud off their arrows with clean linen cloths and returned them to their quivers. The sun sank in the western horizon.

"I don't know why Sen and Hapu are making such a big fuss. The workers just want some time off. They'll work harder if we give them a break."

"I heard those two are annoying your aunt. She's going to Nubia in a few days and doesn't need distractions."

"Do you know she has muscles, Itaja?"

"She looks thinner than usual."

"That happens when you work out. We'll look like that one day."

"With smaller boobs."

"Not yours!"

Playfully, Tuthmosis whacked Itaja around the head. The blow was returned, and the boys fell into the grass where they tussled. Finally, the prince got his friend into a wrestling lock.

"Ow! Stop!"

"Do you surrender?"

"Never!"

Thutmose squeezed harder. Itaja gasped out the words of surrender to end the fight. Getting up, the prince pulled his friend to his feet. They embraced as tradition dictated. Walking half mile back to the training shed, they broke off the main path to run down to the Nile. At the water's edge, they doffed their kilts and plunged into the cool water. Now the sun was just an orange sliver vanishing behind the trees.

"I hope there are no crocodiles out here, Tutty."

"Stop looking on the dark side."

The prince lay on his back in the water. The sky above them was still a pale blue. Stars came out. Sirius, the bright one, gleamed overhead. It was the star of ancient pyramids and calculations, as old as time itself. He felt relaxed and free. A clopping sound reverberated through the warm waters.

"What was that, Tutty?"

The prince trod water.

"Get out!"

He paddled for the shore, with Itaja in tow. Reaching the bank first, Thutmose pulled his friend out of the water. Another clop sounded near to them. Suddenly, enormous jaws rose out of the river. A hippopotamus yawned.

"They kill more people than crocodiles, Tutty," Itaja gasped.

"At least it's not coming over here."

The hippo's ears twitched. Two smaller sets of ears pricked up beside it.

"It's a mother and her calves," Itaja whispered. "That's even more dangerous."

Slowly, Thutmose picked up his quiver and put an arrow into his bow.

"Don't shoot her! What'll the babies do without their mother?"

The prince lowered his bow.

"I was thinking of picking off one of the calves."

"That wouldn't be right. Look how sweet they are!"

Thutmose's hunting drive fizzled away.

"You sound like a woman," he said gruffly. "Come on, it's getting dark."

The hippos disappeared underneath the slowly moving currents as the boys headed home.

***

"Why were you out so late?"

Thutmose gulped. *How does Aunty know?*

"We were doing target practice."

"You were swimming at night!"

She must have spies everywhere. Or else Dusman has a big mouth.

"It was sunset."

"I don't care what time it was. Swimming in the Nile is strictly forbidden."

"Not when it's still light."

"Don't interrupt me. I'm King."

Don't I know it?

"And don't look at me like that. You know very well the throne is no place for a child. But if you're going to be so irresponsible, I'll put you back on it."

"Really? When?"

"Do you know you could have got Itaja killed? He's the son of my vizier!"

"How awful for you Aunty if you couldn't boss everybody about."

Astounded, Hatshepsut said nothing.

"Go to your room," she said at last.

***

99.

Senenmut turned the papyrus over. Its clay seal imprint belonged to Chief Vizier, Useramen. Bracing himself, the royal architect broke the gob of clay. It was a formal letter. He sat down to read. For the eyes and ears of Pharaoh, the letter reported a situation so grave it could overturn the economy. Maybe Hatshepsut already knew. Lately, whenever a delicate matter had to be broached, Senenmut was sought out. It was as if everyone was suddenly afraid of the woman who led the nation. Rolling up the document, he placed it in the folds of his robe.

***

In the royal apartments, Hatshepsut raged. Lord Senenmut accepted the dates offered to him by a servant.

"You shouldn't be so angry. He's just a child."

"Since when do you back Prince Thutmose, Sen?"

"He pulled Itaja out of the water. Remember, it was only a hippo and her calves."

"Hippos are dangerous."

"The main point is that they weren't attacked."

"That isn't the point."

"The point is, he'll rule Egypt one day."

"Precisely! I allowed him to step off the throne to have a life, not to end it."

"If he's going to rule, he needs to develop character."

"I disagree. He needs to stay alive."

"And you need to concentrate. You leave for Nubia in four days. You won't be able to monitor Tutty. Put him out of your mind."

"I've already assigned members of our intelligence department to keep track of him. Do you realise a hippopotamus killed the first king of Egypt?"

"You need to focus on battle."

"You are so right. You are dismissed. I have a meeting with my generals."

***

100.

Senenmut left the royal apartments as hastily as his dignity would allow. Walking down the corridor, he turned into the most private quarter of the royal gardens. The smell of jasmine and incense trees filled the evening air. Inhaling their beautiful fragrance, he relaxed. A full moon was rising. He sat down on a garden bench to enjoy the sight. Slowly, the gigantic ball climbed the inky sky to glimmer over the still waters of Thebes. Outside in the night air, the courtier examined his thoughts. If only people knew the price, he paid for being successful! Most only saw his titles and how far his family had advanced.

He gazed up at the beauty of the yellow moon. Surely the goddess could hear him. Remembering the first kings of the Theban dynasty, he thought of Pharaoh Ahmose, who was named after the moon. Senenmut wondered about those first Theban rulers. They defeated the Hyksos in battle, a victory Hatshepsut was now claiming for herself. The Egyptian monuments left to history would claim many things. How much propaganda had been disseminated throughout the ages and would never be known as such? Like everyone, kings wanted to live forever. Even Senenmut had placed his image in the inner sanctuary of his monarch's mortuary temple. Now, a sliver of immortality had been reserved for the man who had worked tirelessly for his sovereign during his lifetime.

An obese figure came into view. Those stomachs were recognisable anywhere.

"Please join me, Vizier Useramen."

The courtier arranged his robes neatly about his girth. Joining Senenmut on the garden seat, he kept a respectful distance.

"I often walk these gardens, my dear architect, when I can't sleep. Or when I want to think."

"It's a beautiful moonrise."

They sat in silence, absorbing the beauty of their surroundings. Cicadas filled the air with cheerful song.

"I hope she comes back alive."

The words were barely a whisper. Excusing himself, Useramen waddled away. Senenmut felt a chill through his bones. Drawing his cloak about his shoulders, he hurried to his palace apartment.

***

101

Lamplight streamed across papyrus maps. Generals pored over marks which denoted ridges, valleys, and strategic hideouts. Hatshepsut was asking questions.

"I want to know which tribe we should first attack. General Ahmose, you were on campaign with my father. What do you think?"

"Times have changed since the late Tuthmosis rode out to battle."

"The present king of Egypt asks your advice."

"The first tribe we encounter is always important. If it surrenders, the process should be easy. If there's resistance, we must act."

"That sounds like good sense."

General Paneb cleared his throat.

"I respectfully disagree. The first Nubian tribe usually welcomes us, but there is always an ambush at some point. The barbarians inevitably lose, however, their archers take a toll of our army. It's the reason we recruit them, after they've been vanquished, of course."

"How does one prepare?"

"By not taking anything for granted, Your Majesty. We need to be on guard."

The eldest general, Senefer, stabbed the map several hundred miles inland from their planned landing by boat.

"We should be careful of this tribe. They always fight. Up to that point, we should simply be prepared. As our enemies know, a woman rules Egypt. We will need to be extra vigilant."

"I must lead from the front."

"None of us expects you to fight, Your Majesty. There are hills for kings to view the battles. Otherwise, you can stay in your tent until we give the evening report."

"I am King. I will lead Egypt's army."

***

102.

Senenmut stood in Hatshepsut's doorway. His face revealed a mixture of anxiety and determination. A large basin sat in the middle of the room. Armour was stacked against a wall. A doctor dabbed the monarch's bloodied arms.

"You can come in, Sen."

"Why are you covered in blood?"

"They're just scratches. I'm training."

A servant untied the queen's corselet.

"Dear Ra!"

Senenmut turned away quickly. The servant sponged the wounds, coating them with aloe vera and bandages. A dresser flipped a robe over Hatshepsut's head. Her hair was combed in readiness for her audience. Dismissing the servants, she picked up a glass of red wine, laced with poppy, and drained it.

"You must be here on official business to disturb me after practice."

"Hapuseneb saw me yesterday. I also received a letter."

"About our brick workers?"

"They want a week off."

"I thought it was a day."

"The overseers don't want it."

"Why not?"

"The workers worship a foreign god."

"So do the Syrians, Libyans, and Nubians. I don't see the problem."

"But our brickmakers only have one god."

Hatshepsut started to laugh.

"What an impoverished people to have only one! However, are you seriously going to deny them a day off because of a god?"

"It's a Creator god. And invisible."

"Imagine all the resources Egypt could save if we had an invisible god!"

"Our economy would be ruined."

"Give the workers three days off, and plenty of beer."

"But –"

"A happy workforce is a productive one. Ra knows we need the bricks. I'll see you at dinner."

Senenmut departed with a heavy heart. Hatshepsut swallowed another glass of wine with poppy. She remained standing. It was too painful to sit. Suddenly, she realised what it must have been like for her father. Many wives of the previous kings fought in battle. Those kings must have felt a bond with their wives, she reflected. However, her mother Ahmose had not taken up arms and, like Tuthmosis, Hatshepsut shouldered the burden of war alone.

The poppy hit her nerve centres. Pain receded. She sat down and waited. It was like this every day before the evening meal.

And the battle was yet to come.

***

103.

In the dining hall, Hatshepsut's courtiers waited for their monarch. It was already evening. Torches flared in the gardens. Braziers burned incense.

Thutmose turned to Lord Senenmut.

"Where's my aunt?"

"Getting dressed."

"She's an hour late. That's not like her."

Senenmut's lips twitched in amusement.

"You don't think I assassinated her, do you?"

"You can never be too sure these days."

Beckoning one of the servants, Thutmose whispered an order. Ripping his bread violently, he gave the sign for the courtiers to follow suit.

***

Hatshepsut was dozing. Skimming over fields of wheat, she calculated the amount of grain needed for the silos. There must be enough, in case of famine.

Suddenly, her shoulder was shaken. Kalma's face swam into view.

"You're not supposed to touch a king. Even the doctor needs permission."

"You're in pain. I'll bring you some of my medicine."

Hatshepsut pushed herself up.

"The doctor gave me a dose of poppy extract."

"I had your food brought to you. A Syrian mutton dish is on the table next to the patio."

"I should get to the dining hall. I need to preside over the meal."

"Rest up. Your nephew is filling in for you. I'll bring you a potion."

Kalma closed the door behind her. The exhausted monarch fell back and closed her eyes.

***

104.

In the morning, Hatshepsut was well enough to attend breakfast in the dining room. It was the fifth hour of the day. Bread baked over flames in mudbrick ovens. Cooks stirred bean porridge. Chewing indifferently, Kalma sat by a window, picking at a piece of fruit.

Hatshepsut downed her usual morning honey tonic.

"My shoulder still hurts."

"It's only your muscles, Hattie. Archery practice is tough at first. And you shouldn't combine it with sword fighting!"

"How do you know?"

"Itaja is an archer this semester. He tells me all about it. You'll be fine."

"Sen's at the docks, ensuring the chariots are loaded safely on board. Now, don't forget your designs for the Delta palace. I want to see them when I return."

"I've made test mosaics. Eat some porridge, Hattie. It's more filling than a drink."

"You're just like Dad. You know I don't eat breakfast."

"He ate before battle."

"I won't be in a battle for many weeks. Come, it's time to go."

Standing, Hatshepsut pushed her chair back. Picking up a piece of warm sesame seed bread, Kalma followed her friend out of the empty dining hall.

***

A white sun climbed slowly over Thebes. Men carried sacks of flour over their shoulders. Trudging up the gangplanks of the royal fleet, they deposited them in the holds. Hatshepsut stood under her royal pavilion until all the supplies were loaded.

Finally, everything was ready. Courtiers rose to bid their sovereign farewell. She boarded the flagship, and the fleet cast off anchor. Tears streamed down Kalma's face. Senenmut kept his composure.

Neferure was not at the jetty. Still sound asleep in the nursery, she would not rise until after her mother departed the shores of Thebes. A lonely sun kissed the tops of the palms. Kalma retired indoors to work on her designs for a new palace.

Senenmut stood on the jetty until the last ship was out of sight.

***

In the nursery, a distraught little girl was shaking her plaits.

"Mummy said goodnight last night Tutty, but she's not here this morning!"

"She told you where she was going, Nef."

"But why isn't she here?"

"Because she said she was going to Nubia. Now put your toys away, and get your writing kit for your lessons."

Senenmut entered the nursery.

"It's time for school, Prince Thutmose."

"I stopped in to see if the brat was alright."

Infuriated, the boy stomped out. Senenmut picked up the child, who was now crying. Rocking her in his arms, he quietened her. Then, he ruffled her hair and kissed her on the forehead.

"Come on, little one. Mummy's coming back in a few weeks. In the meantime, she would like you to keep up with your hieroglyphs. I've never taught anyone before. Would you like to help me?"

Neferure nodded and put her head on the architect's firm shoulder. It was nice to feel safe from her horrible brother.

***

105

Flat plains loomed before the Egyptian army. The limpid skies of Nubia, which delighted Hatshepsut's eyes on her journey down the Nile, now seemed ominous. Outside her tent, she checked the ground, her chariot wheels, and her horses' hooves. Then she retired inside to don her armour, including the war crown of Egypt. No one assisted her this morning. Taking a deep breath, she viewed her face in a polished bronze mirror. It was as if her father stared back at her. Turning on her heel, she opened the tent flap and marched out.

The army roared its approval. Across the plain, Nubian spears rattled in the morning sunlight. Stepping into her chariot, Hatshepsut was no longer a woman. She was the First Commander of Egypt's Armies. Her job was to lead, fight, and die. And as usual, she thought grumpily, protect everyone else except herself. Grasping the reins, she tied them round her waist.

The soldiers observed her with a mixture of trepidation and curiosity.

"Is she –?"

"Going into battle, Menna? Absolutely."

"Surely not the front line, Arath?"

"Many Egyptian queens have fought from the front. Why not our monarch?"

Hatshepsut's chariot trundled past the first row of cavalry, then the second. Finally, she reached the archers. Moving through the ranks, she spoke calmly, greeting the men by name, and placing courage in their hearts. Noting the sun's position above, Hatshepsut wheeled her horses round and approached the infantry. Men cheered. She knew the enemy could hear the noise. Moving through the ranks she allowed her divine appearance to inspire her soldiers. Unexpectedly, she turned round to face them. The army fell silent.

"No pharaoh has ever had such an army. No one has been more fortunate, not even my father, the mighty King Tuthmosis." A cheer broke out. "Today we fight the miserable Nubians. The fields will run with their blood. Today, Egypt will be victorious!"

She swivelled the chariot round.

"Her Majesty is going to head the army, Arath."

"Now I've seen everything."

Slowly, the Egyptian troops trundled across the plain. Hatshepsut looked at the azure sky. Her father Ra, the sun god, hung brightly overhead. However, Hatshepsut's thoughts were entirely human.

Why did I have to lead? Why didn't I sit on the hill and watch the army like every other king?

The answer was naturally, her nephew, Thutmose. Everything was for him. Icy determination filled Hatshepsut's veins. Picking up her bow, she tested the gut string. Like the warrior queens before her, Tetisheri and Ahmose-Nefertari, she let fly an arrow. To her surprise, it caught a Nubian soldier in the chest.

Amun, I killed him! They're coming for me.

Enemy soldiers descended on the chariot. Arath tipped back his hat.

"Is that our divine monarch?"

Up ahead, the soldiers saw a diminutive figure slashing the enemy right and left. The army was slow in realising the danger to their leader. Eventually, it started to move in to protect Hatshepsut. Undaunted, she continued to hack with her sword.

The things I do for that boy.

Suddenly, Hatshepsut laughed. Leaning over the side of her chariot, she hacked at the enemy forces around its wheels. Horrified at the mad laughing woman, the Nubians fell back *en masse*. The Egyptian army closed around its sovereign. One of Hatshepsut's wrists was bleeding, but still she slashed with her short sword. Vultures circled overhead. Men screamed. Burnished weapons clanked and crunched. The smell of blood seeped into the warriors' nostrils.

By afternoon, the battle was over.

***

106

They worked on a math problem for a few minutes. Dusman hummed a little tune at the head of the class. Itaja put down his reed pen.

"Don't you care that your aunt's in danger, Tutty?"

"Kings go to war."

"I'm sure your aunt would rather be at home."

"Why you don't you mind your own business, Itaja?"

Several men arrived with trays piled with cakes and a stack of empty plates.

"Put them on the shelf," Dusman directed. He turned to his class. "In celebration of our army's invasion of Nubia, we have morning snacks. Line up! You all have five pieces each."

Itaja rushed forward. Thutmose continued to paint hieroglyphs. Dusman pointed to the mixed tray of delights.

"Take the green ones, Itaja. They're delicious! And tell your friend to come up."

Itaja selected his pieces. Returning to his mat, he plumped down his plate.

"Dusman told you to go up."

"I'm writing."

Suddenly, the teacher loomed above him. Placing a plate at Thutmose's elbow, he returned to the head of the class. There were extras, which he now doled out to the boys. Filled with happy conversation, they took their well-deserved break.

"May I talk to you?"

It was Dusman again. Thutmose sighed. He put aside his papyrus sheet. Obediently, he followed his teacher into the cloakroom. They cleared satchels off some of the seats.

"You have military tests this term, Prince Thutmose?"

"I've been practising daily with Itaja."

"Tell me, how do you feel?"

"Confident of winning the Golden Fly."

Dusman nodded. The Golden Fly was a military honour bestowed on Egypt's greatest warriors. The school had its own imitation. Wooden replicas of flies were painted gold by the teachers and awarded to the best cadets.

"And your aunt?"

"You mean King Hatshepsut?"

"Even so," Dusman said agreeably. "But also, your aunt and your mother these days. You must have been sad to see her sail away on the flagship."

"I wasn't at the docks."

Thutmose felt he had farted.

"But you're the crown prince!"

"I was told to attend school after I checked on my sister."

"Princess Neferure?"

"She was crying."

"Your sister is a very lucky girl. We must always remember those weaker than ourselves. I'm glad our future king has such good character. You deserve an extra cake."

***

107.

Wrenching off her muddied helmet, Hatshepsut shook out her sodden locks. Flicking blood and grime over her tent, she took a cup of strong beer from her manservant. A gold drinking basin sat in the middle of the floor.

The royal physician was already present.

"You'll want that attended to, Your Majesty."

He pointed to a gash on her right bicep. Surprised, Hatshepsut looked down. The cut was something she had not noticed on the battlefield. Or felt. Now a wave of nausea swept over her. She wanted to throw up. The pain was so strong, it sang in her ears. It was a terrifyingly large gash, but the warrior in her willed herself to remain calm. The doctor ordered the basin to be filled with cold water from a goatskin.

"We don't have time to heat the water," he explained.

Taking a pouch slung round his shoulders, he emptied a small amount of its contents into the liquid. A servant handed him a spoon. He stirred the contents into a muddy green colour. Taking a pitcher he scooped up some of the contents. Hatshepsut almost gagged.

"I can't drink that."

"No need."

Taking a wad of linen from his pouch, the doctor dipped it into the pitcher, coating it with green herbs. He wrapped it round the wound.

"I look like a mummy!"

"Fortunately, Your Highness won't be one today."

Feeling lightheaded, Hatshepsut wanted to pass out, but knew she had to stay strong. Egyptians were the greatest gossips on earth. The doctor continued an examination of the rest of her body. To her dismay, there was a cut on her leg. Although Hatshepsut thought she had been protected in the chariot, a weapon had sliced through the back of one calf muscle. Fortunately, the cut was not deep. After the longest hour of her life, she was bathed and bandaged. The doctor emptied a vial of poppy into a bowl of wine. Downing it, the monarch began to feel pleasantly warm. She fell asleep on her camp bed under waves of opium rest.

Next day Hatshepsut awoke late. Her arm was not throbbing. Peeking under the bandages, she grunted with satisfaction. The wound had closed. The Nubian blade had not sliced the vein, and her leg felt better. A male attendant entered the tent. He was followed by a Nubian servant girl, carrying a gold tray.

"Feeling well, Your Majesty?" the man asked.

"The wound needs redressing. What's for breakfast?"

"Beans and bread."

"No yoghurt or cold duck?"

"It's a Nubian breakfast. I can send the girl back to the kitchen for Your Highness' choice of food."

"No need. It smells good."

Hatshepsut scooped up the beans with a wooden spoon. The gold spoons had mysteriously disappeared on the voyage. There was a thief on her staff. But she had no urge to complain. The lion in her breast was tamed. She Who Scratches, Pakhet, goddess of war, had retired. The diplomat in her had taken over. Maybe this was how men felt. Senenmut said they could compartmentalise their lives. Women did the same thing with their husbands, ungrateful progeny, and housework.

But war was different. Unlike many of Egypt's kings, Hatshepsut had never attended military school. True, she had been introduced to a military perspective by her father, but it was not the same thing. However, it was no use thinking of the disadvantages of being raised as a princess instead of a prince. Already dubbed the foremost builder of grand monuments in the world, Hatshepsut was now a warrior, like many of her illustrious predecessors. Finishing her beans and bread, she noted it was tastier than the breakfast of the Egyptian royal court.

And now, Nubia was secured.

***

108

It was the third hour of the afternoon. Dusman entered the airy living room of his home. Skylights admitted air and light without the heat of the sun. His wife Henyt, a pleasant woman of around thirty, relieved him of his bags. Embracing, they rubbed noses in a traditional greeting.

"How was your day, Dussy?"

"Wonderful! We had cakes in honour of Egypt's campaign in Nubia."

"I hope you're still hungry. Palace officials dropped off extra flour and meat at noon. Our king must think highly of us."

"I was Hatshepsut's teacher once."

"You're in her good books, which is fortunate for us. Let's get you refreshed for the evening."

Dusman accompanied his wife into the small lobby, where she brought a bowl of water and natron for his feet. Sitting on a wooden trestle, he slipped off his sandals. Dipping his feet into the warm, salty water he sighed with pleasure.

"You're the best of wives. I get so sore these days."

Henyt added more natron and placed a linen towel next to him. Patting his cheek, she left Dusman to his thoughts. After soaking his troubles away, the master of the house took his feet out of the water and dried them. Then, he joined his wife for dinner.

His son, who was studying in a corner, rose to greet him.

"Nehi, where's your sister?"

"Meri's upstairs, mooning over her boyfriend."

"He's not up there with her, is he?" Dusman asked sharply.

"He's not allowed to visit," his wife interjected. "You know that."

Dusman took a seat. Henyt brought him a steaming stew, fragrant with herbs and spices. He looked surprised.

"It's venison!"

"From the palace. There must have been a royal hunt before our king left for Nubia."

"We are indeed favoured, Henyt."

There was silence while the family ate. Upstairs, a sweet lilting tune broke out. Meri sang a love song. Nehi snickered.

"Henyt, how old is she now?"

"Twelve next birthday, Dussy."

"Nearly ready for marriage."

Dusman dipped his bread into the meat juice. His wife offered him a mixture of grilled beans and herbs.

"How is the prince, dear?"

"Becoming a skilled warrior."

"Thutmose is still a child, isn't he?"

"Eight, this year."

"And his health?"

"Better than when he left the Horus throne, but today he said something that bothered me. Our prince wasn't invited to see his aunt off. Can you imagine that?"

"Would you prefer he missed your class?"

"Tutty should be treated as part of his family. He should have been on the jetty to farewell his aunt. Hatshepsut's gone to war. He may never see her again."

"Prince Thutmose is being treated as one of the family. He's a military cadet, which is fitting for a member of a military family."

"It's all very strange Henyt, with his aunt taking the throne. She could have opted to stay his adviser. And Lord Senenmut is too powerful."

Shaking his head, he ladled gravy over his greens. Nehi excused himself, and took a plate of stew to his sister.

"Stop worrying, Dussy. Hatshepsut probably doesn't want her nephew to be anxious on her account. What do you think would have happened if your princely pupil broke down in front of those courtiers? He would never have forgiven her!"

Dusman chuckled.

"You're right. Tutty is very unforgiving!"

***

109

Itaja gave Thutmose a wooden mallet. Hammering with all his might the prince nailed a wicker target to a tree. He stopped and rubbed his stomach.

"Feeling alright, Tutty?"

"I have a stomach-ache."

"There were a lot of cakes yesterday."

The prince pulled an arrow from his quiver.

"Don't remind me."

"Why do you hate your aunt so much?"

An arrow zinged from Thutmose's bow, and sailed above the target to plough into a neighbouring field. The farmer on the other side waved his fist at them.

"I don't hate her!"

"I just asked."

"You shouldn't accuse me of hating our monarch. It's treason."

"You're only human, Tutty. Everyone hates their mum sometimes."

"For Ra's sakes – she isn't my mother!"

Itaja laughed.

"What are you laughing at?"

"You always lose your temper when the throne is mentioned."

He let fly an arrow which sailed perfectly into the heart of the target. Thutmose's ears turned red.

"I'm supposed to be Egypt's king."

"At three? Was a bit young, don't you think?"

Another arrow flew perfectly into its mark. Thutmose gritted his teeth.

"I'm eight now."

"Big difference."

"I have counsellors."

"People who would turn you into a puppet."

"Kings are divine."

"You know, I never noticed before." Itaja walked to the target and pulled out his arrows. The wicker board fell to the ground under his tugging. "But you're an ungrateful idiot."

The prince flew at his friend. Clutching him by the waist, he brought Itaja down onto the soft black earth. Writhing around in the mud the two boys fought violently. After some minutes Thutmose felt a sharp prod in his right shoulder. Swinging around he saw the concerned face of Dusman. Immediately, he sprang to his feet. His opponent's face was firmly wedged in the mud.

Rolling up his perfectly pressed linen sleeves, Dusman yanked the boy out. The exertion was too much, and he fell onto his well-rounded bottom. Gasping, he tried to rise, but fell back next to Itaja. Thutmose reached out with one mud-encrusted arm and tried to assist his teacher. Toppling forward, he landed next to him.

Dusman pulled out a linen kerchief and wiped the children's faces. "We make a fine group."

"Itaja started it."

"I don't care who started it, Prince Thutmose. Don't you realise that fighting is only for the gym?"

"What about war?"

"What about it?"

"You don't honestly expect us to fight at set times."

"Why not?"

"Because we should be prepared for surprise attacks."

"That's war," Itaja added.

"I'm glad you two agree." Dusman rose with difficulty. "Let's go to class."

Obediently the boys followed their teacher into the schoolyard. At the gate, a pair of sentries raised their eyebrows.

"It must have been some workout," one said to the other.

"The crown prince's mother is at the front, you know."

The two men watched the bedraggled group head to class. Dusman led the way to the cloakroom. The boys followed. Pushing aside a mass of school bags and capes, their teacher pulled back the bathroom latch. Several students, who were applying pomade to their locks, viewed the newcomers with alarm.

"Is that you, sir?"

"Time for class, boys."

The bathroom emptied. Filling a basin with water, Dusman placed two pitchers on a wooden bench. He invited Itaja and Thutmose to bathe. The boys poured water over each other, and scrubbed themselves with school issue linen pads.

Meanwhile, their teacher made his way to a cubicle. Outside it, on a ledge, was a full pitcher of warm water. Walking over to a curtain, he pulled it back. A compact mudbrick box, lined with gypsum, served as a shower.

Humming to himself, Dusman picked up the pitcher and retired behind the curtain.

***

110

Itaja and the prince worked hard all day. Dusman sat at the head of the class, instructing his pupils and correcting their work. The fact he had arrived late in a filthy, dishevelled state was noted. By noon, the entire school knew.

Oblivious to the gossip, Dusman bid farewell to his pupils in the afternoon. Watching them make their way to the field for military exercises, he finally turned inside. Then, he cleared the water pots used by the children. Rolling up his papyrus scroll, he placed it in his satchel. The cleaners would swab down the room later with water, and then fumigate it with natron, and sandalwood.

Closing the door, the teacher checked the cloakroom for missing capes, and the bathroom for tardy students. Content that all was in order, he stepped into the blinding sunshine. Suddenly, he was encompassed by people whom he recognised as parents of his children. It was like a noisy market day on the banks of the Nile at Thebes. A barrage of questions slung themselves like well- aimed arrows at his prized reputation. Then, quite suddenly, they stopped.

"Your appearance is fine," noted one parent.

"Most presentable."

"I thought you said he was caked in mud."

"What I want to know, is did my son receive his lessons?"

Dusman smiled innocently.

"All lessons are completed."

The mob started to disperse. Dusman waited until the parents melted away into the shimmering haze of the afternoon. When they had gone, he made his way out of the gate, past the snickering sentries, and down the path to his home. It took only a few yards for him to reach the welcome shade of his house and beloved Henyt.

"You won't believe what happened to me today."

At the end of his story, his wife was less than sympathetic.

"Why didn't you bribe the guards?"

"I'm a man of principle."

"We can't afford to lose this house, Dussy."

"It's ours."

"At the pleasure of the Crown."

"That's right. I'm a teacher to the next king, whose aunt happens to be paying me."

"Whose aunt is our king and has a point to prove. Hatshepsut is going to hear about this incident."

"But she's in Nubia."

Suddenly, a chill filled Dusman's entrails. His wife jogged her head up and down.

"That's right. You're going to have to think of something plausible."

"I saved Itaja from death at Tutty's hands. Our prince had the boy's head wedged in the mud when I got to them."

"Then use that."

"Use what?"

"Put her on the back foot. With an heir like that, Hatshepsut had better watch out for an assassination attempt later in life."

"You really are most political. We've been married for twelve years, and I never saw it before today."

"You may be the provider Dussy, but I'm the matron of this family. It's my job to protect its interests."

"Your mind is evil."

"All I'm saying darling, is please think of something plausible before you get hauled into Principal Tchay's office tomorrow."

With a heavy heart, Dusman decided to soak his feet. Staying longer at his basin than usual, he reflected on the ways of the world.

***

111.

Principal Tchay looked uncomfortable. With a crimson shawl draped over pleated white robes, and tucked into a gold waistband, Dusman was better dressed than most courtiers. Tchay offered his visitor a seat, and poured grape juice into two cups.

"I have reports about you."

"All good, I hope."

"Not exactly." Tchay picked up a cup of juice and sipped it. "You – er, arrived late yesterday."

"I was here before dawn. The boys were doing military exercises."

"When they should have been in class."

"There's a test next week for the Golden Fly award. They were training for it."

"Ah, yes! A most prestigious prize."

"It is the highest award for juniors. Prince Thutmose is expected to win."

"Marvellous! That'll look good for the school. But why didn't you get the boys to class at an earlier time?"

"As you know, the training grounds are large. I didn't know where they were."

"Makes sense."

The principal rummaged through his papyri. Dusman waited politely, a bland expression on his face.

"They say you were dirty and untidy. Did the boys give you trouble?"

"There was a muddy patch on the field. I fell. You know what happens when the field is overused."

"Oh yes! Especially after the horses and chariots. It takes weeks for the tyre marks to disappear."

"Fortunately, I keep a spare robe at work."

233

"Of course, of course."

"I also ensured the boys cleaned up before attending class."

"Naturally. Well – er – that'll be all."

Dusman rose from his seat and left the office. Outside, his pleasant demeanour was replaced by a crinkle between his brows.

***

112

At noon, the pupils set aside their papyri and spilled into the play-ground. Dusman pulled out a loaf of seasoned bread from his satchel. It was wrapped in a coarse linen cloth to keep its freshness. He placed it on his desk. Stuffed with duck, it was one of his favourite dishes.

"Nefer and Pawara, please stay behind."

The boys cast worried glances at each other.

"I'm sorry I didn't do all my homework, sir."

"I know you have a spear throwing test next week, Nefer."

Dusman reached for his spices, which he kept near to him on the surrounding shelves. Placing them next to his loaf, he took out a gold knife and cut the bread into wedges. Shuffling them onto a napkin, he pushed the food towards the boys.

"Help yourselves."

"We brought our lunch, sir."

"Nefer's right. We'll eat ours in the playground."

"Not today, I'm afraid, Pawara," Dusman smiled pleasantly.

"Are you keeping us in?"

"This is detention. Now eat up. My wife makes an exceptionally good duck sandwich."

"What for? I did my homework!"

"You gossiped, Pawara."

The boys goggled at their teacher. Dusman chewed evenly, and regarded the shelf on which rested a new pot.

"I don't understand, sir."

"You understand perfectly well. Both of you spread a story about me turning up to class late, and in a mess."

"How do you know we spread a rumour?"

"I'm an adult. I know everything."

Dusman took another wedge of duck loaf. Unsure how to respond, the boys helped themselves to slices. The combination of seasoned duck and bread melted in their mouths. They were soon engrossed in their lunch.

"I thought it remiss of me not to educate you in the ways of politicians."

"We're *children*."

"You are both sons of aristocrats, Nefer. You are one of Chief Vizier Useramen's brood being groomed for the court. And Pawara is a distant relative of Itaja."

"Unfortunately, it's true," Pawara sighed. "I heard my cousin lost to Tutty."

"There's no shame in losing to a prince. What you both must learn is to never break anyone's confidence."

"What if somebody wanted to murder the king, sir?"

"Does anyone want to murder the king, Pawara?"

"I'm just asking. What if my father came up to me and said he was plotting to kill the king?"

"Then you have a duty to inform the state."

"But how do I do that? I'm just a child. He might kill me."

Dusman finished his last bite, and cleared the desk.

"Time for class," he said.

***

113.

Feet paddling in agitation, a nervous Dusman was in a quandary. The cool of the footbath at the end of the day was no relief.

"There's a plot to kill the king, Henyt."

"Breathe!"

"I am breathing."

"You're jabbering."

"I put a courtier's son in detention, and he told me."

"He was hoping you'd let him go."

"Rubbish!"

"Isn't that what you did?"

"I had to release him after class – you're not listening to me!"

Henyt placed a towel next to her husband on his wooden seat. She retired to the kitchen where she was baking bread. Dusman wiped his feet and padded across the glazed tiles to join her. Henyt took the bread out of her oven and left the loaves on a bench to cool. Filling pottery bowls with condiments, she set them on a low table next to a couch, where her husband rested before dinner. Covered with cedar and over-laid with embroidered blankets, the bench was an extension of the plastered mudbrick wall. Sitting cross-legged, the tired teacher fluffed up a cushion behind his back.

Henyt went to the cellar and collected a jar of beer. In the kitchen, she unplugged it and poured the thick liquid through a sieve into a large cup. Mixing warm honey into the contents, she placed it next to her husband. Dusman took a long draught of the beverage.

"I am worried, Henyt. Should the Crown be notified?"

"That could mean a lot of trouble for us."

Henyt crushed garlic with a pounder, and added it to the herbs for their stew. A door banged. It was Nehi. Shuffling off his sandals in the hallway, he joined his parents.

237

"Dad, is it alright if I take an extra hieroglyphs course next summer?"

"You're asking for more study?"

"I'll be teaching, too."

"It's a good opportunity for him, Dussy."

"Dad, I want to become a scribe for the Royal Treasury."

"I thought you might help me out at Cadet School. Where's Meri?" Dusman suddenly asked.

"Upstairs."

"She's very quiet. Go and check on your sister." Obeying his father, the boy climbed the stairs to Meri's room. "I thought we'd decided Nehi would work with me, Henyt."

"We haven't decided anything yet."

"A boy should follow his father."

"Your son is teaching."

"He's aiming to be a scribe in the palace – of the Royal Treasury, no less."

Henyt left her simmering stew to join Dusman on the stool their son had vacated.

"Don't you want Nehi to have ambition?"

"Of course."

"You should be pleased with his accomplishments. He's a good boy. Do you see how quickly he obeys you, and always shows respect? You should be proud."

"I am!"

His wife returned to the fire.

"Blast! The stew is dried out. Meri will have to eat beans. I do wish you would save these conversations until after dinner."

Dusman drained his beer. Overall, this was turning out to be a most trying day.

***

114.

Thutmose could not concentrate. Scrunching up his papyrus homework, he started again. His entire life revolved around copying hieroglyphs, and archery practice. His shoulders ached. His fingers felt stiff from holding a reed pen all day. It would have been better to stay on the throne. Suddenly, Neferure was at the door.

"Want to play, Tutty?"

"Go away!"

Bursting into tears, the girl ran up the corridor back to her nursery. Looking out of his window, Thutmose gazed at the sun over the Nile. It was his favourite time of day. Sinking into a glow of amber and red, it almost sang above the tops of the palms. Incense trees, recently planted outside his apartments, gave off a faint smell, or so he imagined. Servants lit braziers. Incense purified the palace and warded off mosquitoes. With a heavy heart, Thutmose turned back to work.

Senenmut was at his door.

"Why are you scolding your sister?"

"I can't play with her. Our Golden Fly test is tomorrow."

"Shouldn't you be practising?"

"Coach says my body needs to rest. I also have writing homework."

"Anything I can help with?"

"It has to be my own work." Thutmose attempted a smile. "Thank you, all the same."

The man vanished. If there was one way of getting rid of the sycophant, it was politeness.

"Having problems with sums?"

The prince jumped up.

"Itaja! What are you doing here?"

"I was practising for the spear throwing test, but can't concentrate."

"Neither can I."

"Why aren't you doing archery, Tutty?"

"Coach wants me to rest."

"I came to congratulate you, and wish you the best for tomorrow."

"Save your congratulations until after the test."

"Why? Everyone knows you're going to win."

"I'm nervous."

Itaja plonked himself onto a divan. Selecting a handful of dates from a wooden saucer, he ate quickly.

"We're all nervous, Tutty."

"Everyone's been practising, but I'm expected to win."

"Won't you?"

"Neeja is good, especially with the bow."

"And I'm excellent in hurling a spear."

"Spear throwing doesn't have the same weight as archery."

"No, but I'm good at it. Heck, I just want to pass."

"I envy you."

Itaja rose.

"If you can't concentrate, we could go for a walk. The Nile is beautiful at this time of evening."

***

Itaja was right. The sky glowed gold, and was streaked with red and purple, deepening into the dark blue of night. The boys walked in silence for some minutes, absorbing the warm breezes.

"I'd like to be a scribe, not a soldier."

"At least you can choose what you want to do, Itaja."

Thutmose picked up a piece of rock and threw it. Whizzing high in the air, it smacked the water. Nearby bushes rustled with alert sentries.

"You shouldn't tease them like that."

"I wasn't."

"How's your stepmother?"

"Hopefully dead."

"That's not very nice!"

"What do you want me to say? I don't have a mother."

"You have an aunt who protects you. It's stupid to wish her dead. You'd be on the throne again. Do you want that now?"

"I have no choice about anything."

"You do. She's given you choices."

They sat down in the cool grass.

"What do you mean?"

"You can train for the future. We graduate next week, and then it's chariots."

"That's true!"

"Imagine riding out to battle against the Hittites!"

"Or Nubians."

"You know, I don't ask after your aunt to be rude, Tutty. It's what you're supposed to do. Ask about people's parents, and –"

"I don't have any."

"You have our king personally looking out for you. Nobody else can say that."

"Except Neferure. Brat!" Thutmose tore at the grass. "I'm just an orphan."

"That's true!" Itaja laughed.

Thutmose punched him in the arm.

"You're not supposed to say that!"

"Ow! Must you be so violent?"

"It's my soldier's training."

"You're still technically a king. It's not as though your aunt deposed you."

With a huff, Thutmose lay down on his back. Tiny stars peeked out from the darkening vault above. Suddenly, the pressure melted away. A wonderful future held gleaming chariots and whinnying steeds. Dusman had another vase for him to paint. And Itaja was his friend, even if he was the most annoying person on earth. How that boy could talk! He should have been born a woman, although he did like Kalma. It was wonderful, too. Thutmose knew he, as a prince, could not marry the pretty lady, but with Itaja it was a different matter.

He smiled up at the sky, as his spirit left his body, and he fell asleep in the grass.

***

242

<h1 style="text-align:center">115.</h1>

Principal Tchay nervously turned his reed pen over in his hands. Pawara stood in the office, an insolent look on his face.

"Your teacher thinks there's a plot to kill the king."

"A plot? The king?"

"Don't act the innocent with me, Pawara! Our school is obliged to report it."

"You should."

"Did you tell Dusman there was a conspiracy?"

"Did he say I told him that?"

"Not exactly."

"My father is an important man in Egypt. Perhaps I should have a word."

"No need. I'm sure it was a mistake."

Pawara closed the door on his way out of the office. With the merest hint of a malicious smile, he walked out of the plain whitewashed building, and into freedom.

***

Dusman reflected that being hauled into the Principal's office was becoming a regular occurrence. He waited for his boss to speak.

"I spoke to Pawara today."

"Do you think there's a security threat, sir?"

"I think you've been exaggerating, Dusman."

"If I have, I am truly sorry."

"We won't speak of this again."

Tchay bit the insides of his cheeks. It was a habit he had developed over the years when stressed. Recently, more parts of his mouth were becoming tender. Staring blankly out of the tiny office window grill, he watched a group of children playing in the courtyard.

A royal school for the elite was something he envisioned a long time ago. When he was young, and pulsating with ideas and energy, he put his dream into practice. Many days were spent at court trying to convince the king that it would be a good idea. A place of study and intellectual development, coupled with military development for the youngest, the new school was to produce Egypt's future elite. Nowadays, Tchay was tired, even after a good night's rest.

"Shall I leave?"

"You're dismissed. And thank you."

"For what, Principal?"

"I'm sure something more than bread loaves is cooking in that youngster's household. Don't worry. I'll put spies in place. We have a duty to investigate."

Relief washed over Dusman. He left quickly. There was only so much time a man should spend in the presence of his superiors.

***

116

"Now it's time."

Hatshepsut gritted her teeth. A handmaiden placed the monarch's bruised feet in a basin of warm water. Leaving her mistress to soak, the servant drew the curtain, and retired to another part of the tent to wait.

On her own, Hatshepsut was left with her thoughts, as the pain in her feet ebbed away. The hardest part of kingship, according to Tuthmosis, was being alone. Her father had always repeated the fact day and night until she thought he was losing his memory. When she ascended the Horus throne, Hatshepsut felt it was different to anything she had imagined. Hapuseneb described a similar feeling when he was admitted to the inner sanctum of Amun-Ra.

But, if Hatshepsut thought being crowned supreme monarch would be a sublime privilege, she was wrong. It was far more. The enormity of being a king affected her in a way she could not have imagined. It was as if she was married. Her innate sense of purpose was the reason she had the grace to be alone, and not feel lonely. Perhaps, her father was right about kingship. But perhaps he did not have the same sense of destiny as his daughter.

In her bathtub, Hatshepsut, King of Upper and Lower Egypt, relaxed.

***

After an hour, the attendant returned. Lifting her sleeping mistress's feet out of the bath, she dried them.

"Is it over?"

"Time for sleep, Your Majesty."

With an effort, Hatshepsut rose and made her way to the camp bed. Lowering herself onto the linen sheets, she tried not to collapse outright. The room spun around. Closing her eyes, she fell into oblivion.

Taking handfuls of frankincense and myrrh, the servant threw them into a brazier. Sparks flew. For a moment, the woman felt a rush of wind, as if a bird had brushed her shoulders on its way out of the tent. Shivering, she pulled her shawl tightly around her shoulders. Checking on the slumbering sovereign to ensure she was still only sleeping, the attendant left Hatshepsut to heal.

***

117.

Pounding of the pestle and mortar reverberated through the house as Henyt crushed herbs for her family's bread.

"What did he say, Dussy?"

"That everything was fine."

"You were lucky. Pass me the salt."

Dusman handed his wife a pottery saucer. She took several large pinches, and threw them into the mixture. Then she started pounding again. Deciding to sit on the roof, Dusman climbed the stairs. Passing his daughter's room, he heard her singing a lilting melody of a popular love song.

On the roof, the air was cool. He sat down on a bed. It was used when the nights were too hot to sleep inside. It also doubled as a couch. Presently, his wife appeared with a large beer jar, and a straw. She set a warm bread loaf next to his drink.

"Duck is coming."

She hurried back to the kitchen. Sipping his beer through the straw, Dusman put his feet up on the bed. Resting against the headboard, with a cushion behind his back, he watched the sun go down in a happy frame of mind.

***

Itaja was in a bad mood. The chariot handling exam was taking all day. Moving the horses from their stables onto the track was beyond the capabilities of the bureaucrats in charge. Arguments and papyri flew about with equal volatility.

"How long do we have to wait, Tutty?"

"I would tell you to hold your horses, but clearly that's what is aggravating you."

"Don't joke! Why can't they let the horses out before the examination staff get here? We need to know which horses are assigned to us."

"Patience is what the army is all about."

"It's nearly noon, Tutty. Next thing you know, they'll be having lunch. I'm going back to class."

"You can't miss the first day of the exam. They deduct points."

"If I stay here, I'm going to be dead of sunstroke before the blasted exam starts."

Itaja strode away. Chewing a dry grass stalk, Thutmose moved under a tamarisk tree.

***

Dusman looked up.

"Aren't you supposed to be riding?"

"There are no horses."

Itaja sat down on his study mat, tucked his feet under him, and began a hieroglyph.

"Leave at once!" Itaja, who had never heard Dusman give orders, set his pen down.

"I mean it. Now!"

Reluctantly, the boy left the room. In the yard, the midday sun shone down with relentless ire. Boys ate their lunches under the trees, and talked in a desultory manner. Shading his eyes, Itaja squinted at the green track, still empty of horses. Sighing, he trudged across the blinding expanse of fields. Heat hummed off the grass.

Sweating profusely, the boy finally reached the racetrack.

"Under here," Thutmose waved.

Itaja quickened his pace to where the prince sat under a broad tamarisk tree.

"By Ra, it's hot!"

"You should stop moving, Itaja. Keep your energy for the test."

The boy collapsed under the welcome shade of the tree's spiky branches.

"Why won't the horses come out, Tutty?"

"Lunch! You were right."

"Battle horses should be able to cope without a meal. I wish they'd get this first part over."

"So do I. My aunt's due back next week. I want to get the top prize." Voices wafted from the stables.

"Let them out!"

"It's not allowed, sir."

"I'm their teacher!"

"You're not an army instructor."

"The instructors will be here in an hour to conduct the first part of the exam."

"That's when I let the horses out."

Sounds of splintering wood followed. Thutmose cautiously packed his lunch.

"What are you doing?"

"Getting ready to practise, Itaja."

Emerging from the stables, a triumphant Dusman led the first horse. Harried stable boys followed. Soon, all the horses were on the field. Bridled, they were hitched to chariots. The boys hastily put aside their food and started practising the gallop, trot, and ceremonial pacing required for royal parades.

Eventually, the army instructors arrived. They singled out the prince in order to place him first in the final examination, and then started to grade the boys. The task took up the remainder of the afternoon. By sunset, Thutmose had his winner's sash. Itaja accepted tenth place.

"That was so hard, Tutty!"

Thutmose made a wry face.

"I wouldn't know."

"They have to give you first place. Stop frowning! It doesn't mean you can't handle a chariot."

"The problem is they never give any constructive feedback."

"But do you really want that?"

"Of course I do! I'm going to be heading our army. I want to know if I'm any good."

"You *are* good."

Dusman stood in front of the prince with a serious expression on his face.

"With respect, how would you know, sir? You're not an army instructor."

"I won the Golden Fly five years in a row."

"You studied here?"

"I graduated with top honours. That's why I teach at this school."

"But how could you win the Golden Fly ahead of a crown prince?"

"Your father did not study here. He was not first in line to the throne." Thutmose's face cleared.

"And Uncle Wadj died young! Aunty told me. How good am I, sir?"

"Top of the class. Itaja should be top equal. Your style is not approved of by the army, Itaja. However, on the battlefield, I would keep him close to you, Thutmose. You will live much longer if you do."

"Top equal? You'll have to give me half your sash, Tutty!"

"Not likely!"

Dusman made to walk away. He halted.

"Remember, you're still a king, Thutmose. Although we all address you as 'prince,' your aunt did not change your rank. When you ascend the Horus throne after her death, you will be fully trained and capable of making your own decisions. Be nice to her when she arrives from Nubia next week. She's doing this for you."

Thutmose jumped down from his carriage. Placing his arms around Dusman, he hugged him.

***

On the army's return, Egypt celebrated for three days. Villages and towns from the Delta to Thebes were covered in debris from riotous partying. Although the masses were only allowed as far as the front of the temple, acrobats and dancers performed for them on the streets.

Impassive as a Karnak statue, Hatshepsut presided over the parade of Nubian tribute. Gold, animals, and prisoners passed before her as the victor. After two hours, she began to weary of the long lines. She was also sure the sun was melting the hair fat used by her vanquished foes.

Chief Vizier Useramen was proud of the parade which he had planned. Senenmut sat at a discreet distance behind the throne. Finally, Hatshepsut turned to her right.

"Is that stench from the prisoners, Chief Vizier?"

"It must be the animals, Your Highness. The prisoners were bathed last night."

"They *smell*. Fat and cow's milk. You can't get rid of it."

"How do you know?" Senenmut ventured.

"I was on campaign."

"I can't smell at a hundred cubits, Hattie, unless there's a breeze."

"If you don't be quiet, I'll have you removed."

Hatshepsut summoned the incense bearer to waft frankincense around her. Senenmut fell silent. Two of the officers overheard the conversation.

"Trouble in the royal bedchamber, Arath?"

"Her Majesty was with us in Nubia, Menna. He stayed at home."

"Not his fault."

"Her Majesty's seen action."

"And not just at the front!"

Irritated, Arath looked away.

"You need to show our monarch respect."

"Why are you so offended?"

"All anyone wants to do, Menna, is talk about Lord Senenmut and Hatshepsut."

"We have to pass the time. This boring parade has taken most of the morning."

"That's because our king won a great victory."

"We won it."

"Would you say that if the conquering king was Tuthmosis?"

"He was a great king."

"I need a lavatory."

Excusing himself, Arath left the group. Walking around the compound, he reflected that Hatshepsut's victory was being marginalised, even as she took a pharaoh's tribute.

***

120

Rolling up his plans, Senenmut stuffed them into his satchel. Dawn was another hour away. He made his way to the audience hall. Sitting close to a corner pillar, he took out his breakfast. A bread loaf baked by his servants, was still warm. Stuffed with seasoning and fish paste, it made a nutritious start to the long day. Finishing his meal with milk from a goatskin flask, the architect settled down to wait.

At the eighth hour of the day, two guards entered the hall. Noting Senenmut, they clenched their spears and stood to attention. The throne, which stood on a dais, was dusted hastily by two maids. A red cushioned footstool was placed in front.

When everything was prepared, Hatshepsut arrived with her bodyguards. Taking her position on the throne, she rested her sandalled feet on the footstool.

"Lord Senenmut, I want an update of my latest project."

"Do you require a report, Your Majesty?"

"I need two obelisks, not a report."

"Ramose was despatched to the Aswan granite quarry early this morning."

She indicated the bread crumbs on his robe.

"I see you have already eaten."

"I was about to start work at the office after this audience, Your Majesty."

"Your work ethic is commendable. I shall join you. Perhaps you could show me the plans for my obelisks."

"No need."

Senenmut took the plans from his satchel. Unrolling them, he placed them on the floor. Guards assisted him by standing on two sides of the papyrus. A glow of pleasure lit Hatshepsut's face.

"Chief Architect, you are due for a raise."

Poring over the diagrams for the monuments, she listened eagerly as her courtier described how they were to be manufactured. Wistfully, Hatshepsut recalled Dhey's comment of long ago, questioning her need for the knowledge of building codes, and the angles of obelisks.

***

121

Ramose was accustomed to Thebes in the summer. However, its heat was nothing compared to midday at Aswan's granite quarry. The bearers of his litter put him down with grunts of exertion. As he alighted, two overseers approached. They hovered anxiously behind him, waiting for orders.

Ramose unrolled his plan of the quarry and checked its directions. He walked about and found the corner of the rocky shelf, which was marked in red on his papyrus sheet. He could see the depressions left by the removal of King Tuthmosis' granite obelisks. Waving to the overseers, he pointed to the section of rock above them.

"Cut the new obelisks from above the empty space. We need two."

The men murmured in surprise at the quantity, but accepted the instructions. It was time to get their workmen. Cursing his stupidity for not hiring a fan bearer, Ramose returned to his litter.

***

Fires flared around the rock. Men poured water from the Nile over the hot granite, breaking up the top layers. Sweepers rid the site of broken pieces. Dozens of workers, armed with stones made of hard dolerite, pounded out the obelisks. Ramose watched from a distance. They were keeping the granite wet, but dust clouds still rose into the air. The workers were prisoners, condemned to hard labour. Most of the foremen were Egyptian, although some were foreigners who lived and worked in Egypt.

If he had stopped to think, Ramose might have wondered at the value of human life. Men's hands and arms juddered under the strain of pounding heavy dolerite against unforgiving granite. Conscripted to hard labour, many would be dead within a year. Instead of feeling concern for the men, Ramose turned to his charts. Relieved the operation was set up, he could report to Lord Senenmut without fear of losing his post.

Later in the day, Ramose waited patiently on the jetty to welcome his boss. Boats were never on time in Egypt, and the sun was setting when Hatshepsut's favourite courtier arrived. A sumptuously appointed royal barge glided across the water to the dock. Men threw ropes from the boat to those waiting on the jetty. Chief Royal Architect, Lord Senenmut, descended the gangplank at a brisk pace. Lean and tanned, he was all business.

"Daydreaming, Ramose?"

"I was thinking about our pharaoh's obelisks. We are making good progress."

"First day?"

"And both obelisks."

"That *is* good news!"

Ramose conducted a brief tour of the quarry where he confirmed the progress of the stone monuments to his distinguished guest. As the sun set, the pair retired to a mansion for the king's men. An evening meal of plump pheasant, and baked pigeon, was accompanied by platters of cucumbers, lettuces, and steamed leeks.

Senenmut, who was fond of his vegetables, tucked into the leeks. Southern wine was the best part of the meal. Imported from Mycenae, the beverage was diluted with water, but still potent. Night fell. Alabaster lamps were lit. Their orange glow projected images carved within their interiors, onto the walls.

After dinner, Senenmut related his adventures down the Nile. There was nothing of particular interest, but Ramose pricked up his ears when the royal architect changed the subject.

"Hatshepsut will remain sovereign of Egypt."

"What do you mean?"

"Co-regents move aside for their adult sons. Hatshepsut isn't going to do that."

"Does that mean the manufacture of more obelisks?"

"Your job is secure, Ramose."

Towards midnight, the two retired to their bedrooms. Fresh sheets covered fleece-lined mattresses. Ramose washed his face and hands, said a prayer, and climbed into bed. Strangely, he did not feel uneasy at Senenmut's news. Two or three decades of one ruler was a comfort. He would travel up and down the Nile, checking on the building of monuments for many years to come.

Then Thutmose would ascend the Horus throne as an adult. Trained in the army, he would be the first generalissimo of Egypt. Nothing could be more soothing in its continuity. Much like the Nile lapping close to the window. As for the gossip that Hatshepsut and Senenmut were lovers, it was none of his business.

Ramose fell asleep.

***

122

Dawn broke over Aswan as Senenmut accompanied Ramose on an inspection of the quarry. Pale fingers of a watery yellow sun bleached the sky. The stone was freezing to the touch. Workmen huddled in groups. Covered with thin shawls, they drank beer and ate bread.

Lord Senenmut tapped the hard granite with his cane.

"You chose well, Ramose."

Peering into the crevasse between living rock and the new obelisks, the chief architect checked columns of red marks on the granite. Every few inches showed a day's work. Where each man sat, marks were made to record his daily contribution. Senenmut calculated the workers' rates of progress. Judging by the speed of their work, the obelisks would be ready in record time.

In the grey light of dawn, the workmen packed away their plates and mugs. Debris from the breakfast was cleared by young boys. Then, walking to the oblong granite shapes, which would become obelisks, the labourers started pounding with their dolerite pounders.

It was time to leave.

***

Back at the state villa, the host and his guest drank pomegranate juice, and snacked on dates. The royal inspection was completed, and a boat was docked at the jetty. Both men felt they were running out of conversation.

"My ride to Thebes is finally here, Ramose."

"I trust Her Majesty will be pleased with the report."

"You have made excellent progress."

Ramose waved his guest off at the banks of the Nile. With nothing to do, the chief of operations stayed home where he spent the afternoon listening to a comely lute player. Back at the quarry, clouds of dust rose. Granite blocks took shape. Petty thieves, prisoners of war, and criminals laboured under overseers, skilled with shouts and sticks. They were ahead of schedule.

***

123.

Senenmut did not return to Thebes. Instead, he stayed outside Aswan in a village with his brother Ity, and his wife Alath. Neither had been presented at court, and their home was a place of refuge for the busy architect. Senenmut particularly enjoyed the company of his nephews and niece. The twins, Amenhotep and Pere, were five years old, and learning to read and write. Their sister, Meret, was more interested in painting the pretty hieroglyphs than understanding their meaning, but she could still keep up with the writing classes.

The children provided Senenmut with hours of joyful companionship. During the day, they made time to play ball games or *senet*, at which Amenhotep excelled. Alath was a superb cook. She prepared tasty snacks to assist with the learning, and replenish reserves of her children's energy after a spirited game of stickball.

Instead of working in the Theban court, Ity had chosen a simple scribe's life. The local council employed him. Leaving early in the morning, he returned in the afternoon for lunch and a nap. Towards evening, he ate a light meal and left home again for a short stint at the office. Later, Ity returned, and always with a special treat. There were tasty pastries, wine or delicious fruit, which the family consumed together on the roof in the warm evenings. Sometimes he even brought back toys, or a new paint set for the children.

One evening, the stars rose in the sky, and a full moon shed its light on the roof where Ity and Senenmut conversed by a fire. Incense burners kept the mosquitoes at bay. Her week's weaving done, Alath was playing a lute by the light of an oil lamp. All three children were fast asleep, having spent the afternoon playing in the fresh air.

"You've done well for yourself. Remember, there's always a place for you at Thebes, brother."

"Aswan is home for me, Sen."

"I must admit, I'm envious of your life."

"But you're the most prominent official in Egypt!"

"I have no family of my own."

"You have us."

"I can't have my own wife and children."

"I don't understand."

Senenmut looked at his brother.

"You really don't know?"

"Marry. Be happy. What's stopping you?"

"I work for a monarch who is a woman."

Ity filled his thin bread pancake with humus and lettuce. Senenmut reached for the date wine.

"Hatshepsut is young enough to give you a child."

"That would create a public scandal."

"What about an arranged marriage for you to someone of her choice? It would appease Her Majesty's jealousy."

"Not an option."

"Is your career so important to you?"

"I love her. Besides, she has a bad temper!"

Ity laughed and shook his head. Remembering his own courtship, it was Alath's sweet disposition which had been her chief attraction. Perhaps pharaohs were different to mortals. Maybe Hatshepsut was indeed She Who Scratches, Pakhet, the lioness goddess of war. There were rumours of her plans to fight again in Nubia. He ate his sandwich.

Lord Senenmut savoured the moment. Time away from the Theban court, with its internal politics, was a blessing. Nothing was promised in this world, not even one's life. Certainly not for the men in the quarry.

***

124

Weeks turned to months. Ramose continued to work unhindered at the quarry. Senenmut tutored his nephews and niece in his brother's village. Meantime, the twin obelisks were pounded and polished to perfection. A team of skilled sculptors engraved hieroglyphs to the king's glory. Copper, gold, and silver were smelted together to form electrum for gilding the tips of the monuments. After seven months, they were finished.

A message was sent to Senenmut. The boat captain ordered a messenger boy to deliver the news. In another week, the architect would be free to supervise the transportation of the monuments from the quarry to Karnak.

Now Senenmut knew he had to make time with his family count. He played with his nephews every day, even carrying them piggyback through the surrounding fields of barley and wheat. They climbed date trees and shook the fruit to the ground, which Meret ate greedily. In the afternoons, all the children played stickball in the shade of the tall palms. Afterwards, they would run to the Nile, and splash in the shallows before dinner.

Finally, on the morning of his departure, the architect felt ready. Swinging his legs out of bed, he set his feet on the bare whitewashed floor. Suddenly, the happy guest realised he was going to miss the simplicity of this mudbrick room with its brightly coloured rugs. His eyes swept across the chamber which had been his home for over half a year. Smiling at the decorative stones, collected from the desert and placed on the furniture in pretty, rustic designs, he contemplated his wardrobe. It was just a plastered and whitewashed hole in the wall but, like everything else, felt like home in a way the palace never did.

Taking a breath, Senenmut did his morning stretches. His heart was heavy, and his body felt like the granite blocks of the quarry he was due to inspect. Breakfast was subdued. Up since dawn, Alath served traditional round bread loaves, piping hot from the oven. Today they were stuffed with goat cheese and sweetened with honey.

When the royal boat messenger arrived in the hallway, it was finally time to say goodbye. Meret wailed. Amenhotep cried. Pere bawled his eyes out. Alath was unable to comfort them. Ity put on a brave smile, and escorted his family to where the royal barge waited. It had arrived from Aswan in the early morning, and was tethered to the muddy shore, where it waited for its illustrious passenger to embark. Senenmut reflected that in this part of Egypt, there was not even a jetty. It was a rural outpost, a backwater. If only his family could live with him in Thebes!

"Come back soon, Sen."

"Think about the palace, Ity. There's a free home and education, waiting for you and your children. I shall be back this way after Aswan. I could pick you up for the journey north."

"We are simple people."

Ity embraced his brother. Senenmut boarded the barge and waved farewell. The river craft drew away from the shore into the rapidly flowing Nile. Pere followed, wringing his hands, and calling out between sobs. Amenhotep ran after him to pull him back. Finally, Senenmut's family receded into the distance. It was replaced by a bucolic landscape which flowed past on both sides of the vessel.

The ship's captain greeted Senenmut.

"Wine, Your Lordship?"

A boy stepped forward with a carafe and two gold goblets. The wine was a deep yellow, which meant it came from the king's vineyards. Hatshepsut had doubtless stocked the boat with the finest of everything. Senenmut accepted the drink.

"We will dock at the quarry port by midday. To the gods and your success, Lord Senenmut!"

"You don't know how empty success is until you have it, Captain Meryre."

Bemused, the captain led him to the living quarters at the back of the boat. Cradling his cup, Senenmut entered the cabin. Red damask curtains, embroidered cushions, and ebony furniture lined a luxurious interior. Sitting on his comfortable bed, the architect drained his wine. His muscles unwound and relaxed. He placed the goblet next to a pitcher of fresh pomegranate juice. Drawing the blind, he settled down to sleep.

***

It was early afternoon. Dressed in his best kilt, Senenmut emerged from the coolness of his cabin. A youth was on hand to serve him fruit juice and a slice of watermelon. Meryre appeared at his elbow.

"We won't be long, Your Lordship."

"You put a potion in the wine, Captain."

"I trust you had a restful sleep."

As they sailed into port, Meryre took his position on the bridge. Expertly supervising the crew, he negotiated the craft into the position reserved for royal barges. Finally, they were docked in Aswan. Ropes were thrown to men onshore, who tethered them to palm wood posts. Captain Meryre arranged for Senenmut's luggage to be carried down to the waiting porters. "We will see you next week, Your Lordship."

Senenmut climbed into a waiting chariot. Flicking his whip, the driver sped along the dusty lanes to Ramose's house. It was time to load the obelisks and head back to Thebes.

***

265

125

Overseers bellowed instructions. Sweaty workers hauled ropes attached to sledges. Men poured water in front of the great sleds, and tried not to trip on ropes, or bump into their fellow workers. Inching along, the gigantic granite slabs departed the quarry. Senenmut bit his lip.

"What are they doing, Ramose?"

"Loading the barges."

"They'll sink." Senenmut waved to an overseer. "Turn the obelisks around!"

The overseer obeyed and stopped the crew. Confused, Ramose waited. Huffing with exasperation, Senenmut marched up to the barges. Calling the overseers into a huddle, he pulled out a map. On it, he revealed a sketch of the obelisks stacked on the barges, nose to end. Immediately, the men understood.

Rolling up his map, Senenmut called for his litter.

"Where are you going?"

"Back to the house, Ramose. Keep up the good work!"

***

Crunching across the quarry, the obelisks made their way to barges bobbing in canals specially built for the purpose. Once the granite was loaded, the craft slid further out into the Nile, to avoid being beached. There, it waited in outer anchorage until morning.

At sunrise Senenmut donned a long, beaded robe. He downed a cup of water. Then he collected his satchel with his architect's plans. Grasping his favourite walking stick, a gift from Pharaoh, he joined Ramose in the hall of the villa.

House staff were gathered to see them off. He and Ramose took chariots to the quay. They boarded the royal barge, on which Captain Meryre greeted them. Servants laid out a deck table with food and drink.

"We also stocked red wine, Lord Senenmut."

"Captain Meryre, I shall commend you to Her Majesty. What will you have, Ramose?"

"Breakfast."

Meryre indicated a platter of fruit and cheese. Ramose nibbled on the food. Sipping his drink, he made his excuses, and repaired to the cabin to rest. After seven months, he was free of the commission and glad of it.

Senenmut turned to the captain.

"You've chosen a happy life, Captain Meryre."

"Sir?"

"You don't want worldly promotion. You'd rather ply the waters until old age. Your family means more to you than duty to our sovereign."

"I will do anything to serve Egypt."

"Balderdash! I have a brother who is the same as you. He turned down life at court. I even threw in a free home and education for his children as a bribe. He would have none of it. You are both wise, unlike me."

"There is no more capable man in Egypt than the Chief Royal Architect."

Shrugging, Senenmut looked over the ship's rail. Captain Meryre joined his men in order to watch over their work as they navigated the boat past sand banks, and into the open waters of the Nile.

***

126

Outside the palace offices, Vizier Ptah-hotep enjoyed the shade of a portico.

"How was Aswan, Lord Senenmut?"

"Hot."

The vizier chuckled.

"Walk with me?"

They made their way under the portico to the vizier's office, where Ptah-hotep called for beer.

"This is incredibly good, Vizier."

"My wife makes it."

"It reminds me of home."

"Your parents' place?"

"Brother's. I stayed with him in Aswan."

"You were missed at court."

"I didn't miss court."

"You don't have to tell me. Last month I asked for ten days in the Faiyum, just to get away from this place."

"To visit your family?"

"First wife's – yes. Ordinary people, happy people."

Ptah-hotep offered his guest a honey-and-fig pastry, sprinkled with crushed almonds.

"I know this!"

"It's from the south, eaten throughout Egypt. Except for my house. My third wife is from Crete. I believe you know our son, Itaja."

"He's at school with Prince Thutmose."

"He applied for a scholarship, you know. Wanted to stand on his own two feet. Smart lad." Ptah-hotep chewed for a few minutes. "Have you thought of marrying?"

"Impossible."

"What are you afraid of? A beheading?"

"My marriage would spell demotion."

"Her Majesty was married. She would understand."

"I disagree."

"But even our divine monarch takes lovers."

Senenmut choked on his pastry.

"More than one?"

"Oh, yes!" Ptah-hotep laughed.

Excusing himself, Senenmut made his getaway. Taking a chariot, he left the palace and headed to his private home. Located outside the main city, he had bought it to separate himself from the demands of the royal court. Its location was still close to his place of work, and accessible by chariot ride.

Situated on the edge of an estate, with palm trees and a variety of wildlife, its birdsong replaced the palace intrigue of a thousand courtiers climbing the ladder to Pharaoh's favour. Even Hatshepsut did not know about her beloved courtier's hideaway.

Inside the vestibule, Senenmut gave his servant his outer robe and staff. Entering the living room, he settled in a comfortable chair. Beer was set at his elbow. A manservant lit the oil lamps, and placed lumps of incense in a brazier. Adding more wood, he bowed to take his leave.

"Your week's wages have a bonus, Maya."

The extra wood made the fire crackle merrily. Lumps of incense sent a fragrant but definite warning to mosquitoes. Relaxing in his chair, Senenmut sipped his beer and wracked his brains. Hatshepsut always made him feel as though he was the only one. Come to think of it, she made everyone feel important. It was an art mastered by royalty, he reflected. Kings met multitudes, but always made the individual feel valued. As a commoner, Senenmut had no such skill. He always thought Hatshepsut's charm was real.

Not one to lose himself in sorrowful introspection, he decided to go to sleep. His bedroom was comfortable. Senenmut had allowed for an extra chest of clothes, but it was not like his sumptuous palace apartment. Nestling under the sheepskin blanket, he reflected the mattress had a curve of a bed slept in too long. Closing his eyes, he was surprised to feel no humiliation or shame.

The Chief Royal Architect for Upper and Lower Egypt fell asleep.

***

127

The evening sky flushed orange and gold. Hapuseneb hurried past the main gates. Still wearing his white robes from the evening service, he padded past the obelisks, through the narrow gate, and sat at the base of a stone plinth. Nobody was there. Taking a deep breath, he contemplated the evening. He loved the sun as it smacked into the obelisk tips, and fell in waves of gold upon the stone statues of Pharaoh Hatshepsut.

Recently, things had been piling up. His wife, the children – the heat. A neighbour of his had a dog who was terrorising the cats. Hapuseneb had imagined his own household was pet-free until his youngest, Meryte, had rushed to him one day, crying. Her kitten was being barked at by the yellow dog across the street. She held up a small stripy bundle. Her father soothed her, and suggested she go to the kitchen, where her mother would put out a saucer of milk.

Later, he spoke with his wife, Abar. To his surprise, he discovered they had no less than seven cats! It wasn't the extra mouths to feed. As High Priest, he took home the choicest cuts of meat from Amun's offering tables. His wife had not betrayed him, either. Their children smuggled in the mother cat who proceeded to have kittens.

But it was all too much. On top of everything else, he felt overwhelmed. King's recruiters were bothering the neighbourhood by removing fit young men from their families. Police turned up in their street at the beginning of the week. Fortunately, they were only there to apprehend drunkards during the upcoming Festival of Opet. The festival celebrated the second month of the flooding season of Akhet and was one of Egypt's favourite celebrations. Hapuseneb's house was on the main route leading to the Temple of Mut at Karnak. Close to work, his home was also near the celebrations. He would have to get ready for a week without sleep.

Stars came out. Small at first, they increased in size as night set in. The click of a watchman's stick by the lake reverberated across the temple. Then he saw it in the mauve shadows. It had been sitting there all along. A black-and-white cat blinked at him. It meowed a greeting. Suddenly, the priest had a revelation. His home was blessed by Baastet, the cat goddess of luxury and sweet ways.

A strong, warm feeling enveloped him. He rose from his place and hurried home.

***

128.

In her office, Hatshepsut spent the morning poring over building plans. Her chief architect made his appearance an hour before noon.

"My mortuary temple must be bigger than that of King Montuhotep."

"It will be the grandest monument in the world, Your Majesty."

"I'm building an empire. My temple must be impressive. I want gardens at the front, and more statues."

"It will be done as Your Majesty commands."

Hatshepsut scrutinised Senenmut.

"You look different this morning."

"Your presence gives strength to her humble servant."

"Angling for another raise, are we?"

"Only Your Highness' instructions for her Temple of Eternity."

Dismissing him, Hatshepsut called for Vizier Ptah-hotep.

"I see you've spoken to Lord Senenmut."

"He sought my company. The rest was easy."

"He's more polite than usual."

"Then I have done my duty."

"Has he a new lover?"

"For that information, Your Majesty will require an update from the royal intelligence unit."

"I don't spy on friends."

Ending the meeting, Hatshepsut retired to her apartment for a rest. Sending for Kalma, she changed out of her formal attire and waited for her only friend.

***

129.

Kalma was pleased to get away from a fresco project that was going wrong. Hurrying to the royal wing, she set down her gift of a glass perfume bottle on a table. Then, before the servant could assist, she poured herself a large glass of water.

"How's the mortuary temple going?"

"Getting bigger every day, Kalma. I also have a new hobby."

Hatshepsut ushered her visitor onto the patio. It fell away into flower beds, and a vegetable garden.

"Since when did you become a gardener, Hattie?"

"It relaxes me."

Cool winds blew in from the Nile. Kalma sat in a patio chair. Her friend took the other.

"These seats look worse for wear, Hattie!"

"We used them as children, remember? My late husband kept them in his garden."

"I could give them a fresh coat of paint."

"It might make Lord Sen jealous," Hatshepsut chuckled.

"And how is he these days?"

"Very formal. Perhaps I have offended him."

"You are grumpy these days."

"He's never complained about my moods before. All I know is he's changed. Not that I care."

"I thought you liked him."

"I was married, Kalma. Once was enough."

"I won't say anything about the burden of the throne and your many lovers." Hatshepsut's eyebrows shot up.

"Is that what they say?"

"Of course! But you knew that."

"How is your mother faring?"

"She's getting old and forgetful." Kalma drained her water and moved onto pomegranate juice. "But she and Dad still love each other."

"A marriage of love that lasts forever. It sounds wonderful. As for me, perhaps I should use my palace intelligence unit to find out what ails the mighty Lord Sen."

"So long as you don't use your spies on me."

"They spy on everyone. I don't know anything until I ask. But they always have the information at hand."

Kalma pointed to the new gardens.

"I want the grand tour."

***

Montuhotep's mortuary temple rose from a rocky cul-de-sac. Senenmut and his team gathered on the flat valley floor paved with black basalt. They were deciding on the position of Hatshepsut's grandest monument.

"There's plenty of space here, Ramose."

"Not for your project."

"We'll remove part of the cliff."

"That'll make it twice the size of the previous king's monument!"

Senenmut turned to his colleague.

"When I've finished, Hatshepsut will be the only monarch you will see here."

***

True to his word, Senenmut built a temple so large it eclipsed anything in the rocky cleft. Ramose visited once every few months and was always taken aback by its sheer size. Gangs of workers and their foremen dotted the site. Builders rubbed shoulders with stonemasons and artists. Clouds of limestone dust accompanied the noise of chiselling and hammering.

In March, during the harvest season of Shemu, Ramose watched as steps of a grand staircase were laid out. In July, during the second inundation month of Akhet, he watched in wonder as temple terraces rose out of the cliff. Towards the end of the year, during the season of Peret, when crops grew, he was stunned to see statues of Hatshepsut as the god Osiris, standing on the same terraces.

One afternoon, Ramose visited Senenmut in his office on the site.

"Has Her Majesty inspected her temple, yet?"

"Not until its completion, Ramose."

"This monument's grandeur will have come to the attention of envious courtiers by now."

"What do you mean?"

"I would get ready for an unscheduled visit, Senenmut. Tidy the place up a bit. Play the gracious host."

"You amuse me. Why the concern?"

"This temple needs to be seen."

"And there are rumours I am not the only lover of our sovereign."
"I didn't say –"

"You want your job security, which you have through my post."

"I didn't mean –"

"But you do say, and you do mean." Senenmut laughed easily. "Don't worry, Ramose. You're right. We need to keep our jobs. This place will be as clean as the virgin rock on which it will become the greatest monument of all time."

Embarrassed, Ramose took his leave. As he walked off the site, he thought he could hear faint laughter, tinged with bitterness.

***

130.

Downing their tools, the workmen clambered up a rock face. They took shelter from the sun in an unfinished tomb. High up in the cliffs, they would have plenty of warning if any unwelcome visitors tried to disturb them.

"What will it be today, Nebamun?"

"Date beer, Djau."

"And you, Paare?"

"The usual. And put more jugs out."

Soon, fifteen men squeezed into the cool shelter. Clay jars were assembled on the stony shelf. The self-appointed bartender filled pottery mugs with brew. Then, he pushed the beers across to his clientele, who paid him in vegetables and bread.

A dishevelled youngster stood at the entrance.

"I don't have anything."

"Bring your drawing skills to that stela, Samuel, and it's on the house."

The lad peered up at the writing. It was a tricky climb to the roughly hewn rock, but he managed it. Below, he could hear the men using foul language. Assessing his audience correctly, the boy swiftly drew a profane cartoon. Hopping down off the rocky ledge, he reached for a jug of date beer.

"Not so quick, lad. We must assess your work."

Samuel grasped the jug firmly by its handle.

"No need. Unlike this brew, my drawing will be remembered for all time."

Dumping the contents of the beer down his throat, he ran away.

"Hey!"

Djau chased after the youth. A blast of hot air caught him in the chest at the tomb's entrance. Squinting to no avail, the proprietor saw nothing. The lad had vanished. Grumbling to himself, Djau retreated. He decided to climb up to where the youth had penned his cartoon, but the area was already jampacked. Guffaws echoed through the stone chamber.

"Quiet! Do you want to alert the hills to our club?"

Pushing through the crowd, Djau examined the drawing. Executed in quick, sure strokes was a sketch of a man conjugating with the pharaoh. Senenmut and Hatshepsut were drawn in black ink. Then Djau noticed something. It was a not a man making love to a woman. The member on the king was something to be proud of.

"Clearly the boy hasn't a clue our king is a lady," he announced.

"She's no lady, Djau!"

The cave rocked with laughter.

"Don't you get it? Samuel thinks Senenmut likes men."

Paare was the first to stop laughing.

"Maybe that's what the younger generation thinks."

"Or maybe he really hates the overseer."

"Now I remember! I saw that young man getting a telling off. It was about two weeks ago. He dropped a load of bricks outside the temple."

"I remember, too! The bricks squashed some incense trees. There was quite a ruckus."

"He deserved that beer, Djau."

"Where does Samuel come from?"

"Over the hill from Karnak, in the village of the bricklayers."

"Tell him he's welcome to our drinking den. And this week, help him carry his bricks. Make sure the overseers stay away from him. They're getting mighty generous with their sticks!"

"It might be an idea to keep him clear of the incense trees, too."

Masculine laughter filled the room. Climbing down from the stone shelf, they went on with their afternoon drinking.

***

131.

It was late afternoon as the friends strolled across the Theban valley. Hatshepsut cocked her head to one side.

"I can hear something, Kalma."

"No, you can't."

Despite her confident retort, Kalma shivered. It was rumoured this part of the Theban valley was haunted. Men from long ago had died in it while protecting their king, the valiant Montuhotep, with whom they were now buried.

"What do you think, Kalma?"

The artist cast her eyes to the left, towards the temple of Montuhotep.

"Your boyfriend copied your neighbour."

"My temple's larger. Come and see the paintings."

The women wandered through the halls.

"I love the Anubis chapel, Hattie."

"The Hathor wing is my favourite."

"I hope you didn't bring me here to paint a wall decoration for the goddess."

"The temple is incomplete."

"It's going to take years and years to finish. I'll be an old lady by the time I complete the work."

"I want you to return to the Delta. More extensions have been added to the palace." Kalma did not respond. "What's the matter? Don't you want a commission? The Crown will give you another house if you want."

The women left the chapels and made their way down the vast staircase. Sitting on one of the enormous solid stone bannisters leading up to the temple, Kalma loosened her hair. A mild breeze blew the fragrance of incense trees across the temple.

"We have been together since childhood, Hattie, but don't bring me to a place like this again."

"Why not?"

"This entire space is dedicated to your divinity. It makes me uncomfortable."

"Do I have to lose Sen and my best friend in one year just because I'm filling in for my nephew?"

"You won't lose me. I acknowledge your divinity. It's the custom for kings. This place is too much, that's all."

"And to think I was going to have you executed for treason!"

"This has inspired me to work on that Delta palace of yours. But I want a palace of my own, Hattie, as a reward for being exiled to that swamp!"

***

280

PART IV

132.

A decade later, the project was still incomplete. Thutmose was eighteen. Itaja was in the adults' royal military school for professional soldiers, and Ptah-hotep had taken a fourth wife. One evening, Hatshepsut decided to confront the problem. On the pretext of a temple inspection, she selected her ceremonial chariot and favourite driver. Wearing a cool linen dress, and carrying her sceptre, she made her way to the mortuary temple.

Drawing up to it, Hatshepsut quickly scanned the construction. Scaffolding reached up into the cliffs, some of which had been removed. A chapel was cut into the living rock. Gigantic tiers protruded from the cliffs and fell in waves, hundreds of feet across the valley floor.

Moving up to the main staircase, the driver slowly reined in the horses to a stop. Men hurried forward to place wooden steps close to the carriage for their sovereign's descent. A nervous Senenmut took his place, and waited at the temple entrance. Leading his sovereign slowly through the pillars of the first tier, he allowed her to absorb the details.

Hatshepsut looked down at the mortuary temple below.

"It's magnificent."

"The temple reflects Your Majesty's glory."

"I see you why positioned me next to the great king, Montuhotep."

"His accomplishments are dwarfed by your grandeur."

"I selected this spot because he unified Egypt. But I am pleased to have surpassed him, at least in the art of building monuments."

"All of Egypt bows before you."

"There is still a lot of work to be done."

"I admit the gardens need to be put in place. Substantial greening will be necessary."

"I visit every few months when you're not here. I know what needs to be done. This project is progressing at a slow pace."

Senenmut swallowed. He had waited so long for an inspection from the woman he loved, and for whom he had built the greatest monument in Egypt.

"Your Majesty is always correct."

"Perhaps I could assist by sending a trading expedition to Punt."

"You are most kind."

"Thutmose will be Egypt's ambassador. After all, he is now an adult."

"Prince Thutmose is the perfect choice for a diplomatic mission."

Darkness fell. Torches were lit. At nightfall, the temple was a striking sight. A warm orange glow soaked the limestone cliffs. Half-finished mummiform figures of Hatshepsut threw stark shadows across the terraces.

After an hour, the formal inspection was concluded. The sovereign returned to her chariot. Her dozing driver jumped up to take his place at the reins. Whinnying, the stallions tossed their black manes. Eager to stretch their legs, they galloped across the desert plain towards the palace.

A relieved Senenmut patted his brow with a linen handkerchief. He had been wise to listen to Ramose all those years ago.

***

133

Lotus perfume filled the audience room. A vizier and a scribe stood in attendance to witness and record the formal meeting. Thutmose stood to attention. Hatshepsut marvelled at how muscular he had become over the summer.

"I summoned you, my nephew, because I have a job."

"I am willing to do Pharaoh's bidding."

"Egypt is sending an expedition to Punt."

"What is its nature?"

"Trade. You're to be my Royal Ambassador of Upper and Lower Egypt."

"When will I be leaving?"

"In ten days."

Thutmose bowed to his aunt and backed out of the chamber as protocol demanded. It was time to pay his respects to Kalma.

***

Dusk fell over the Cretan home. Kitane poured cups of hot grape juice, mixed with spices and honey for her family. Kalma was in the studio with Nashuja, arguing over the details of a palace mosaic. Ever since visiting the royal Delta residence a few weeks ago, father and daughter had disagreed on how it was to be decorated.

Kitane seated her visitor and gave him a drink.

"You'll enjoy the trip, Tutty."

Thutmose wrinkled his nose.

"Unless we drown."

"Nobody's died on a trip to Punt."

"It's a plot to get rid of me."

"It's the only opportunity you'll get to travel there."

"What's your point?"

"When you become sole Pharaoh of Upper and Lower Egypt, you will know the country and its rulers. It could be useful."

"I don't see how. My aunt isn't leaving Egypt to meet people. Why should I?"

"You will know which products to import to this country when you sit on the throne again."

"I'm not a merchant."

"Your mortuary temple will be rich in incense and baboons."

A canny glint lighted Thutmose's eye. Rumblings from the artists' studio indicated a volcanic argument brewing between Nashuja and his daughter.

"Say goodbye to Kalma for me."

He finished his drink and returned to the palace to prepare for the voyage.

***

A few days later, Thutmose visited Itaja at the royal barracks. His oldest friend shuffled from one foot to the other.

"I can't come, Tutty. You know I'm in military school."

"Next time, perhaps."

"We could visit Crete together."

"We'll take a trip after you graduate. I'll be Egypt's foreign ambassador for a while."

Itaja became serious.

"As you know, I'm part Cretan. Promise me when you become king you will treat our fair isle kindly."

"You will always be my friend."

Before Itaja had time to reply, the prince was gone.

***

Pacing her room, Neferure waited for wine to be poured for her guest. The female server was nubile and young, and Itaja was clearly entranced.

"You're dismissed," she said curtly the girl when she had finished her task. "So, what is your complaint about Thutmose?"

"He answered me like a politician."

"That's typical of him these days."

"You're supposed to be on his side, Nef. You two will be married soon."

"I am on his side. I don't want to lose Thutmose to illness in that wretched country of savages."

"You won't. He's strong."

"Do you know that I now have lessons on how to be a king?"

"Hatshepsut has to cover all the possible outcomes. Tutty could die of a cold, or malaria at home, just like his uncles, and then where would we be?"

"Being Great Wife will satisfy me, but unfortunately, Tutty is the only royal male in this family."

"His aunt has done a good job of keeping him alive, so far."

A worried look crossed the princess' brow.

"Do you think Mummy might be deliberately endangering Tutty? Did Kitane say anything?"

"I wouldn't worry, Nef. If your mother wanted her only nephew bumped off, it would have happened a long time ago."

"You should go with him, Itaja. Keep him safe. We can always pull strings to hold your place at the military school."

***

Dusman was putting furniture back in place when the prince entered his classroom. The teacher's hair was grey, his shoulders stooped, and his stomach was flabbier than Thutmose remembered. Two royal bodyguards stood to attention in the doorway.

Suddenly, the older man's face broke into dimples. Arms akimbo, he waddled towards his ex-pupil.

"Prince Thutmose!"

"I wanted to say goodbye, sir."

"I heard you were travelling to an exotic country by the sea."

"I'm visiting Punt."

"It's an important trading partner."

"I'll bring you back a gift."

"Come back alive, Tutty. And no big cats, please. I hear panthers are partial to human."

Embracing his former student, Dusman wiped his eyes.

"I'll bring you back an incense tree, sir. Aunty's ordered dozens for her mortuary temple. I'm sure she can spare one."

Dusman brightened then, reaching for his linen handkerchief, he blew his nose. With a royal officer's salute, Thutmose turned on his heel.

***

Dawn broke over the deep blue of the Red Sea. A mainsail billowed overhead. Thutmose crossed his legs under him as he sat on a hatch. Shaking his reed pen, which had accumulated sea spray in its bristles, he wrote out an exercise. Fond of poetry, he set his eyes dreamily on the horizon. It was enough to put him into a state from which a divine flow of words emanated.

"I didn't know you wrote for fun, Tutty."

Annoyed at the break in his concentration, Thutmose looked up. A bronzed youth blocked the morning sun.

"Itaja!" Casting aside his writing equipment, the prince hugged his friend. "How did you get aboard?"

"Our captain had orders from your aunt. You don't think I could just stow away, do you?"

Thutmose pulled him down onto the hatch cover beside him. The friends stayed locked in conversation until noon, when they were called into the royal cabin for lunch. Over slabs of freshly caught bonito and vegetables, they discussed the voyage ahead. In a week's time, they would be in Punt with an opportunity to see one of Egypt's popular trading spots.

When the sun slid below the horizon, Itaja retired to his cabin. Thutmose also felt the effect of the sea's ozone. It refreshed, and simultaneously made one ready for bed earlier than when on land. Who knew, he thought sleepily, as the lights were snuffed out by his servants, he might bag a wife or two for the voyage home?

***

134

Thatched houses on stilts emerged from the jungle before the eyes of the Egyptians. Vines hugged tree trunks thicker than the temple columns at Karnak. Soaring a hundred feet into the air, they formed a leafy canopy which housed colourful birds, snakes, wild cats, and indigenous tribes.

Itaja moved close to the prince.

"I saw a python, Tutty! Fifty cubits long."

"Where?"

"Up a tree, to the left of those huts."

Twisting about, Thutmose saw lianas, and an African juniper tree. A highly patterned, sleek python peeked out from the leaves. Making a mental note to capture it later, he kept pace with the expedition guides. The prince's bodyguards moved in close to his person as they approached a clearing.

Huts on stilts loomed up ahead. Thutmose noted they had the advantage of height over danger from intruders. It would take seconds for an archer to let fly a poisoned arrow.

Itaja leaned forward.

"There's no one around, Tutty."

"Sssh!"

Thutmose and Itaja marched at the head of the party with their guide. Further back, the Egyptian crew followed with trading goods. In the tenth hour of the morning, it was already hot and humid. Slowly, they made their way uphill. A circle of dwellings, interspersed with makeshift pathways, greeted them at the end of their journey. Directly in front was a large, conical thatched hut.

Guides motioned everyone to stop. They beckoned to the crew. Placing reed mats on the flat earth compound, the Egyptians laid out their wares. Soon, brilliant beads of purple amethyst sparkled in the heat, next to blocks of bright blue lapis. Carnelian and jasper contrasted with volcanic glass from the Western Desert. Bolts of fine linen were produced. Men sloshed the contents of wine jars into earthen cups. They were set aside for thirsty buyers. A Puntian guide, who was with the Egyptians, stepped forward to speak in the native tongue. Thutmose and Itaja knew they were not alone. Invisible eyes from every home were fixed on the newcomers.

Eventually, a slender black figure from one of the tree huts, slid down a rope into the compound. He welcomed the visitors in the same tongue spoken by their guide. An Egyptian offered the newcomer a clay cup filled with wine. The man smacked his lips in appreciation.

Suddenly, Thutmose and Itaja heard stirring above them as people slid down vines from their homes, and flooded the compound. Chattering and laughter filled the village. Now there was movement in the largest hut. A bearded middle-aged man emerged, followed by his household, including his enormous wife. Her pendulous folds were not simply reserved for her stomach. Even her legs and arms carried plentiful fat rolls. Itaja chuckled, but compassion rose in Thutmose's heart.

"That must be the royal couple. Stop making fun of the queen, Itaja. She has an illness."

When the king reached Thutmose, he offered him a gold dagger inlaid with lapis lazuli. Some of the Egyptian crew stepped forward, and presented a gift of coloured linen.

"Welcome, Prince of Egypt. I am King Perhau, and this is my wife, Queen Ati."

Surprised and flattered at being greeted in Egyptian, Thutmose made a reply in the language of Punt. Rehearsed the night before, a short phrase of address rolled effortlessly off his tongue. Noticing he had mastered the accent, the king and queen acknowledged their guest with pleasure. Then, in a genial mood, the Egyptian royal party followed them inside.

There, the visitors were given beer. Unlike the Egyptian variety, it was more potent. Thutmose sipped it slowly, and waited for the food. A feast of roast boar, pheasants, beef, and mutton followed.

"They must have known we were coming, Itaja."

"Look at the pork falling off the bone! It's been at least eight hours in an oven." King Perhau dabbed his lips with a linen napkin.

"The meal was cooked underground. We build a pit and steam the food. It is a traditional method used for special feasts. Good results, you'll agree."

"Even the Egyptian court would be hard pressed to put on such a spread."

"You are kind, Prince Thutmose. And you are right. We knew you were coming."

"I gather it's because Pharaoh notified you last month."

"Pharaoh's notification has not reached us yet."

"King Perhau has an extensive knowledge of the seas."

"You're a diplomat, Prince. It is the custom to enjoy our hospitality for a few nights.

We will stock your vessel with provisions for the journey home."

"In return for your hospitality, I invite Your Majesties to accompany me to Egypt's court. There you may meet my king."

Pleased with Thutmose's answer, King Perhau ordered musicians and dancers. The Egyptians took part in the revelry, stamping their feet, and clapping in time to the music. Snakes slithered into the jungle. Panthers vacated their branches to retreat further away from the village. Knowing he had won a diplomatic victory, Thutmose stayed vigilant. Keeping an eye on the Egyptians, he ate and drank sparingly, while making pleasant conversation with the king and queen.

***

135.

Thutmose and Itaja inspected their quarters. Two adjoining rooms were separated by a large living and dining space. Bowls of fruit sat on ebony tables. Each man had an attendant to wait on his needs.

"Inviting our hosts to Egypt was clever, Tutty."

"We're now guaranteed to get home safely."

"Was that your idea or your aunt's?"

"Hers."

"You see how she protects you!"

"I see she wants a good deal. And King Perhau does not want to appear before Egypt's monarch with less than the best."

"I am surprised you allow him to address you as a prince."

"I'm usually addressed the same way in Egypt. No country has two kings. It's best to leave our host in his ignorance. Any explanation would cause confusion."

Retiring to their separate rooms, the men prepared for bed. Spending an hour in prayer, Thutmose waited until Itaja was asleep before checking the doors and windows. Sentries were stationed around the house. To his relief, Thutmose noted his bodyguards were included with the men who stood watch.

***

Excited chattering heralded a new day. Yawning, Thutmose rolled to one side to see a large baboon next to his bed. Shrieking in fright, he leapt up to bump his head against the hut's wooden pole. Running into the living area, he encountered his bodyguards having breakfast. Immediately, they grasped their weapons, but it was no use. Horrified, they watched as the baboon bared its red bum before vanishing. Thutmose rubbed his head.

"It must be sunrise."

Shaken, he returned to his room where he donned a kilt. Then he joined Itaja and his men, who were now all awake. An African maid in a long gown, with plaited hair, arrived with goats' milk. She offered a bowl to Thutmose, who drank. More women, wearing only fibre skirts, trooped in with breakfast. An array of fruit, hot beans, porridge, and warm bread sent tempting aromas through the hut.

Itaja looked discomforted.

"Where is the royal taster, Tutty?"

"We don't need one."

"I insist on a taster trying this foreign fodder. Your mother would order it as a precaution."

"Quiet! You're embarrassing us. Just enjoy the maidens. I've got my eye on one or two."

"I forget, one day you'll be Pharaoh and have a hundred wives."

"Two hundred!"

"We still need a taster."

Finally, a royal taster from King Perhau arrived to sample the meal. Impatiently, Thutmose dismissed the man and began to eat. His friend barely touched his food. Donning a Cretan belt, which accentuated the slimness of his waist, Itaja left the hut.

The visitors' accommodation had stairs, rather than a ladder. At the bottom of the steps, two guards greeted the foreign guest. As he walked through the compound, its flattened clay felt pleasant underfoot. Itaja knew he was being watched. He felt eyes bore in his back, and on every side. In front, lay the forest and the sea. Even from here, he could smell the salt of sea air.

When he passed through the gates of the compound, Itaja was suddenly aware of being followed. Turning, he noticed a young boy. His manservant, by the name of Pura, was also following some way behind the lad. Conversant with several languages, including the Punt dialect, Pura was talking with the boy, who spoke in an agitated manner.

Despite walking fast, Itaja could not lose the pair. After several hundred yards, the unwanted duo caught up with him.

"Who is the lad, Pura?"

"King Perhau ordered him to follow you wherever you go."

"He sounds like a spy. I'm headed for our boat."

The boy waved his arms and spoke in Egyptian.

"Long way, long way. Too far, too far."

"I can see a mast from here, lad."

In a rush of Puntian dialect, the youth pleaded with Pura.

"King Perhau expects you to stay in the compound, Itaja. The boy says the jungle has many tribes. They have poisoned arrows and blow darts."

Itaja did not need to be told twice. Turning on his heel, he followed Pura and the lad back to the compound.

***

Thutmose brushed his teeth with a twig toothbrush. Itaja washed in a basin, anointed himself with olive oil, and combed his long tresses.

"Itaja, you'd make someone a great wife one day." A deftly thrown comb nicked Thutmose's left ear. "Ow! That hurt."

"In Crete, our hair is our pride and joy. Unlike in Egypt, where you shave it off and only preserve it for wigs."

"It's all about hygiene and lice."

"I don't have lice."

Taking a gold tie from his waistband, Itaja caught up his hair in a ponytail. Thutmose rinsed his mouth with natron to freshen his breath. Then they left their quarters. Outside, in the compound, mounds of resin were displayed. Scribes were ready to record the day's events. The people of Punt were ready to trade.

On a high platform, Prince Thutmose began a long speech. Listing the items of jewellery brought to Punt by the Egyptians, he exaggerated their value. King Perhau's vizier replied with an equally long speech.

294

At its end, the king clapped his hands. Itaja drew a breath. An array of valuable products, including incense trees, resin, and tame baboons, were marched before them.

As Thutmose watched the display, he knew his aunt would be pleased.

***

136

"That was a success!"

Itaja untied his hair and shook his locks out. Stripping off, he jumped into a tub and poured perfumed water over his head and body. Meanwhile, Thutmose stretched out on a couch. His face was strained.

"I'm worried about the expedition."

"These are serious negotiations, Tutty. It's normal to fret."

"Do you think my aunt hopes for my demise? It's not safe here. The customs alone are a trap. I nearly called the queen a fat cow, instead of praising her as a woman worth many cows."

"You know why your aunt has the throne."

Thutmose sat up and clasped his hands.

"Maybe she knew I was born to be a warrior, rather than a king. Aunty sent me to military school."

"You'll be our *king*. By the way, I heard Hatshepsut is going into battle again." "When?"

Itaja dried himself off with a towel.

"After we get back. My guess is she's terrified of any possible threat to Egypt." "Nonsense! Aunty's heartless as a stone sphinx."

"Your callousness towards her is interesting."

"If she wants to go to battle, it serves her right for stealing my crown."

"You know why she goes to war? To protect and expand an empire for *you*."

Thutmose rolled his eyes and stood up.

"It's time to join King Perhau."

***

137.

It was winter and Hatshepsut needed a shawl. Pulling her robes about her for warmth, she stood on a rocky promontory. Ayn Sukhna was a well-known port. Ropes and boxes were stored in its caves. Seafarers had used this place from the time of the first pyramids. Even Montuhotep, whose mortuary temple was next to hers, had once moored a fleet here.

Lookouts stationed themselves along the shoreline. Servants set out seats, and erected colourful awnings. Many of the courtiers went for a beach stroll.

"Can you see any sails yet, Sen?"

"They are due late in the afternoon."

"I have a feeling it will be very soon."

Senenmut made no reply. In his experience, it was the best tactic. A lookout suddenly pointed.

"Ships!"

Everyone turned to see a flotilla of vessels. On the shore, men at the jetty readied for docking. Shouts floated over the waves as the ships slowed. Hatshepsut could see exotic cargo tied down to decks. Livestock peeked out from tarpaulins which blew in the strong wind. Most fantastic of all were the baboons sitting on hatches, and swinging from masts. One was even perched on the prow of the main ship.

"I can see him!"

Hatshepsut waved excitedly to her nephew. The ships docked quickly. Thutmose's vessel was the first to anchor. Before the gangplank was lowered, the prince jumped ashore with a parcel clasped tightly to his chest. Reaching his aunt, he rubbed noses with her in the traditional Egyptian greeting of affection.

"How handsome you look!"

Handing his aunt the parcel, he watched her open it. A green ceramic vase appeared. Thutmose pointed to its painted exterior.

"I decorated it for you."

Eagerly, Hatshepsut turned it about in her hands. On the vase were drawings of strange faunae and flora. Natives in traditional garb were surrounded by trees so high they threatened to leave the pottery.

"It's a record of your trip!"

Handing the vase to an attendant, the monarch turned to her nephew's ship, where pandemonium reigned. Baboons cavorted about the decks. She clapped her hands with delight as she watched the sailors trying to catch them. Much to their indignation, the creatures were rounded up, screaming and chattering to anyone who would listen.

Then the holds opened. Men transferred myrrh trees into paniers, which they carried on their shoulders. The gangplank sagged as precious cargo was unloaded onto the jetty. Hatshepsut counted thirty-one myrrh trees.

"Those are for allocation to the mortuary temple, Lord Senenmut."

The Royal Architect of Upper and Lower Egypt inclined his head. Thutmose observed, with some amusement, that the courtier never spoke a word in public unless necessary. An attendant carrying a tray of resin was next to disembark. He took up his position in front of the tree bearers. Then, the oddest pair Hatshepsut had ever seen, stepped onto Egyptian soil. A slim bearded man, followed by his wife, so fat she required a donkey to ride up to the royal pavilion, emerged from the vessel. Hatshepsut gathered it was the royal couple who had travelled from Punt to Egypt.

Everyone took their positions. The man with the resin tray followed the odd pair. In turn, he was followed by a team of men who carted the myrrh trees. Thutmose took his place on a throne next to his aunt. When the delegation gathered at the pavilion, an officer of the court stepped forward.

"Your Majesty, King Hatshepsut, I present King Perhau and his wife, Queen Ati of Punt."

Puzzlement crossed the visiting queen's face. She turned to her husband.

"Where is the Egyptian king?"

"Hatshepsut is Pharaoh, filling in for Thutmose until he comes of age."

"A woman? I've never heard of such a thing!"

"Follow my lead, dearest."

The visitors paid homage and moved up to the dais, where they sat on two thrones, slightly lower than that of the Egyptian royals. Glancing up at the sun, Thutmose calculated they were ready to break for the midday meal. His body needed exercise, and he was looking forward to a chariot ride.

At lunch, he caught up with Itaja in a pavilion set aside for young army officers. The men chose their cuts of meat from platters arrayed in tables at the front. More informal than the royal tent, it provided excellent grub.

Taking a pottery bowl for the main meal, and a reed basket for bread, Thutmose joined Itaja in the queue.

"Missing the sea yet, Tutty?"

"I'm hunting this afternoon. Want to join me?"

"I have another engagement."

"Suit yourself."

Helping himself to slices of goose, the prince spotted Kalma across the room. He nodded his head in acknowledgement, but she dropped her eyes. A secret smile played at the corners of her mouth.

***

The royal tent was the place to be out of the blazing heat. Hatshepsut changed into a flowing robe. Senenmut sipped pomegranate juice.

"What an extraordinary expedition, Sen!"

"I'll have the myrrh trees transported to your temple tomorrow."

"Wonderful! When will it be finished?"

"We're landscaping the gardens now."

"Are the terraces completed?"

"We'll build and put in the gardens at the same time."

"Good. It will ensure the project is finished quickly."

Hatshepsut opened the tent flaps. The sun was setting. Her nephew would be at his vespers.

"You need to stop thinking about that boy."

"Thutmose is the reason I work ceaselessly."

"And you're the reason I work."

"It's what I expect of my subjects."

Stepping outside, the monarch's bare feet scrunched shells in the sand. Senenmut joined her. Gazing into the dying sun, his thoughts were on the mortuary temple. Hatshepsut turned to him. Kissing her favourite courtier lightly on the cheek, she patted his shoulder. Together, they watched the sun as it sank over the sea.

***

138

It was the third day of festivities, and Thutmose was bored. At the end of the ceremony, he yawned as he made his way to the luncheon tent. Itaja sat next to him.

"Your aunt is giving you credit for the expedition."

"And she likes my vase."

"Not to mention the wealth you accumulated for our country."

Ladling gravy over a piece of goose, Thutmose took a bite. By contrast, Itaja's plate was piled high with food.

"Are you coming to the track after this?"

"I want to digest lunch first, Tutty."

"Why don't you eat less? You'll be able to exercise afterwards."

"I'm a firm believer in a hearty lunch, especially when it's free."

Wafting into the tent in a cloud of perfume and draperies, Kalma joined them. Kissing Itaja on one cheek, she sat down to share his food. Thutmose glanced at the pair.

"How is your wife, Itaja?"

"I don't have a wife."

"That's not what you told me in Punt."

"Don't tease. I have a *family*. Like you."

Finishing his lunch with a smirk, Thutmose excused himself and left the group. Making his way back to his tent, he passed piles of incense along the shore. Tethered baboons sat on panther skins. Screaming and eating fruit, they watched over the gold and ivory. All the cargo would be heading to Thebes in a few days.

Back in his tent, the prince stuffed extra clothes into a bag. Grasping a full jug of water, which stood next to his bed, he poured it into a waterskin. An acacia box also stood by his bed. From it, he selected a ball of myrrh gum. Chewing happily, he left the room.

Outside the soldiers' tents stood several chariots, all parked in serried rows. Horses stood by eating sandy grass, waiting to be taken to the stables. Selecting two, Thutmose hitched the steeds to a light chariot. He cantered to the port barracks, which consisted of one building. Tethering his horses, the prince patted their glistening necks. It was hot, but a coastal breeze would dry them in moments. Swinging his satchel over one shoulder, Thutmose made his way to the track.

He noticed the same one was used for horses and archery practice. The port authorities were nothing, if not economical. Thutmose winced. It was times like these he wished he was on the throne. Spitting out his gum, he carefully tucked it in between wads of linen. There was nothing worse than chewing gum on the track.

Running slowly, he felt his muscles warm up. If this was his military barracks, he thought, there would be separate tracks for horses, archers, and runners. Maybe even a royal track where he could exercise alone. He knew that personal space was important. Hatshepsut's strategy was to retire to her study. During her reign, which included her nephew's, two governments had been formed. Staff had been appointed and demoted. It was her father who had given his daughter her first insight into the palace's royal administration. Within that office she drew strength from his memory.

Thutmose reached the first corner. The inside track was a bit bumpy. Used by both runners and horses, it could prove dangerous. He resolved that when he became king again, it would be level. For now, being out here, he was at least free. Running at full speed, the prince covered the length of the field. Then he turned. A flash of light blinded him. His blood grew cold. Stopping short, he felt his ankle twinge. A chariot with galloping horses headed straight for him. Thutmose realised he was completely alone, without his sword. Before he had time to gather his wits, the charioteer pulled up in front of him. The man dismounted and threw himself into the dust.

"Pharaoh requires Your Highness' presence."

***

139.

Pacing her tent, Hatshepsut was about to burst a vein.

"You could have been killed!"

"I was running."

"Where were your guards? You could at least have taken Itaja."

"He's courting Kalma."

"What are you talking about?"

"They're getting married."

"She's my age!"

"Kalma is beautiful."

"And another thing. You're to stop collecting women! I've heard about your harem. You are not a ruling king, yet." Thutmose looked up at the ceiling. "Don't roll your eyes. Look at me when I'm talking to you."

"I'll be the next King of Egypt with a working harem. I can't help it if you don't use it."

Hatshepsut stopped. Despite herself, a smile creased the corners of her mouth.

"Just make sure you're always protected. I didn't go out to Nubia for myself."

"No, you went for Egypt," was the sarcastic retort.

"I went for you!"

Senenmut was standing in a corner of the tent.

"He doesn't understand."

"You're right." Hatshepsut composed herself, and turned to her nephew. "Unlike you, my boy, I have no military training. I'm not accustomed to killing my subjects, even if they are foreigners. But I'm safeguarding the throne of Horus for you. And this afternoon, you jeopardised your safety."

Noticing a tear in his aunt's eye, the prince quickly bowed.

"I will take guards with me in future, Aunty."

"You may go."

"You're an ungrateful boy," Senenmut whispered as the prince passed him.

Thutmose knew it was a trap. If he reacted his aunt would never forgive him. Instead, he continued on his way. Outside, he paused and inhaled deeply. Walking across the mudbrick path, the prince allowed his feet to stamp out their impatience. His right ankle started to ache. Cutting across the beach he returned to his tent. There, his manservant applied a compress of aloe and herbs to the throbbing ankle.

Afterwards, exerting his willpower, he pushed Senenmut's offensive comment out of his mind and turned to his homework. An acolyte in Amun's temple now, Thutmose was a conscientious student. Reading and memorising several hymns, he prepared for the week's services. At sunset he rose, drank a glass of date wine, and watched the sun disappear over the horizon.

The prince had not given way to his temper. He had not told Lord Senenmut what he thought of his conniving ways. Nor had he been uncivil to his aunt's messenger. The poor man had instructions to ride directly towards him at top speed so that the prince would understand the terror of an assassin. But, Thutmose reflected, he had let his guard down with his aunt. It was because she was more familiar to him than anyone. However, discourtesy to one's elders was frowned on by Amun, and the gods whom he served. As his country's future ruler, Thutmose resolved to be more disciplined.

Picking up his satchel with papyrus copies of the hymns, he filled it with bread, a bottle of wine, and a vial of water for the god. Making his way to worship, he ensured his chariot was followed by the appropriate security, including an armed personal bodyguard.

***

<h1 style="text-align:center">140.</h1>

Back in Thebes, a game of *senet* filled the hours between morning court and the evening's activities. Engaged in the pastime they had loved since childhood, Kalma and Hatshepsut tossed their ebony sticks to establish how many moves to make. Chatting pleasantly, they shifted their pieces on the familiar squares of heaven and hell.

"Your mortuary temple is the biggest in Egypt, Hattie."

"It has to be."

"Your lover has created the foremost memorial of any king."

"Don't be vulgar. It's not all for me."

"I know, I know! Tutty must inherit a powerful kingdom. Though, I wonder if he'll outdo your feats of building."

"I have to do better than any man, Kalma. If this country isn't properly controlled, my nephew will never be allowed the throne, let alone any of his heirs."

Kalma threw her sticks.

"Don't be so touchy! I'm not the enemy, you know."

"You will be if I lose."

***

141.

Hatshepsut looked up from her desk. Since her return to Thebes, there were constant interruptions.

"What is it, Vizier Useramen?"

"We have a problem, Your Highness."

"Be quick about it. I have spear practice soon."

"The brick workers want a day off to worship their god."

Hatshepsut put her reed pen down.

"So, you have cleverly put it on me, Vizier. How many days do they want this time?"

"Your Majesty, with respect, your reputation is the king who bends Egypt's back with heavy loads."

"We both know it's propaganda. I asked you, how many days this time?"

"One."

"I don't see the problem. It's not even a matter for the king. Why are you bothering me with it?"

"They have a different god from us, Your Majesty."

"We all have the same gods."

"Their god is different."

"They work for us. Egypt has a million gods. I'm sure we can accommodate them.

Anything else?"

"No, Your Majesty."

"Good. You're dismissed."

Hatshepsut pushed her scrolls to one side. It was time to see her nephew.

***

Thutmose gazed across the Theban school field where he had spent five years of his life. Every year as a youngster, he won the Golden Fly. Walking to the main range where the old copper target stood, he inspected its punctures. Thutmose now taught archery to cadets. He excelled in the chariot riding, which was just as well. As Egypt's future king and Chief Commander of the Army, he would need it on campaign. It was not simply a tool for battle, but necessary as a rallying point for his troops.

The prince had also acquired an ability to relate to the common man. Men could look into his eyes and feel his warmth as he patted them on the shoulder, or commended them for their work.

"Thinking?"

"Aunty!"

The pair embraced.

"I was thinking, too. We need to get you involved in more royal duties."

"What did you have in mind?"

"You need to know about our allies."

"You want me to travel again?"

Hatshepsut put her hand on his muscled forearm. They walked around the field, chatting like mother and son.

***

142

All week grain and produce travelled north. Senenmut supervised the provisioning of the ships to Crete. At various Nile ports, they were subjected to screening and product control, before being released.

Vexed, Captain Meryre unburdened his feelings to his chief officer.

"Why does our royal architect have to stick his big nose into everything?"

"King's orders."

"If Hatshepsut were a man, this wouldn't be happening. Lord Senenmut has every major post in Egypt. He took me away from my nice job in Aswan. It's almost as if he was King!"

"It's standard procedure. Prince Thutmose is travelling on the flagship."

"What's that got to do with my holds being inspected, and the crew repacking everything? That man is a blasted nuisance. At this rate we'll never get out to the Nile, let alone to Crete!"

"Be patient. Prince Thutmose is Egypt's next king, after all. There are worse things than losing a few days."

Grumbling, the captain stomped off to the main hold, which was being inspected yet again for stowaways. His chief officer calmly chewed a dry cracker. Knowing the future King Thutmose was on the flagship rather than their vessel, reassured him of Amun's beneficence.

***

News after dinner was always well received. Better for promotion, too. Taking the private path from his apartments to Hatshepsut's office, Senenmut arrived in his best attire.

"I trust this a good time for you, Your Majesty."

"On formal business, I see. Be quick about it. I was about to spend time with a friend."

"Prince Thutmose's ship for is ready for Crete."

"Waiting in the north?"

"At Thonis."

"How big is the fleet?"

"Twelve ships, Your Majesty. It's a trading expedition."

"When does he leave?"

"In two days."

"I had better give him a blessing for the voyage. You did well, Lord Senenmut. There is a bonus in this month's wages. When Thutmose returns, I will gift you land in Akhmim."

"Your Majesty is most gracious to her servant. I shall come back later."

Bowing, the courtier backed into the corridor. The office doors closed. Righting himself, he saw Ptah-hotep waiting.

"Do you also have an appointment, Vizier?"

"More like a social engagement."

With no betrayal of emotion, Senenmut continued on his way.

***

143

It was early morning at sea. Thutmose felt chilled under his covers. Noise on the upper deck, combined with the rolling motion of the ship, forced him out of bed. Donning a thick waterproof cape, he joined the men. Once outside, he wished he had stayed below decks. An icy squall hit the boat and spikes of rain stung his face.

Officers frantically pulled up the sails to their skipper's shouts, while the crew rowed. Wrapping his cape about him Thutmose stood still, his legs spread apart to take the rocking of the boat. Finally, the squall abated. Clouds rolled away as they neared land. Gulls circled, riding up high under the currents, before swooping to devour fish in their wake. Bright sunlight contrasted with the choppy deep blue of the Mediterranean.

The Cretan navigator pointed.

"The harbour's up ahead, sire."

Squinting, the prince's eyes made out a faint shoreline. Foam-crested waves danced around them as the royal Egyptian fleet sliced through the ocean. Behind them, Thutmose noticed, there was no trace of any storm. Instead, the sea merged with the horizon.

For the past few days, the ocean had been a friend, encircling the fleet. The prince loved the feeling of being the only one in the world. At night, when the moon came out, there was silence on the deck, with only the sky and sea for company. Now, after their first storm, the excitement of docking at Crete was palpable.

Thutmose turned to the navigator.

"Is your wife waiting?"

"Everyone's family is on the jetty, Your Highness. King Minos will greet us, before we go to our homes."

A pier leapt into view. Unlike Egyptian docks, it was a solid wooden affair holding hundreds of ships. Taken aback, Thutmose gawped. An enormous palace rose above the shore. Covering acres, it soared in a white mass. Its columns of red and patterns of blue-and-gold reminded him of Kalma's paintings. The fleet pulled in at a steady pace, and the mooring process began.

On the docks a spectacle stunned the Egyptian visitors. Women with long curly tresses stood in the sun. Men also boasted long hair, which was carefully oiled and combed. They wore bright colours in striking patterns. Groups of women wore yellow dresses and crimson bodices, which contrasted with others clad in shimmering blue skirts and emerald jackets. Their male counterparts wore a variety of robes, kilts, and stylised loincloths. Their tanned, slim bodies were as slender-waisted as those of their womenfolk. In the middle of this crowd, on a gold throne, sat the king in a robe of red, and sandals of gold.

Thutmose retired to his cabin to change. When all the ships had docked, the Egyptians were ready to be greeted by the welcome party. As he made his way down the gangplank, the prince's new leather boots squeaked. The first thing he noticed was the state of Crete. It was spotless. There was no muddy riverbank to catch aristocratic sandals, or ooze to seep through the toes of a barefoot crewman. Here, one stood on a jetty of white rocks, cut and assembled to cater for a professional fleet of seagoing vessels. Cretans were renowned as the greatest sailors in the world. Even here, Thutmose mused, his boots crushed seashells underfoot. Turning, he noticed the deep oily blue of the sea lapping over a rock wall which protected the shore. Above, the clear sky reminded him of Egypt. Sunshine and happiness, Kalma always said when remembering her home.

Local ladies began dancing. Their men started to sing. An ancient patriarch walked up to Thutmose. With great ceremony he led the foreign delegation to the Cretan king. When the prince was nearer to the throne, he noticed King Minos was middle-aged. He did not smile. The hat he wore appeared heavy. Perhaps it was crushing his skull like the coronation crown Thutmose remembered from his childhood. Rhododendron columns with pale pink, white, and cerise flowers flanked the king on both his right and left. He spoke in a stilted fashion.

"Welcome, brother, to King Minos' palace."

Thutmose acknowledged the Cretan king through an interpreter. Gold and semi-precious jewels were offered to the guests, together with embroidered linen, and Cretan wine. Speeches were made. Thutmose noticed the sun did not burn as it did in Egypt. Finally, they all turned to the enormous palace, to walk up winding pathways into its gaping maw. Trying his best to be nonchalant, the Egyptian prince was secretly overwhelmed by the high ceilings and painted frescoes. His officers were not so restrained. They commented and stared in equal measure. Sumptuous hangings, and highly worked pottery, with bright patterns of black, white, and red, contrasted with the blue of the sky and sea.

Perfectly coiffed women, and dignified men, served refreshments. The visitors devoured delicious sea food, and a strange clear liquid which burned and warmed the stomach. Eventually, they were led to their rooms to rest.

Thutmose sat on his great state bed and looked out to sea through an enormous window. A woman hovered in one corner. Perhaps she was a maid, but he was unsure. He asked for a drink. The woman obliged by handing him a cup filled to the brim.

"Do you speak my language, lady of Crete?"

"Fluently, Your Majesty."

"Are you a royal servant?" She smiled mysteriously. "I must tell you I am very tired."

The woman disappeared. Not knowing whether he had caused a diplomatic incident, or averted trouble for his country, Thutmose tried to enjoy the sea view with his cup of wine.

Sometimes, he reflected, it was best to travel light.

***

<h1 style="text-align:center">144.</h1>

Breakfast was held in a vast dining hall. King Minos presided at one end. Thutmose was seated next to the king. Itaja was behind him, while the captain and his crew dined with a group of elite Cretan courtiers. Breakfast consisted of fish, yoghurt, and bread.

As they ate the Egyptian prince admired the collection of blue vases on display in the hall.

"Your vases are magnificent, King Minos. The blue is something I've not seen in my country."

"They're made of glass."

"Not clay?"

"It's a luxury product and entirely man-made. We normally import it from Greece and Ur."

"Perhaps Egypt should do the same."

"It would be my pleasure to give you some to take home, Prince."

After breakfast Thutmose accompanied his host on a tour of the palace. Giant jars, filled with wine and oil, stood in underground cellars. Gardens of flowers and fruit trees surrounded the vast complex. Wild trees dotted the hills. A constant breeze ventilated the rooms and swept across spacious balconies. Minos' home held so many rooms and terraces that Thutmose and Itaja began to think it resembled a city.

At mid-morning, snacks of honeycomb, and thin pancake bread were served with white wine imported from Egypt.

"I hear you hunt, Prince Thutmose."

"I like nothing more."

"Except to paint vases."

"You are well informed."

"Not as well as you. I understand Hatshepsut has ears everywhere."

"Egypt needs a firm hand."

"Especially with a woman on the throne."

"Putting a toddler in charge was not the best idea for Egypt."

"It's the sign of a weak nation. Bad for the economy, too."

"Hatshepsut is only minding Egypt's throne. I will rule one day."

"For now, your aunt is a strong monarch. Crete is happy to trade with Egypt."

"I will be pleased to let her know."

"I'm sure. Now, we have something prepared which is different from a hunt. Bull leaping."

Visions of Kalma's frescoes danced before Thutmose's eyes. Itaja dug him in the ribs.

"I should like that very much."

"For now, I will leave you to retire until this evening."

Free for the afternoon, the prince repaired to his chambers. Changing into a kilt of a coarse weave, he stuck a dagger into his belt. Calling on Itaja, the two left the palace for a walk in the surrounding hills.

"I'm impressed by your country, Itaja."

"Uncle Didikase is in a neighbouring village."

"Kalma's relative?"

"My uncle married her aunt."

"And now you are courting Kalma?"

"I asked her to marry me three months ago."

"Why haven't you moved in together?"

"In Crete it's customary to have a wedding celebration first."

"In Egypt there is no such ceremony, but I would like to give you both a gift."

"It's gracious of you. You're welcome to attend the wedding, Tutty. It's a celebration with lots of people. Others will be there with presents, so you won't be out of place."

"I was thinking more in the region of land near the palace. If you prefer a section in Akhmim, it could be arranged. Aunty is gifting Senenmut with a parcel, but I can't imagine you wanting to be his neighbour."

"I'd rather be poor!"

Their laughter rippled through the trees. Boughs sighed and creaked above them in the wind. Eventually, the men came to a depression in the landscape. Negotiating wild olive tree roots, they jumped to the level below the palace.

Before them lay a grove of trees planted in a circle. As they approached Thutmose laid a hand on one of his daggers. An entrance opened within a dense grove of trees. Suddenly, the prince smacked his hand into Itaja's torso.

"Stand back!"

Teetering on the edge of a large cave, the men took a step backwards.

"It's a sacred cave, Tutty."

"Who, by Ra, would plant trees next to a cave, plunging hundreds of feet down?"

"Cretans."

Intrigued, Thutmose continued walking to his right. Pushing back branches, he peeked through. Shafts of light streamed from above the trees into the cave. It was a glorious place, with odd configurations everywhere. Stalactites rose from the pool below. Ridges of yellow and red rock dripped water.

A path led into its interior.

"I'm not going down there, Tutty, unless we have a guide."

"It's fascinating. Look, there's even a god's shrine!"

"*Goddess*. They worship the Earth Mother. The groves are for dancing. It's a place for serious worship."

"How can anyone dance in this death trap?"

"The dancing area will be at the back. Let's walk round. We can visit the cave another time."

But Thutmose had already started to head down the path into the cavern. Taking his sandals off, he tucked them into his belt. Gingerly making his way down the sloping path, he waved to Itaja to follow him. About twenty feet down, the men saw a shrine cut into the rock.

Ceramic vessels of scented oil and wine sat next to tiny earthenware objects representing dancers. Wearing bodices pulled in at the waist to accentuate their bare white breasts, they held snakes which writhed up their arms. Long Cretan skirts fell in layers down their bodies.

"I recognise Kalma."

"If I wasn't so afraid of falling to my death, Tutty, I'd punch you in the head." "I heard she dances."

"And with your aunt, no less."

It was Thutmose's turn to feel his temperature rise.

"What are you implying?"

"My future bride told me. They've been doing it for years. To be honest, I think Kalma dances while your aunt sits dreaming under the poppy spell."

"Are these secret rites exclusive to women?"

"Male initiates can join. But not with Kalma and your aunt. You don't have to worry about being surprised with another sister!"

Deciding it was best to ask no more, Thutmose continued his descent into the cave. At the bottom Itaja began to feel uneasy. It was cold. Water dripped from rocks around them. Rays of sunlight faded over the pool as the sun moved.

Thutmose halted.

"Let's go," he said.

They climbed up the rocks. Faint sounds of pipes echoed through the cave behind them. Without pausing, the friends kept climbing until they reached the entrance. They hurried past the tree fringe which hid the cave.

"Someone was down there, Tutty."

"A worshipper, perhaps."

"Or a spirit."

Thutmose snorted. Dusting his palms, he went to check the back of the grove with Itaja. Here the trees curved in on one another. They were so densely packed there was no sign of an entrance. Walking around, Itaja selected a spot.

"Here it is."

"But there's no opening!"

"Believe me, it's marked."

Itaja parted the branches. Thutmose followed. They found themselves on a neatly trimmed lawn. Around four sides, trees were packed densely so that it gave one the feeling of being in a forest. In the middle was a mound.

"What does a grove dance involve, Itaja?"

"Poppy is taken to worship the goddess. That mound represents Earth. I don't know any more."

"You don't dance?"

"Not at all."

"Not even with Kalma?"

"She dances with other Cretan men."

"Don't you worry?"

"It's not my business."

"Why be nosy?" Thutmose said sarcastically.

"A piece of advice, Tutty. Give your lady freedom and she'll stay forever."

Looking about him, the prince noted that the grove, with its neatly trimmed grass, was peaceful. It could have been anywhere. Even paradise.

***

145

Rising early on the morning of the bull leaping ceremony, Thutmose visited Itaja's apartment. There was no sound from inside. Entering the bedroom, he pulled the sheets off his slumbering friend. There was no response.

"Wake up!"

"I haven't been to bed."

"We aren't on holiday, Itaja. Drink with your mates when we get back."

"Who said anything about drinking? I was with a girl."

"But you're engaged."

"Says the future pharaoh with a hundred wives."

"That's different."

"How so?"

"You're a commoner."

"I'd be careful what you say, Tutty."

"Even Grandfather didn't use his harem."

"I didn't know that."

"He wasn't born into royalty. And neither were you."

"I attended a grove ceremony."

"Which makes it fine to commit adultery?"

"It's mandatory to take a woman."

"What are you going to do when Kalma continues dancing?"

"She dances alone. It was different when she was young, of course."

"Rubbish! Kalma was always chaste. I'm angry with you, Itaja."

"Maybe you're in love with her yourself."

"You need to show your future wife respect."

When Itaja was washed and dressed, the two made their way to separate chariots. Cretan drivers took them to a stadium where they sat in the royal box with King Minos. Thutmose calculated several thousand people were in attendance, including most of the court and the city's residents. Peasants ate fresh cheese and bread, which they chased down with warm Cretan wine. Ladies of the court gossiped, while strong farmers' sons showed off their tanned bodies, and long hair anointed with olive oil.

Finally, a large black-and-white bull was led onto the field. A hush fell over the audience. A lone acrobat approached it. Thutmose leaned forward. Standing quietly for a moment, the man looked into the bull's eyes. Then he reached forward and grabbed both horns. Leaping over its back in one lithe motion, the acrobat landed on his feet. The crowd roared.

Impulsively, Thutmose cheered. He nudged Itaja.

"Have you ever seen anything like that?"

"Quite often at Uncle Didikase's village."

Several acrobats followed. The crowd sang and threw flowers. For several hours, the foreign visitors looked on at a spectacle which involved tumbling, dancing, and singing. Towards the end of the show, ten bulls entered the arena. Acrobats tumbled over them effortlessly, and joined a line of dancers. The Egyptians leapt to their feet. King Minos looked benevolently at his awe-struck visitors. He leaned over to Thutmose.

"It's not a hunt, but as you can see, most enjoyable."

"I've never seen anything like it."

"Visit again, Prince. You are always welcome in our fair isle."

"Your Majesty must also come to Egypt."

"I will send a delegation with those glass vessels you admire so much. It will give us an excuse to visit your fair land."

The next day at the jetty, King Minos and his court farewelled the Egyptians. Thutmose's boots felt broken in as he scrunched shells underfoot. Then, all twelve ships set sail on the blue sea under a cloudless sky, back to Egypt.

***

146

Hatshepsut's office was dark. A single lamp flickered on her desk which was piled high with foreign correspondence. Incense burned to keep mosquitoes away. Thutmose was announced by her guard.

"How was Crete, dear nephew?"

"Successful."

"I heard you enjoyed yourself."

"Itaja came. Did you know he and Kalma are to be married in Crete?"

"You can't go. I'm have appointed you General of the Army."

Thutmose swallowed.

"That's unexpected."

"You've wanted to lead our army since you were a toddler. Why do you think trained you for the job?"

"I rather thought you'd stolen my throne."

Hatshepsut chuckled.

"Are you pleased?"

"It is my honour to serve Egypt."

"I want you to be prepared for what happens after my death."

"Are you ill, Aunty?"

"No, but when I die the neighbouring nations will give you trouble. It always happens at the beginning of a new king's reign. In your case, you might not only keep the dogs at bay, but be able to extend the empire."

***

Itaja's room in the barracks resembled a prison with one bed and a table. Despite the surroundings, the young officer was bubbling with excitement.

"Is that what she said?"

"I'm sorry I can't come to your wedding, Itaja."

"You're General. Congratulations! Where does that leave your aunt?"

"She's still Chief Commander."

"In the meantime, you'll gain experience."

"My first task is to promote you to 'Major'."

Thutmose clapped his delighted friend on the back. Steering him out of the military barracks, he led Itaja to the palace. There they sat by the fishpond and sipped wine throughout the afternoon.

***

Frowning, Senenmut tasted his goat's milk. It was sour.

"How long have you been hunched over those papers, Your Majesty?"

"All day. Did you hear about Thutmose?"

"I'll wager he enjoyed being promoted. Must have been music to that boy's ears."

"He's a man now."

"And a general at that. Do you think it's wise?"

"Do you suspect him?"

"All the time!" Senenmut laughed. He became serious. The lines on his face had recently become more pronounced. "He's never forgiven you the loss of his throne."

"I can't help what he thinks. Thutmose has survived to adulthood. I did my job as his guardian."

"You've done more than your job. You're a great monarch."

They left the office. Statues of Hatshepsut surrounded them as they made their way down the long corridor to the dining hall. A setting sun shone through the windows.

"Isn't it a pity they can only depict me as a man these days?"

***

Thutmose, commonly known as Tuthmosis the Third (or "Great"), became Egypt's foremost warrior king. It is not known whether he

321

visited Crete. However, the two countries were trading partners. What is known is that the king enjoyed painting vases in his spare time.

While some have postulated that Hatshepsut was the queen who drew Moses from the Nile, there is no proof.

Twenty years later her monuments were destroyed. Statues of the female pharaoh were defaced, hacked to pieces, and thrown into pits. Her name was erased from Egypt's list of kings.

The prime suspect was Thutmose.

***

EPILOGUE

All was white and luminous, like the pearly interior of an oyster shell. Thutmose knew he had died. And there she was in the corner, chatting to the ambassadors and courtiers he remembered from his youth.

It did not take long for Hatshepsut to recognise her nephew.

"You destroyed my monuments, Tutty."

"It was for my son, Amenhotep."

"After everything I did for you."

"He can't be seen to descend from a matrilineal line."

"Hogwash! It was good enough for you, the greatest military commander of all time."

"I might be surpassed by my son. Amenhotep is adept at clubbing foreign kings."

Peering over the balcony through the clouds, Thutmose seemed to be looking for something.

"Did you commission that thug to wreck my monuments?"

"I was too sick to make any decisions, Aunty. And so here I am." He essayed a smile.

"I don't fancy spending eternity with you."

"The feeling is mutual."

Walking past her, Thutmose left. Unsure of where to go in all the whiteness, but knowing he did not wish to be within an obelisk's width of his aunt, he kept going. Suddenly, a door opened ahead. He walked through it into the sunshine.

A tall man, with conspicuous wings, handed him a key.

"What's this?"

"The key to your house, King Thutmose. Show it to the man waiting at that door." The stranger pointed to a blue door a short way ahead.

"Where's Anubis?"

"He doesn't exist."

"Nice wings. Goose?"

"I'm an angel."

Squaring his shoulders, Thutmose proceeded to the blue door. Another man appeared. On seeing the key, he stood aside. The door swung open. Egypt's king stepped over the threshold. Although it did not resemble a house, the Egyptian king felt at home. The floors were a curious mixture of white and rainbow, but felt stable underfoot.

On a gold table floating nearby, he found his favourite wine, a simple loaf of Egyptian bread, which he often ate on campaign, and cheese. Satisfied with his victuals, Thutmose took them to a couch. Recognising the blue and yellow colours of his reign, he sat down and started to eat. After a while, he noticed there was no one anywhere. It was the state he always preferred in life. After sitting in perfect peace for some time, he finally decided to look around.

The house was filled with never-ending rooms. It must be a palace, he thought. One door led outside. He gasped. All the animals and plants he had ever owned or seen, were stretched out before him. Herds of elephants trumpeted. Lions roared. Birds swooped through thick foliage. He recognised baboons from Punt, incense trees, tulips, crocuses from Syria, and even the poppy which killed battle pain.

He rushed down the steps and found himself walking through fields of flowers, his heart completely free.

***

Biography

Sharon Janet Hague is a lawyer and writer with an interest in ancient Egypt. Holding a master's degree in Egyptology from the University of Manchester, she pens articles for various publications, including Nile Magazine.

For more on the author you may visit her website at:

https://sharonjanethague.com

***

www.ingramcontent.com/pod-product-compliance
Lightning Source LLC
Chambersburg PA
CBHW010509100726

47902CB00011B/2137